THE SWORD AND THE CROSS CHRONICLES

ADORATION

OLIVIA RAE

ADORATION
Copyright © 2018 by Denise Cychosz
ISBN: 978-1-7320457-0-5
All rights reserved. Published by HopeKnight Press

No part of this book may be used or reproduced in any manner whatsoever without written permission except in case of brief quotations embodied in critical articles and reviews.

Please Note
This is a work of fiction. Names, characters, places and incidents are either the product of the author's imagination or are used fictitiously, and any resemblance to any actual persons living or dead, business establishments, events or locales is entirely coincidental.

For information, please contact:
oliviarae.books@gmail.com

Cover Design by Kim Killion, The Killion Group, Inc.
Interior Formatting by Author E.M.S.

Bible Passages are from the King James Version

Published in the United States of America.

Books by Olivia Rae

The Sword and the Cross Chronicles

SALVATION

REVELATION

REDEMPTION

RESURRECTION

ADORATION

DEVOTION
(coming soon)

Contemporary Inspirational

JOSHUA'S PRAYER

Contact Olivia at
Oliviarae.books@gmail.com

For news and sneak peeks of upcoming novels visit:
Oliviaraebooks.com
Facebook.com/oliviaraeauthor

For my son-in-law, Stephen,
May your feet always take the right path.

And to the glory of God

*A special thank you to my cheerleader,
Betsy Norman.*

*Without your daily morning email
I would still be on page ten.*

One

*For there is nothing covered, that shall not be revealed;
neither hid, that shall not be known.*
Luke 12:2

*April 5, 1199, Châlus, France
Close to midnight*

LARGE BLACK CLOUDS FILLED THE AIR, HIDING THE moon's soft glow. The camp lay quiet, all waiting to hear word of their leader's fate. Not wearing his chain mail, King Richard had taken an arrow between the neck and his left shoulder nine days earlier while foolishly walking the perimeter of Château de Châlus-Chabrol. A barber was called to remove the arrow, but his skills were not adequate and the wound festered until the skin oozed puss and turned black. Some prayed for a miracle, so the king could live on. Others counted the days and hours, certain His Majesty would shortly meet God.

Casting his eyes to the dark, brooding heavens, Darrin Longbeard waited outside his king's tent. A sentinel gave a curt nod and Darrin raised the flap and entered the modest shelter. A foul order of urine, sweat and blood greeted his presence; he struggled not to cover his nose and mouth as he edged forward to his king's pallet. The strong and virile man who had taunted and marched over the French no longer existed. Instead, on a soiled bed lay a withered soul with a plum-black hue stretching down the skin of his arm and traveling up his neck. Sir Theo had not lied; the king was dying.

"Longbeard, are you here?" King Richard whispered, waving a shaking hand toward the entrance.

"Aye, Your Majesty." Darrin rushed toward the bed and dropped to one knee, taking the king's wavering hand. "I am next to you."

Richard gave out a long, raspy gasp followed by a pause. The hair on Darrin's neck rose, as he feared this could be the Lionheart's last breath. But then the cracked lips moved and the king inhaled sharply. "Are we alone?"

Though the room possessed a single tallow, the light cast no doubt they were the only occupants. "Aye, we are alone."

"Good. Good." The king took another rough breath and then turned his glassy grey gaze toward Darrin. "It is time."

"Time for what, my lord?"

A rattle grew in Richard's chest, his eyes closed and his grip on Darrin's hand softened.

Was this it, then? Was his king leaving this earth? Darrin leaned closer. Short, shallow breaths escaped Richard's lips. "Your Majesty, time for what?"

The crusty eyes opened again and gazed into Darrin's. "You must claim Château du Vent Doux. You must return home."

For a moment, Darrin stilled and a short flutter of elation rose in his chest. He feared to give voice to the desire he had held deep in his heart for ten years. "Are you sure?" he whispered, fearing the king might have spoken the phrase in his delirium. "You may still need me."

"Needed you." A hoarse cough rose in Richard's throat. "I'm dying. I fear I will not live past the morrow."

"Your Majesty—"

Richard raised his hand. "We all know what is to come." Again the king paused, his eyelids growing heavy, but then he rallied and tried to rise up on his elbows.

Quickly Darrin placed a strong arm of support at his king's back. "Here, lord. Rest easy."

ADORATION

Richard shook his head, then motioned with his chin. "See there. On the table." Another gravelly cough left his lungs and a spittle of blood appeared on his lips. "That is my missive giving you back your lands."

Temptation grew within Darrin to let his king's head fall on the bed and rush to see if, indeed, the words were written on the parchment. But Richard seemed all the more urgent, as if he still had more to say.

"You must promise me..."

A violent fit of coughing seized the king, every gasp of air a struggle, and Darrin worried each one would signal the end...of life. He eased the king's neck and head down until they gently touched the pallet. "Sleep now, Your Majesty."

Richard's eyes closed as his breathing labored until it slowed and became steady. Seconds dragged by and Darrin inched away, not wanting to disturb the king's much-needed rest. A small twig snapped beneath Darrin's boot as he made to stand. Richard's eyes flew open and he reached out and grabbed Darrin's hand with a mighty strength.

"Promise me...promise me..."

"Anything, lord." Darrin gripped the king's hand with equal strength and bent down again. "You only have to ask. You fulfilled your half of the bargain—I will have my lands." He nodded to the document on the table. "I am your man. Your will is all I desire."

The king's shadowy grey eyes held Darrin; the monarch struggled to speak. "There is one more thing. Faith...Faith... You must marry her."

Darrin had to resist the urge to pull his fingers away from the king's hand. Faith who? Slowly his memory gelled and he realized what the king was asking of him. They had been talking about his home, Château du Vent Doux. There resided the only Faith he knew—Faith de Saint-Marie. Why would the king want him to marry the very woman who helped steal his home? Nay, this could not be true. King Richard asked too much.

"Do you speak of Lady Faith de Saint-Marie? If so,

I cannot." Darrin shifted his gaze to the ground.

Richard's body began to shake and another series of coughs rumbled and reverberated around the small tent.

Gently, Darrin placed a hand on the king's good shoulder. "Ease, Your Majesty, we can talk about this tomorrow."

A thunderous "No!" filled the air, followed by choking and retching. Again, slowly, Richard's breathing became normal. "Now."

Not wanting to upset him further, Darrin settled with both knees in the dirt. "Speak then. I will listen."

"The château is yours only if you marry Faith."

What cruel joke was this? This had never been part of the bargain when they left England. Ten years earlier, Darrin fled his home all because that girl and his uncle falsely accused him of murdering his father. All done to seize control of Château du Vent Doux. Now Richard wanted him to marry the liar?

"My king, I am certain she is the one responsible for my father's death. How can you ask such a thing of me?"

Richard's face scrunched up in an angry twist. "She did not. She could not. She is my daughter."

By all that was holy, this could not be true! The pain must have made the king mad. All knew he had an illegitimate son, but a daughter as well? Again Darrin's mind tripped back, more than twenty years ago. It could be true. Faith had come to their keep when she was four summers old with a young nun and a letter from King Richard. His father had been ordered to take the girl in as his ward. But his father had always claimed she was a distant cousin of the king, nothing more. Could his father have lied to protect Faith?

A gurgle came from the king's throat and fresh blood dripped from his lips. Darrin quickly reached for the basin next to the bed and wiped Richard's face with a cool cloth.

Like a strike from a snake, Richard grabbed Darrin's hand. "She is legitimate."

He hesitated and stared at the man lying on the pallet.

Surely the poison from the king's wound must be destroying his brain. Darrin shook his head. Faith, the girl who sang off tune and helped him catch frogs, who had almost been like a cousin until she betrayed him, was King Richard's legitimate heir?

Ridiculous.

"Your Majesty, you are confused. Rest now. We will talk later," Darrin said, easing his hand from the king's grip.

"No. No. Listen to me." Richard took a heavy breath. "When I was young, I fought with my brothers..." More coughing, more choking.

Darrin could not watch the struggle. "Aye, all know when you were sixteen summers you fought with your brothers against your father. Do not tax yourself with the past. Your father forgave you. 'Tis all forgotten."

The king gave a weak wave. "My troops were destroyed. I ran to Château de Taillebourg while my brothers fought on."

"Your Majesty—"

Color flushed the king's face. "Speak again and I'll take your head."

Some of the old fiery monarch clearly still remained. Wishing to keep his head intact, Darrin ceased his speech.

Again Richard pointed to the table. "There is another document I just had completed. Go read it."

Darrin made his way to the small table and indeed there were two parchments. One addressed to his uncle and another addressed to that very vile woman, Lady Faith de Saint-Marie. The letter to Faith gave an extraordinary account of Richard's time at Château de Taillebourg. If true, while there, Richard had become enamored with a peasant girl who tightly held on to her virtue. In his lustful desire, he badgered a priest, Father Dubois, to marry them. The priest, having strong ties to Richard's mother, Eleanor of Aquitaine, and King Louis VII of France, agreed to the union. After the war was lost, Richard crawled back to his father's side and confessed all. Being a second son, Richard hoped King

Henry II would approve the marriage and would seek sanction from the pope.

But that did not happen. One night while Richard slept, his father sent mercenaries to find and kill the priest and Richard's bride. According to this letter, a fire was set and all documentation of the marriage was destroyed. The mission had been a complete success.

Darrin turned back to his king. "Your Majesty, if the records were destroyed, there is no proof of this union. And if your wife was killed, how could Lady Faith be your child?"

"Read all of it," Richard choked out.

Again Darrin focused on the missive. The priest got wind of the situation ahead of time and had a servant switch clothes with Richard's wife, whom he sent with a monk by the name of Klein to the Abbey of Sainte-Marie-des-Dames. There the woman gave birth to a girl. The girl was given the name Faith de Saint-Marie.

By the holy cross, if this was true and it could be proven, then...

"I did not know of the child," Richard rasped, "until four years later."

"You have proof of this?"

Richard slightly shook his head. "Nay, lost in the fire."

"Then this still could be a ruse."

"Come here and look at me."

Darrin made his way back to the bed and looked down at his king.

"My eyes, her eyes—the same. My temper, her temper—the same. Brother Klein would not lie."

Darrin looked down at the document in his hand. "Your Majesty, according to this, you only saw her once before you sent her to my father. How could you know of her temperament?"

Richard held up a feeble hand and tried to make a fist. "She met me with this. When I was little, I greeted strangers the same way."

ADORATION

A flash of remembrance surfaced in Darrin's mind. Indeed Faith could be stubborn at times and she did hold her hand tightly in a fist when upset. He could still see her standing in front of the magistrate declaring his guilt—chin held high, eyes chipped like grey granite, her pale hair cascading down her back and her right hand firmly fisted. But none of this was evidence that she was Richard's heir.

"This letter will give some proof if she wishes to pursue the throne. You will marry her. Be her protector. It is so written," the king whispered.

Surely Richard had lost his mind. If Faith went to Prince John with this paper in hand, her head, along with her husband—her protector—would be rolling around in a basket. "This is foolish. I cannot. Let my uncle be her defender. For I hate her."

Richard's eyes grew heavy and filled with sadness. "Aye. I know. I wish there was another choice. Your uncle has been shifting his allegiance to the French."

Not surprising, Darrin thought. King Phillip had a way of winning more hearts than his father, King Louis, had before him. And Darrin's uncle, Adrien de Gascon, always managed to worm into any court where he could hold the most power. What would his uncle do if he learned of Lady Faith's heritage? No wonder King Richard was worried.

"I can't be there to protect her. You must. To rule or not is her choice. You will stand by her side. Those are my terms. Look, there is more." The king closed his eyes and inhaled deeply.

Going back to the table, Darrin picked up the other parchment. Indeed, to reclaim his lands and have his name restored, he must marry Lady Faith de Saint-Marie. And make sure she conceived within a year's time. *Was Richard out of his mind?* "Not only do you want me to marry her, but you want me to get her with child? You ask too much. Why me? Why not Sir Theo or some other trusted knight? Find another. Why did you not seek a royal union earlier if this is what you wanted?" Darrin knew the answer to the last question without the king's reply. Richard had still hoped for a male heir, and if that did not happen, he would have fought on until he broke the French backs. After regaining the peace, he would have bullied King Phillip into accepting Lady Faith as his heir and, if God willing, her son as the future king of England.

"Enough. Time is running out. You will keep her safe. You will protect her. You will marry her. You will impregnate her. If this does not happen, your land will be given to another. You gave me your vow to be my man," the king sputtered.

Darrin gritted his teeth. Aye. He had. And he could not deny a dying man's wish.

Two

*Better it is that thou shouldest not vow,
than that thou shouldest vow and not pay.*
Ecclesiastes 5:5

STILL RILED BY THE KING'S DECREE, DARRIN LEFT the tent with both sealed documents in hand. Every time he passed a campfire, he was sorely tempted to drop the missives into the flames. How had this happened? Years earlier, he had been resigned to live the fugitive life in the English forest with a bunch of rogues and thieves. No wonder King Richard jumped at the bargain they struck back then—return of Château du Vent Doux for service in His Majesty's army. Darrin slapped the papers against his thigh. Somehow he had become the king's secondary plan for his daughter.

Sir Theodore de Born rose from sitting around one such fire and frowned as Darrin approached. "How is our king?"

Darrin motioned to Theo to follow him as they headed for their own tent. "Not well. Prepare to leave. We will be heading to Château du Vent Doux east of Nantes near the Loire River."

"I have heard of the place. This is our king's orders?"

Darrin paused. Keeping his past a secret was no longer possible. He filled Theo in about the contents of the letter to his uncle, but did not offer information about the other document, which contained the identity of Lady Faith.

Theo gave out a low whistle. "I always wondered why Richard would treat you, a thief and a rebel, as equal to his knights. Now I know. You are a knight, Sir Darrin de Longue, the scoundrel who killed his father and then ran away. The story is infamous."

Entering their tent, Darrin gritted his teeth, grabbing his sword and bow. "I did not kill my father."

"Five years ago I would have called you a liar. But not now. You have watched my back in many battles. If you were indeed a slimy, killing coward, you would have run from the field and let me and others die."

Darrin placed his weapons on a makeshift table and filled his quill with arrows. "Thank you for that glowing appraisal of my reputation."

"Of course, you speak like a turd—*glowing appraisal*. Who uses such words?"

"Someone who values an education of the mind as much as he does knowledge of his sword."

Theo grunted and sat down on his pallet, scratching his full beard. "I have no need for learning as long as I have my sword." He then stared at Darrin as if he were a stranger. "A lord and a knight. I knew there was more to you, but I always figured you were like me, a second or third son with few prospects. Well, God does have a sense of humor. An heir with his own château. Unbelievable."

"Not quite a lord. You saw the other terms. If I do not fulfill them, then the château and lands will be taken away. Mayhap given to you."

"The king did not tell you who the other choice might be?" Theo tilted his head and sharpened his gaze on Darrin.

"Nay, and I have no intention of giving up my home."

Theo shrugged. "Then it does not matter who the other man is."

"Even if it is you?" Darrin filled a sack with the rest of his belongings.

"The king said nothing to me."

"Nor would he." Darrin held up the missive for his uncle.

"No doubt whoever drew up this document also has the other—in case I fail."

"Then don't fail." Theo leaned back on his pallet. "Because if you do, and I am Richard's second choice, I will throw you out on your arse."

"A true friend. Who could want for more?" Darrin started to roll up his bed. "Get up. We must leave, now. Sir Rollin de Tosny and his men, plus a few of our own, will be going with us."

Theo sat up. "Blast. The king must indeed be dying if he is allowing Sir Rollin to leave. I'll never understand what King Richard sees in him. The man shows up a year ago with less than a fart to recommend him, and the next thing you know, he's the right-hand man of the king."

"Saving King Richard's life might have had something to do with that."

"Ah, any of us would have done the same thing had we been near him. Knocking the king out of the way and taking an arrow above the knee... 'Tis nothing."

"Nothing? Look at our king now. He's dying from an arrow wound."

Theo never moved a muscle as he watched Darrin prepare for departure. "So where was Sir Rollin when the arrow came this time? We could have been relieved of his boastful blubbering instead of losing our mighty king."

Darrin looked around the tent and then down at Theo. "Get moving. I'll tell Gouch to get the men ready."

Theo stood and stretched. "Marvelous. We get to take your merry band of misfits with us too."

"Would you want any other?" Darrin asked, heading to the tent entrance.

"Nay. I trust that scum with my life."

Darrin paused at the entry. "This is King Richard's last command. Things may well change on the morrow. I'll not return even if Prince John asks me to. The château is rightfully mine. I'll not leave it, but I can't ask you to stay if you do not wish so."

Theo bent over and began rolling up his own bed. "Aye, I know. No matter. I swear my allegiance to you. I'll stay until you tell me to leave." He then smiled. "Or something better comes my way."

Darrin nodded but held a sober mood. Very soon, all would be different, when John ruled the realm. What Theo did not know, the future ruler could change as well. Darrin had little doubt that the witch Lady Faith would be more than eager to change her title to Queen Faith. However, one problem remained. He had no desire to stand by her side in court or anywhere else.

"Find Sir Rollin. I believe the king wishes to see him before we leave. I'll meet you and him by the horses before daybreak." Darrin quit the tent, knowing the future held many doubts.

Hours later, after readying his men, Darrin met Theo and Rollin outside the makeshift stable. The dark night swiftly turned to a light grey. Soon the day's rays would be upon them. Every morn for the past week, Richard had the tent flap raised so he could see the morning light. Mayhap today would be his last.

"We are all set," Sir Rollin said, brushing a speck of dust off his black tunic.

Given the rushed circumstances, the man still looked impeccable. His cropped black hair waved and curled about his ears, giving his strong chin with its perfectly clipped goatee a gallant look. No wonder the women flocked to him. Sir Rollin would come off the battlefield looking like he had just stepped out of a rose garden. Theo teased Rollin and called him "Blossom" because his penetrating blue eyes, rimmed with hazel, drew women to him like bees to a flower. Even so, no one could fault the man's skill with a sword. He was quick and accurate, and few of his opponents felt his strike until they lay on the ground, blood oozing from their throats.

"Come on, Blossom. Get your arse up on your horse. We have much to travel this day," Theo chided.

Aye, the pair were a contrast. Theo had managed to grow a thick, wiry beard since he arrived in France. His sandy-brown hair had become a mass of long, greasy strings hanging around his face. Some said the drastic look started the day Lady Eleanor de Taine rebuffed his offer of marriage and chose Sir Hugh de Maury instead. But truth be told, Theo wanted to look like a madman when he went into battle. He was even known for taking the edge of his sword and twisting it upward through a man's chest, while Rollin would take a strike anywhere he could give a lethal thrust. There remained yet another contrast between the pair; when Theo walked off the battlefield, he was a mass of sweat, mud and blood. Yet Darrin trusted Theo to a fault. There was no other knight Darrin wanted by his side in a fight or sitting by a fire, passing idle stories.

Darrin maneuvered his horse close to Sir Rollin's mount. "We travel to Château du Vent Doux. It is located—"

"I know where it is," Sir Rollin said, adjusting his chain mail.

For a moment, Darrin thought to question Rollin, for few knew of the château, but then the knight was raised in these parts. He looked straight ahead and gave no further comment. His thoughts were probably with King Richard—none of them would be seeing him again.

"Let us go, for it could take us more than four or five days to get there and that is if the weather is good." Darrin left Châlus flanked by the contrasting pair of knights.

They had not gone two days before word had reached them that the king was dead. More than ever, Darrin feared the future, for no man knew the workings of Prince John's, now King John's, mind. The man was said to be calm but then could strike with a cruel and bitter vengeance. What would he do if he knew Richard might have a legitimate heir?

With no other directive, the small band marched onward

to Château du Vent Doux—Château of the Gentle Wind. Darrin grimaced. Once they arrived, the château might have to change its name to Château des Tempêtes Tumultueuses—Château of Tumultuous Storms. Even with the challenges that lay before him, Darrin had a hard time containing his excitement. Finally he would be returning home.

The château was truly a beautiful place. The Loire River gradually curved north of the castle and soft planting fields covered the southern lands. A gentle breeze kept everyone cool in the summer and the winds were never fierce in the winter. Darrin inhaled deeply, as if he could smell the stunning spring flowers that swept over the meadows at this time of the year. Indeed Château du Vent Doux held more charm and grace than all the Norman castles combined. He gave his mount a swift kick, not wanting to wait to see his home.

The journey had taken six days and they arrived on a sunny spring afternoon, the meadows full of blue, yellow and purple wildflowers. The echo of children's laughter greeted them as they approached the keep and small village from the south. The moment their horses were spotted, the merriment died, and the children and other villagers disappeared. Shouts reigned from the château walls. A row of archers appeared above Darrin's men.

He held up his hand, slowing the men. Darrin took the document for his uncle from a secured saddlebag and handed it to Theo. The other document for Faith lay under Darrin's tunic, away from prying eyes. "I shall go on alone. Take the parchment. They will, no doubt, drag me from my horse once they discover who I am. If that happens, it will be up to you to deliver this message to my uncle. Make sure our men are ready. I don't think my uncle will give up the château without a fight."

Theo nodded and then divided the men into two groups. Theo would go in after Darrin with one group and Sir Rollin would follow with the other. Hopefully, King Richard's colors would be honored, but Darrin could not be sure.

Especially if his uncle had given his allegiance to King Phillip of France.

Darrin pulled up the hood of his chain mail and pushed his mount ahead, pausing outside the fortress walls. "I am Sir Darrin de Longue. I demand you open the gate."

The chatter inside bounced around the keep and drifted on the wind until it reached Darrin's ears. It did not take long for his uncle's dark head to appear over the château's stone wall. "How do I know what you say is true? Darrin de Longue is a coward and a villain who fled these lands over ten years ago. Why would he return?"

"I am he, and I have a message from King Richard." Darrin shifted in his saddle, hoping his uncle had not yet received word about the king's fate. Ever so slowly, Theo and his men rode forward, carrying the king's colors. Being prudent, his uncle, without a further word, opened the gate. Darrin rode in with Theo at his back.

Surprisingly, his uncle did not pull Darrin from his horse and slap him in chains. Instead the older knight stared at him with speculative eyes and folded arms. "Drop your hood so I may see if it is truly you," his uncle commanded.

With a brush of a hand, the chain mail fell from Darrin's head, exposing him to the archers positioned above him. His uncle stood still and let his gaze drift over Darrin before moving upward to his men.

"Careful, Uncle. The king would not look kindly on the man who killed one of his most trusted knights."

Again his uncle's gaze dropped to Darrin's face. "You are indeed my departed wife's nephew. You have the same muddy hair and straight jawline of your father. None of this I doubt. What I do not understand is how you came into the king's service. I have always thought King Richard fought with noble men, not murderers."

The words were spoken to dig under Darrin's skin, to force him to action. But he was not the young, rash man who fled ten years ago, and what better time for Sir Adrien de Gascon to learn that lesson. Darrin leaned forward in his saddle. "I have been in the king's service for the past five years. I am here at his request. Sir Theodore, bring forth King Richard's missive."

Theo rode forward, dismounted and handed the document with the king's seal upon it to Darrin's uncle. The older man mumbled as he read the letter. Then he paused and became silent, his eyes never leaving the parchment, as if he were rereading the words over and over again.

Finally, his uncle raised his head. "This cannot be true! Archers—"

"Before you give that command, look around you. What do you see?" Darrin waved a hand about the château. Some of Theo's men had disappeared into the crowd while others stood near steps where his uncle's men stood. Theo, with his sword drawn, was less than a hand from his uncle. Sir Rollin and his men had Darrin's back.

"Why, you…" His uncle rushed forward and tried to drag Darrin off his horse, but Theo was quicker. He grabbed Sir Adrien, took away his sword, and placed a blade beneath his throat.

Darrin dismounted and came within a hand of his uncle's face. "I should have had you gutted before I left. For I am certain you had my father killed."

Laughter rang out. "Go ahead. Kill me. Then send word to King John. See what he will have to say."

So his uncle did know King Richard was dead. But King John had not called a halt to their mission, which meant he may have known about his uncle's increasing loyalty to the French. In all certainty, Darrin believed neither man had knowledge about Lady Faith's legitimacy. Otherwise, his uncle would have put an arrow in Darrin's heart before he even entered the château.

Darrin motioned to Theo to drop the weapon from his uncle's neck. "You will leave this keep with all your men and you will not return. For I swear, if you do not, I will kill you."

"You wait and see. King John will feel differently about this once he hears from me." His uncle spit in Darrin's face.

The insult set Darrin's gut rolling. He wiped his face, and then he drew his sword. "Hand Sir Adrien his sword. We shall settle this now."

"What are you doing?" Theo said in a low voice. "Do you want to have this place teeming in blood?"

"I have waited years for this. Give him a sword," Darrin roared.

Theo hesitated, then turned to Sir Adrien, ready to give him a sword.

A loud cry came from the great hall stairs. "Stop. Stop this insanity."

Time slowed as Darrin focused on the familiar voice. The voice that sealed his fate ten years ago. The voice that sent him to the English forest to live as a common criminal. The voice that unknowingly forced him into the king's service for the past five years. The voice he longed to put to an end to with the single thrust of a blade.

There, standing on the steps, dressed in a light blue overgown with a sheer veil covering her soft, pale golden hair was the most hated—Lady Faith de Saint-Marie.

Mayhap killing his uncle could wait. Darrin tightened his grip on his sword and headed for the stairs.

A firm hand landed on his shoulder. "Hold. Think. You made a vow to our dead king," Theo whispered.

Darrin eased the grip on his weapon and pointed the blade toward the ground. With his will sorely tested, he bowed toward the witch, who had descended the stairs. "It has been a long time, my lady."

She stood close. Too close. Her soft grey eyes searched his own. "Indeed it has been, Sir Darrin. I hope the years have been kind to you?"

Truly? She asked about his welfare? Like she even cared. He wondered what scheme she was hatching in her mind this very moment. Her gaze flipped tenderly to her uncle. Darrin had his answer. She wished to save her lover.

"Fear not, my lady. I'll not shed blood here this day."

Then he turned and glared at his uncle. "Unless Lord de Gascon does not leave within the hour."

Like a shrewd tactician, she slipped between the pair, leaving the soft scent of lavender in her wake. "Come now, surely you cannot expect a man to leave his own home?"

"He has others. Besides, this is not his home anymore. He will never lay his head on any pallet in Château du Vent Doux again," Darrin pronounced.

A slight blush filled her cheeks before she dropped her gaze to her feet like a shy virgin. Darrin wanted to laugh.

Faith turned toward his uncle. "Sir Adrien has rights—"

"Give her the missive," Darrin ordered, looking at the crumpled document in his uncle's hand.

The letter fell to the ground. Without a word, she crossed the bailey and picked up the missive. With great pleasure, Darrin watched her scan the document just as many times as his uncle had. The meaning of what was to come drained the color from her face, her eyes wide with bewilderment and her delicate pink lips parted. He expected her to shriek with agony at the prospect of marriage to him.

But she didn't...

She smiled. What game did she play now? No longer was he a foolish young man. He was a seasoned knight who could inflict disastrous pain. Did she think she could best him at a game of wits? Oh, but she would learn who held the upper hand.

"I am sorry, my lady. But unfortunately the words are the last wishes of King Richard. These lands are mine and we are betrothed. I am just as repulsed by the upcoming nuptials as you are. Nonetheless, it will happen."

The smile slipped away and Darrin rejoiced at the small victory.

"Why, you insufferable beast. I should have your head for insulting Lady Faith," his uncle roared.

Darrin laughed. "I cannot take honor where there is none. Now collect your possessions and go." He turned and shouted to his men. "Do not leave Lord de Gascon's side until he is far from the château."

"Fear not, Lady Faith. I shall return and deliver you from this monster," his uncle yelled over his shoulder as Darrin's men dragged him away.

The stress on Faith's face shot more triumphant glee through Darrin's body. He came up beside her and bent his head until his lips were next to her ear. "I promise you," he whispered, "you will never be in your lover's arms again."

Her gaze shot to his and her cheeks flooded with color and her hand curled into a tight fist. His assessment of the relation between Faith and his uncle had been correct. But the pleasure Darrin expected to flood his soul did not happen. Instead, he found his gut ached as if stabbed by a sharp dagger.

Three

And they rewarded me evil for good, and hatred for my love.
Psalm 109:5

A DREAM? OR REALITY? SHE COULD NOT BE SURE. How often had she prayed and wondered what happened to Darrin de Longue? Faith took a deep breath and willed the hand at her side to uncurl. She stared at the man before her. The angry set of his jaw, the coldness in his hazel eyes and his rigid demeanor belonged to a stranger, not the young, carefree man she had once known. He meant to hurt her with his cruel words. But oh, how she wished to comb his tawny locks away from his furrowed brow and beg his forgiveness. However, such an action would not be welcomed. 'Twas too late for any reconciliation. She had sealed her fate with him all those years ago.

And yet, if the parchment she held in her hand spoke the truth, then she would be bound to Darrin forever—as his wife. Another dream she had toyed with since she was fourteen summers old. However, in those musings, Sir Darrin de Longue had acted the part of an adoring and loyal husband. The spiteful man before her would most likely be a loathing and vindictive adversary all the days of her life.

Unless she could reason with Darrin, make him understand why she had to betray him and side with Sir Adrien when Lord Jean de Longue died. Not an easy task, but one she must accomplish if she wished to have any type of a life with Sir Darrin, the new lord of Château du Vent Doux.

She cleared her throat and tried to think what words she could utter that would soothe his vengeful spirit. None came to mind. She slightly bent her head and prayed. *Heavenly Father, Please help Darrin. Calm him and give him peac—*

"What is this? Are you praying?" he scoffed. "Oh, lady, there will be no heavenly intervention here. We will be yoked to each other until God mercifully takes one of us."

Her heart dipped to her toes; he interrupted her prayer. The boy who revered God above all things had truly disappeared. *And you are responsible for this.* She could feel her hand begin to curl into a tight ball and the simple action brought a savage smile to his face.

With all her internal strength, she uncurled her fingers and clasped her hands in front of her and looked him straight in the eye. "My lord, I was not praying for myself, but for you."

"For me?" He stepped back, his face full of astonishment.

"Aye. It is clear you have suffered much over the years. I pray that our Heavenly Father will give you peace and perhaps a little understanding."

"Understanding," he bellowed. "Lady, spare me your feigned sympathy and piety. You know naught. Best you spend your hours preparing yourself for our marriage."

She looked down at her hands, held so tight, turning white. She took another patient breath and fought for control. "You could be civil about this. I have every intention of fulfilling King Richard's wishes. I will marry you."

His eyebrows slanted downward, his eyes scanning her face as if looking for some nefarious trait. She could not blame him. Would she act any differently if the situation were reversed? She stood her ground and held her tongue. Pushing him to anger would be detrimental.

Suddenly, he swept into a deep bow and then rose to tower above her. "Excellent. Then ready yourself. For we shall be wed this very eve."

A fluttering flash of fear and excitement grew in her stomach and washed over her flushed skin. "So soon. But we have no priest."

"Oh, lady, you are so wrong." Darrin called over his shoulder. "Father Chabot, where are you?"

A small man dressed in a brown robe with grey hair and a slight limp came forward. "Here, Sir Darrin."

"King Richard has thought of everything, my lady. We have a priest." Darrin then swept her with his gaze. "The marriage will take place at dusk. For I will not wait a moment longer to regain what is rightfully mine." And with that, he strode away to the stables with a few of his men in tow.

There she stood, her hands clasped. Slowly she let them drop to her sides. Her right hand began to curl in the folds of her gown. Her knees quaked. Her days of being a maid had come to an end. This eve she would be married to Sir Darrin de Longue, who seemed to be driven by the devil. *God have mercy on her.*

Getting his uncle's men out of the keep and along the road had taken longer than Darrin expected. Thankfully, Sir Rollin had offered to escort Sir Adrien de Gascon and those loyal to him across the Loire River and away from the château. Sir Rollin promised to keep a watchful eye on Sir Adrien until the wedding vows were completed and all legal rights of the château would once again belong to Darrin. At least for the time being. Then if his uncle wished to contest the validity of the marriage, he would have to make his case to King John. All this would take time. Time to build up his defenses. Time to get Lady Faith with child.

Until then, Darrin planned to squeeze the truth about his father's murder from Lady Faith de Saint-Marie. King Richard's other missive rubbed against Darrin's chest. The king had ordered the document be delivered to Faith, but he did not specify a time. So then what was the hurry? To Darrin's way of thinking, he would first force a confession out of Faith—that she and his uncle had conspired to murder his father. Since she was a woman, the task should be simple; she would crumple easily. He could almost taste the victory.

With his name cleared, he'd wait for the birth of his child. And just as quickly take the child away from her, keeping his child safe from her wicked grasp. Then he would hand Richard's letter to her. Darrin closed his eyes; he pictured the scene in his mind. Of course, her face would glow with anticipation at being Queen of England. She'd hatch some foolish plot in her mind and then he would suggest she find a new champion to fulfill her dreams of becoming queen. He'd be the noble one...even signing away any royal rights he would have being her husband. If she protested, he would remind her of her confession. Death for murder or life with someone else. She'd leave him so fast, good riddance.

When she would make her proclamation as Queen of England, John and his barons would crush Faith and her new lover with one decisive blow.

But what of the child? He'd be an heir to the throne. Darrin pulled a hand through his hair. How could he keep his child safe? *Blast! Could things get any messier?*

Then there was his pledge to King Richard. He had loved his daughter. The king had always been a fair man to his soldiers and had treated Darrin as a true knight instead of a fugitive. He had given Faith's well-being over to Darrin. Now he planned to dishonor Richard's trust and memory.

Darrin shook his head. How low had he sunk? Yet he could not see another way.

"Are you fearing your nuptials? You look positively ill," Theo stated as he came to Darrin's side.

"Nay, I am fine."

Theo sniffed the air. "The sun is almost set and you smell like a dung heap. Your bride might swoon before she says her vows. And for certain, she won't let you near her smelling like a sweaty ox."

Darrin laughed and slapped his friend's back. "You smell

yourself, you mangy dog. When is the last time you bathed?"

Theo shrugged. "A sennight ago. Maybe longer. Would you like me to dunk my head in yonder well before I show up in the chapel?"

"Who says you are invited to the dismal affair?" Darrin jested as they made their way through the bailey.

Adjusting his sword at his side, Theo gave Darrin a sidelong look. "Oh, you want me there. For I am the only one who will have your back."

So true. Apart from his own men, there probably wasn't a single soul within the keep who was pleased he had returned.

As the skies turned a glowing red and purple, the pair made their way into the great hall, where a warm fire blazed in the hearth. There, sitting on a wooden chair, was a nun of middle age, mending a tunic. Her open smile drew Darrin to her side.

"Come, Theo, there is someone I want you to meet." The knight followed a few steps behind as if he were in battle, watching the enemy.

The nun placed her handiwork on the bench and held out her arms. "Sir Darrin, how wonderful to have you home. It has been too long." She gave him a hug and held on tight for a few moments.

Darrin pulled his friend forward. "Sir Theodore de Born, I would like you to meet Sister Agnus Bernadette Louise Marie Verna.

Theo bowed low.

"We simply call her Nun," Darrin added.

"A perfect name," Theo said politely.

Nun laughed. "Aye. The other is quite a mouthful and every conversation would become all the longer if it was used."

Seeing Nun again produced good memories of Darrin's youth. The moment she had arrived, she became an indispensable member of the keep. Darrin's mother had died suddenly when he was six summers, and instead of hiring someone to take care of him, his father let Darrin run wild about the keep. After he had caused mayhem for two years, Nun arrived with Faith and immediately things began to change. When he wasn't training with his father, Nun used a firm hand to rein Darrin in.

Once in a while, she would speak about her life at the abbey. As a young maid with a quick mind, the sisters of Sainte-Marie des Dames had given her an education. She could read and write, something not all sisters were privileged to do. It was because of her that he had become an educated man.

The good sisters had taught Nun other skills too, which Darrin wasn't fond of at all. Under her instruction, he learned to clean the rushes and scour the pots. Nothing swayed her from making Darrin a well-rounded man. Not even when he protested to his father. Sir Jean de Longue would not intercede. Nun had his full authority. Darrin could also be found sweeping the corners of the keep or serving the evening meal.

Even in the forests of England, her words rang in his ears. *In order to be a fair and good lord, you must also be a good servant to others.* No matter how hard he tried to block them out, those words were etched on his heart and mind forever.

"So tell me, Nun. Did my uncle give you as much leeway as my father did when it came to running the everyday duties?"

Nun's lips thinned and her stance became rigid. Clearly his teasing question was not taken as a laughing matter. "Your uncle took a more traditional role and my duties have been as they should have been all along. Seeing to the welfare of Lady Faith."

Of course. No matter how fair-minded Nun had been in the past, Faith's well-being always came first.

"Well, then, I would say you have done a splendid job," Theo interjected. "For never have I seen a more graceful and lovely woman."

Nun smiled and nodded while Darrin wondered if the dirt in his friend's ears had made its way to his brain.

"She is as kind and generous as she is beautiful," Nun added.

Darrin bristled. Lady Faith might be comely, but she was not kind. She was a viper and a witch. Often in the past, when he tried to sleep in the English forest, he had wondered how a sweet nun could have raised such a harridan.

Darrin grunted and looked about the hall. "Where is Lady Faith? Should you not be assisting her or is she already in the chapel?"

All joy left Nun's face and it was the first time he noticed the fine lines on her forehead. "We were hoping you might change your mind. Perhaps you should wait a few days before proceeding with the marriage? Get reacquainted with Faith again? It has been a long time."

All vestige of decorum fled Darrin's body. "We will be wed this day. In fact, this very moment. Where is Father Chabot?" he bellowed.

The hall grew silent and the priest rose from a trestle table with a slight tremble. "Here, lord."

"Why are you not in the chapel preparing for my nuptials?" Darrin asked in a low voice.

"Do not blame him." Nun looked nonplused, as if time had not changed their circumstances. As if, once again, she controlled Darrin's actions. "I made the decision. It seems ludicrous to rush into something so—"

"These are the last wishes of King Richard. They will be carried out now. Go and inform Lady Faith she will meet me and Father Chabot in the chapel."

For a moment, it seemed as if Nun would defy his order, but then, with a stiff back, she made her way to the stairs. "I shall inform Lady Faith of your wishes, Sir Darrin." The whole sentence came out in a scolding tone.

Aye, Nun had not changed. But he had, and better she understand that now.

"I think you could have handled that a little better," Theo said.

Darrin answered the comment with a cold stare. No one, never again, in his own home, would gainsay him. Without a word, Darrin strode from the hall and into the cooling evening air. No longer were the skies a beautiful pinkish-purple. They were dark with heavy, menacing clouds. A few drops of rain hit his cheeks and a rumble of thunder could be heard in the distance.

Aye, this was a perfect eve to be yoked to a she-devil. A perfect evening indeed.

Four

*And said, for this cause shall a man leave his father
and mother, and shall cleave to his wife:
and they twain shall be one flesh?*
Matthew 19:5

HARD RAIN PELTED THE ROOF AND LOUD THUNDER echoed through the keep and drowned out any sound within. The roaring fire in the great hall hearth had become a few glowing embers. The place seemed deserted since all within had retreated elsewhere, not wanting to upset the new lord.

In the chapel, the light from the sconces cast an eerie glow on the stone walls and the dampness in the windowless room chilled Faith to her toes and she could not stop her shaking.

Earlier Nun had promised to stop this insane marriage, at least for a while. But Faith knew Darrin would not be deterred. It had not surprised her when Nun entered Faith's chamber and informed her of his orders. Quickly she donned a heavy cloak as she had not taken the time to refresh herself.

Now she stood here waiting and wondering how this had all happened. Undoubtedly, Darrin had become bitter and resentful. Yet from young on, his honor had always faithfully guided him. If King Richard said they should marry, then Darrin would fulfill those wishes. Why the king cared if she married anyone, let alone ordered her to marry Darrin, puzzled her. Why would a royal she had no knowledge of ever meeting care about her? Even when he lay dying?

So she waited, with Nun to her left and Father Chabot before her, for Darrin, his lordship, to arrive. Faith wrapped her cold hands in her cloak and hoped he would come before her whole body turned blue, for they had been standing here at least an hour, mayhap more, and her thin slippers were unable to keep the chill away.

Nun proclaimed the whole thing ridiculous and marched over to the chapel door. On the other side, she found a guard refusing to let her pass. "This is nonsense." Nun stamped her foot. "Where is Sir Darrin? How dare he make us wait. Lady Faith may freeze to death."

Faith had to hide her smile. Though it was indeed brisk and the walls were moist, she had never known anyone to freeze in the chapel, especially on a spring eve.

The guard shrugged and quietly closed the door. Nun grumbled, returning to her spot, readjusting the cape on Faith's shoulders. "Are you warm enough, child? Woe to Sir Darrin if you become ill."

"I'm fine. Think on it. How many hours do you kneel in this very chapel?"

Nun frowned. "That is different. I am used to a tougher life. From young on, long before I came to the abbey. Long before you were ever born."

Often Faith had asked about Nun's past, but the woman would always wave off and say her life held no importance except to serve God and the Church. Besides, Nun would never divulge any truths about her life in front of Father Chabot.

So they stood. Silently. Waiting for Darrin.

Faith looked at the stones beneath her feet. One marked the grave of Sir Jean and next to his was the grave stone of Darrin's mother, who died so young. Faith closed her eyes, hoping her fate would not be the same.

Finally the chapel door swung on its hinges and the very man strode to stand next to her without saying a word, his eyes straight ahead. Behind him stood the unkempt knight called Sir Theodore de Born with his hand on the hilt of his sword.

"Let us begin, Father," Darrin barked.

Immediately Father Chabot started the ceremony. When he heard the deep exhale of Darrin's breath, the priest picked up his pace. Before she knew it, all stared at her, waiting for her consent. 'Twas the first time Darrin had deemed to glance her way since he entered the chapel. First she nodded.

"My lady, you must give your consent out loud," the priest said quietly.

Her mouth seemed too dry as Darrin glared at her with cold, impatient eyes. She cleared her throat. "Aye," she squawked.

Within moments, the ceremony was done and he turned and left without another comment.

Father Chabot gave her a sympathetic smile and motioned to the door, which stood open and unattended.

"I should find me a switch and give that boy a whipping," Nun said.

"Shh. He is no longer a child, but lord over us all," Faith replied, putting her hand on the shorter woman's shoulder.

"Mayhap then he should learn how to act like a lord instead of an overbearing villain."

Indeed. Darrin's behavior was quite wanting and their futures were forever tied together. *Please, God, soften Darrin's heart. Make him the man you intend him to be.*

Prepared and groomed, Faith sat by the small hearth in her chamber in a white shift with a warm coverlet draped over her shoulders, waiting for her husband. Nun prattled on, obviously trying to distract Faith from what was to come. Was this her new life? Always waiting for Darrin? Mayhap not. They were both thrown in an unwanted situation. Him more so than her. Once they spoke, perhaps they could come to some understanding. Tonight they would set things right. Then all would be…well.

"Now there is nothing to be afraid of. I am sure Darrin will be tender and gentle. I am sure that you will be able to find the kind lad he once was." Nun poured a goblet of wine and handed it to Faith. "Here. Drink this. It will ease your nerves."

Faith took a small sip and placed the wine on the wooden table next to her. "I am not afraid."

"Nor should you be," Nun said, her eyes full of fear. "Too bad you do not care for each other, because then it could be…" Her gaze drifted off and Faith mused as to what Nun might be thinking about.

Gently Faith reached out and took Nun's hand. "I can endure anything as long as you are near."

The older woman's eyes misted and filled with sadness. A sadness Faith realized had always been there lurking behind a strong resolve. A sadness so deep Nun never spoke of it. Her past must have been awful indeed.

Nun patted Faith's hand. "I have been with you since you were a babe. I'll stay by your side as long as you wish."

Faith started to reach up to hug Nun when the door flew open and banged against the chamber wall. There stood her husband with a heavy odor of wine permeating from his body.

Nun stormed over to stand in front of him. "You come to my lady's chamber like this? Why, you insufferable clod. Go bathe yourself and clear your head."

Sir Darrin towered over Nun. A fierce scowl settled on his face. "Hold your tongue, woman," he shouted.

Faith cringed, but then Nun threw back her shoulders and held her ground.

"I'll not let you touch Lady Faith in your condition."

"What my wife and I do or do not do is none of your affair," he spat out.

His words evidently stymied Nun as she did not snap at him again.

"Now get out of here," he growled. "For I wish to speak to Lady Faith alone."

Nun opened her mouth, ready to fight on.

Faith stood and quickly came to the older woman's side. "It is fine. I wish to speak to my husband in private as well."

No one moved, but slowly some of the rage left Darrin's face and Faith let go of the breath she had been holding.

Nun frowned and glanced at Faith. "I think that is unwise. Are you sure this is what you want?"

"Aye." Faith put a gentle hand on Nun's shoulder. "He will not harm me. Will you?" She looked directly at Darrin, though he did not give comment. Her heart ached. He had become stubborn over the years. "Will you?" she asked again softly.

His frown drew farther south than Nun's, but he gave a curt nod.

Nun looked at him, then at Faith. "I think this is a foolish idea, but if you wish it." She then glared at Darrin. "If you harm one hair on her head, I'll find a large stick and remove the skin from your back."

For a brief moment, the frown on Darrin's face faltered and a hint of a smile shone. Was he remembering how often Nun would threaten so when they were children? He did not answer, but stepped aside.

Nun lifted her head high and walked toward the door. She then turned back and pointed her finger at Darrin. "I'm warning you." With that, she quit the room, leaving the door wide open.

With one hand, Darrin slammed it shut.

But then he did not move. He stood with his hands crossed over his chest, staring at her with his lower lip protruding in a very deep scowl. She couldn't help it—she smiled.

"What are you so happy about?" he asked gruffly.

"Oh, I was just thinking about a time when we were young."

The scowl on his face deepened. "What time?"

She clasped her hands and lowered her head because she could not hide the merriment the thought gave her. "I remember when you were ten summers and I was six and I was picking flowers outside the château wall."

"So what is so amusing about that? You were always picking flowers."

"You came to me with two wooden swords. You demanded I fight you. I had never held one and you were very adamant and impatient. You kept readjusting the sword in my hand. Then you kept banging mine with yours. Over and over you kept hitting my wooden sword. My hands and arms ached from fighting off your attack. Finally, my temper got the best of me. I bashed the sword over your head and punched you in the nose. You had the same look on your face then as you do now." She covered her mouth, fearing she might giggle.

He didn't comment, though his eyes became narrow slits.

"I am sorry. That wasn't a very kind thing to remember."

"Kindness is not one of your strong attributes, my lady."

Of course, anything she said would be met with anger. She had betrayed him. If the situations were reversed, she would probably feel the same way. "You have a right to be upset with me, but let me explain."

He rushed forward until his face was less than a hand from hers. "Upset? I am not upset with you. Let us call it as it is. If I had been permitted, I would have sent you away with Sir Adrien. I loathe you. I despise you. I would rather be married to the whole French army than wed to you."

She put a hand to her chest, fearing a faint at his cruel words. "I had no idea…"

His face twisted into an ugly sneer. "Surely you do? You were always a quick study. So you just said—you knocked me to the ground and humiliated me when I was young. You always knew how to get the upper hand."

"What are you suggesting?" Her right hand began to close in a fist.

"At fourteen summers, you were a young maid, ripe for the plucking. You lied to save your lover, my uncle," he snarled.

She stepped back at his vile words. "No. That is not true. Your suggestion is lewd. Never have I lain with Sir Adrien. Never have I lain with anyone."

Darrin let out a puff of air and rolled his eyes. "Spare me your tales. I do not want to hear more of your lies. Lady, do not think to weave a web around me. I'll not fall into your trap. We may be husband and wife, but that is in name only and for the breeding of children." He reached for the bottom of his tunic and pulled it over his head, revealing his bare chest. "Which we will begin now. I shall be quick and then I shall leave you in peace."

The warmth of a blush traveled over her body. She closed her eyes and turned away. "Please. Can we not talk first? Your rapid actions and coarse thoughts are those of a vile villain."

He grabbed her arm, turning her, forcing her to look at him. He leaned in and the smell of wine on his breath knotted her stomach. "Aye, lady. You are right. For that is what I was until King Richard found me. Living in the forests of England with scoundrels, fiends and the vilest of men. For five years I lived with them as their leader. The chief of sinners."

Oh, poor Darrin. With her free hand, she reached up to gently brush a lock from his forehead. What tortures had he suffered? "I am so sorry. How awful it must have been."

He released her immediately and stepped back. His eyes briefly filled with a deep sorrow, then they turned hard as he set his jaw. "Don't. I'll not fall for your tricks." He sat down on the bed and pulled off one boot.

"Stop. We must speak and pray before we begin in this sacred union."

Darrin put his hands on his thighs and snickered. "Lady, there is nothing holy about this. You read the decree. I need to get you with child within a year's time or I will lose my lands. I promise you, once done, I will leave you alone forever. What you do after you bear the child, I do not care."

"But that is not what God wants. He says a man and woman should become one, forsaking all others. At the least we should pray before our union."

"I do not care what God wants. And I'll not pray. Ever."

His flippant answer took her aback. What had happened to the boy who would follow priests around when they came to visit, begging them to recite scripture? "What has happened to your faith in God?"

Darrin turned his head and glared at her. "It left my body the same day I fled Château du Vent Doux. And it will never return. Never."

An ache bloomed inside her for the pious man long lost and now encased in a hard heart. Oh, how he needed prayers. Her prayers. And as the Lord said without ceasing. She bowed her head. *Dear God, soften Darrin's thick heart.*

"Stop it. I'll not have you pray for me. Stop it this instant and come to bed." Darrin yanked off his other boot, stood and jerked back the bed coverlet.

She shook her head. "Nay. I cannot. Shall not."

"Why?" He put his hands on his hips. "Are you afraid I will hurt you?" He took one hand and motioned to the deep and jagged scars upon his chest. "Or is this not to your appeal?"

Quite the contrary. True, his chest carried several angry war scars, but those did not deter from the pleasing muscular lines. She dropped her gaze to her slippers. "You are not unpleasing to me. That is not the reason."

"Then pray tell, lady. Why would you deny your husband his conjugal rights?"

She lifted her chin and gazed directly at him. "I cannot sleep with a man outside the Christian faith."

He looked at her as if she were a pot of stew gone bad. He then lifted his gaze to the ceiling and shifted his stance as if contemplating every word she said. Finally, he focused on her with his penetrating hazel eyes. "Do you play me for a fool?"

"Nay. I do not. I cannot sleep with an unbeliever even if he is my husband."

He let out a short laugh and shook his head. "You pick a fine time to become a devout Christian, or is that only when it suits you? Does your hatred of me run so deep that you must strip me of my home a second time?"

How could he think such? Truly he did hate her. The ache inside her turned to a sharp stab. "I do not hate you. I want you to keep Château du Vent Doux with all my heart. But I cannot sleep with you. Not as you are. Perhaps if we pray, God's grace will start to soften—"

"I'll not pray," he shouted. "I'll not bend my knees to a God who let my father die and disgraced and discarded me. I stand before you not by God's grace, but by my own will. I stand before you because I have fought to get here. No one but me has done this. And you will not stand in my way of securing what is rightfully mine."

Pain and suffering rippled across his face, ripping her insides into tiny pieces. She desired to take him in her arms and brush away his hatred, but he did not want empathy or sympathy from her. Least of all from her.

"Then you will force me?" she asked quietly.

The room became deathly still. A war of agony and resentment played in his eyes and shuttered through his tortured body. Finally his shoulders slumped. He grabbed his tunic from the bed and put it over his head. "Nay, lady, I'll not force you this eve." He then bent over and picked up his boots and made his way to the door. "But I'll not be denied forever." He turned to leave and called over his shoulder, "And I'll not pray to get what I want."

Five

Thy fierce wrath goeth over me; thy terrors have cut me off.
Psalm 88:16

FOR FOUR DAYS, DARRIN SPENT HIS TIME inspecting every aspect of the château and its grounds. He examined the great hall, the stables, the larder, the buttery, the gatehouse, the battlements, the bailey, the smithy, the armory, the cellar, the storerooms, the crops, the fortress walls, and even the garderobes. He checked all but one of the bed chambers; he did not enter Lady Faith's room since the night of their wedding. Her words constantly rang in his ears. *I cannot sleep with an unbeliever.* He almost said sleeping had nothing to do with it, but that would not help the situation. Nor did the thought of forcing give much appeal. Without being able to resolve the problem, he decided to push it out of his mind for the time being.

Thus he turned his attentions to the château, where everything seemed to be in impeccable condition. Undoubtedly his uncle had planned to live out the rest of his days here. The thought brewed a bitterness inside Darrin. The results could not be denied. Château du Vent Doux was in better condition than when his father had run of the place. Darrin should have sent up a prayer of thanks, but he had not prayed in years and he had no intentions of beginning now. Certainly not now. Not when Lady Faith desired so.

The thought of prayer brought up another area of the castle he had only visited briefly. The chapel. As he remembered, the place had been quite damp and dreary on his wedding day. Just as it had been when he was a boy. Apparently his uncle did not spend a lot of time in prayer either. One thing Darrin and his uncle had in common. But the chapel would serve its purpose to those who wished to use it. Theo had told him that Nun and Faith frequented the chapel daily. How dare she act pious when she was naught but a liar and schemer? *I cannot sleep with an unbeliever.* Bah. More lies and tricks. Nay, she tried to pull him off guard. 'Twas just some diabolical plot. Only this time, he would have the upper hand.

He gave a heavy sigh. Though he had yet to figure out what that upper hand would be. Still there had been rewards. He stood on the battlements and overlooked all that he now possessed. His years of suffering and paying homage to others had been magnificently compensated. All was perfect...almost perfect.

A frown settled on Darrin's face once again as his mind pictured Faith, his wife. Once he knew his future was secured, then he would have his revenge on her. He played the scene again in his mind. He would take his child away from her the moment it was born. Then he would give her the letter from King Richard. No doubt she would squeal with delight over her good fortune and forget all about her child. She would demand that King John should hand over the throne. King John would then strike her down where she stood. A fair death for a fair lady.

Fair. Aye, Faith would catch the eye of any knight. Slender but not overly much. Neither too tall nor too short, but the right size, where a man could hug her properly. Pleasant features, but... Who was he kidding? Her features were striking, even more so than they were ten years ago—when he had noticed she was no longer a child, but a woman. Her chin had the right curve to cup in a man's hand and kiss her plump red lips. Pale hair, which rivaled the heavenly angels, shimmered gold and silver in the sunlight. Though King Richard had claimed that he and Faith had the same eyes, hers shone brighter with a light grey-blue aura. Darrin shook his head. He must be wary, for Lady Faith could steal a man's heart.

A slap of approaching footsteps on the hard stones drew him from his unsettling thoughts. "Good morn to you, Theo." Darrin lifted his face to the warm spring sun. "I believe we are going to have a fine day."

Theo looked up at the sun and grunted. He had been sullen ever since returning from making sure Sir Rollin was indeed tracking Sir Adrien. Theo had hoped to find Sir Rollin derelict in his duty but found no fault. "We have a couple of problems."

"Of course." Darrin sighed heavily. "Out with them."

"Which do you wish to hear first? The problem with the sheep or the problem with Gouch?"

The man's name made Darrin's mind trip backward. When he arrived in England ten years ago, he had nothing but the clothes on his back, and slowly he lost most of those as he sold them for food. In desperation, he went to the forests and started living off as many rabbits, squirrels and other small game as he could snare. Wanting more, he whittled a large stick into a spear. He caught more game, larger game. What he didn't eat, he sold at the local villages. When he had enough coin, he purchased a bow and made most of the arrows. He made a warm cloak from deer skins and bartered other skins for spun tunics, breeches and a pair of good boots. He survived, avoiding the king's men and the many lords who claimed to own the forests and all the game within.

"What's the scoundrel done now?" Darrin asked.

"He got drunk last night and he started chasing the smithy's daughter around the bailey."

In the forest all those years ago, Darrin came across a group of skinny runts who were tied by long ropes and forced to run behind the king's horsemen as common villains. From the looks of their gaunt, dirty faces and bare feet, they probably were caught in search of game to eat. Not thinking clearly, being outnumbered ten to one, Darrin aimed his bow at the king's guard. He struck two before they figured out his position. He took off in a run, not seeing that some of the poachers used the distraction to drag their captors from their horses, choking them with the long ropes.

In his haste to retreat, Darrin stumbled over a large tree root and crashed to the ground. The pursuing horseman dismounted and drew his sword. But the blade never touched Darrin's skin. One of the poachers came up behind the horseman and stabbed him in the back with a stolen dagger.

Gouch saved Darrin's life. Thus began a new friendship and a new way to survive, with others.

Darrin's mind returned to the present. "Please tell me he didn't catch her?"

"Nah, Niles caught up with Gouch and bashed him a good one over the head before he could harm the girl," Theo answered.

"Good. Tell him if it happens again I'll throw him in irons." Darrin folded his arms across his chest, but Theo did not leave.

"It isn't the first time. Seems Gouch has been sniffing around her since our arrival. The smithy is very concerned. He swore if he catches Gouch even looking at her again, he'll take a hammer to him."

Darrin washed a hand over his face. "Send him to me. But before you do so, what is the other problem?"

Theo folded his arms across his chest. "We have a thief."

"Aye, most of the men who came with me from England are thieves." Darrin chuckled.

"This one is stealing your sheep."

Darrin could not see Theo going around counting sheep, so the knowledge had to come from him from a different source. "Who told you this?"

"The shepherd who takes your sheep out to the fields each morn and then brings them back to the pen each eve. He claims two nights ago he counted fifty sheep, but in the morning the gate was open and there were only forty-nine sheep in the pen."

"Only one sheep left the pen?"

"Aye, so the shepherd says." Theo shifted his gaze past Darrin's shoulder to the fields beyond the keep. "He then said the next day the same thing happened. The gate was found opened and another sheep went missing."

"Interesting. Then put a lock on the gate and give the shepherd the key."

Immediately Theo's gaze shot to Darrin's face. "You know as well as I if the gate was truly found open, more than one sheep would have wandered away. The shepherd is the thief and he foolishly thinks you will believe his story that someone else is stealing your sheep."

Darrin smiled. "If we entrust the shepherd with the key and he is the thief, then he cannot steal another without betraying himself. And if it is someone else, then the shepherd will be ever watchful, not wanting the blame to fall his way. In fact, give him the keys to all the pens. The goats, pigs and any other farm animal that needs penning, except the horses. Those shall still be held by the stable master."

"Are you mad?" Theo said. "Those are usually held by the château steward."

"Of which we have none. Or if there was one, he has gone with Sir Adrien. Now, find some locks and keys and give them to the shepherd. His elevated role will ensure his loyalty."

Theo stroked his long, tangled beard. "Aye. No wonder you are a lord. A wise plan."

Wise or not, there was no other idea that came to Darrin's mind. "Now fetch Gouch and then go to the smithy to see if he has any locks with keys."

Theo nodded and left.

Again Darrin's mind tripped back to England and his band of thieves. He taught them to fight and hunt like warriors. They finally settled in the forests, surrounding a keep owned by Sir Hugh de Maury. Being a fair-minded man, Hugh allowed Darrin and his men to hunt freely and steal a chicken once in a while. They became good friends.

More than good—the greatest of friends. He'd still be roaming that forest if Hugh hadn't gotten married. 'Twas then Darrin met King Richard and the bargain had been struck—service in the king's army for return of Château du Vent Doux.

Before Darrin could think more on the past, Theo returned with Gouch. The latter looked down at his boots knowing full well his fate hung in the balance.

"Well. Do you wish to tell me what this is all about?" Darrin demanded.

Gouch looked over his shoulder at Theo. "Can we talk in private?"

It took all of Darrin's strength not to throttle the man where he stood. Instead Darrin took a patient breath and nodded to Theo, who tried to unsuccessfully hide a smirk as he made his way to the battlement steps.

"All right, Gouch. We are alone. What do you have to say for yourself?"

"I-I love her."

Over the years, Darrin had heard many rash comments come out of Gouch's mouth, but this was by far the most foolish. Pure folly. "Love her. You don't even know her."

"I know, but the moment I laid me eyes on Monique I knew I loved her. She's the most beautiful maid I have ever seen."

A vision of Lady Faith crossed Darrin's mind. "Be careful. Beauty sometimes holds the heart of a viper."

"Aw, that's not true when it comes to Monique. Her smile is so sweet and innocent, it just isn't possible for her to have an evil thought."

Darrin shook his head. He hoped Gouch would not suffer because of his infatuation. "It is apparent you are smitten with her, but I have seen you chase after women before."

"This isn't the same."

"And how is that?"

"I want to marry her."

"What?" The man had gone mad. Darrin took a closer

look at Gouch. His body was caked with a thin layer of dirt. A thick beard covered most of his face and he had hair filthier and stringier than Theo's. No one knew for sure what he looked like under all that hair. As a matter of fact, no one had a clue on his age either.

"I swear I'll die if I can't wed her. You have to talk to the smithy for me. Tell him I'm not crazy."

The way Gouch stood there wringing his hands, one could easily believe he was cracked and a mite loose in the head. Darrin put a hand on Gouch's shoulder. "You must admit this is very sudden. Have you even spoken to her?"

"Aye, twice. She has the voice of an angel."

"I see. And what did you talk about?"

"I asked if I could have a drink of water from a jug she was carrying. She said, 'aye,' and I said, 'My thanks.'"

Darrin waited for Gouch to continue, but the grubby man remained mute.

"And?" Darrin encouraged.

"And that was it."

"You two said nothing more?"

"Nay. Not the first time."

"And the second time?"

Gouch smiled, showing his stained teeth. "I lifted a bushel of cloth from a cart for her and she said, 'Many thanks.'" Again Gouch stood there not adding another word.

"No other words?"

"Nay."

"Yet you wish to wed this woman?" Darrin ran a hand through his hair. Never in all the years they had been together had Gouch ever acted so irrational. Not in the years they poached the English forests and not in the five years they fought gruesome battles against the French. Yet within four days of meeting some maid, he acted like a simpering green lad.

Gouch sniffed and wiped his grimy nose. "I just don't know what to do."

As Darrin tried to puzzle out a way to reason with Gouch, a willowy figure came toward them.

Lady Faith.

She stopped right next to Darrin.

Blast!

Not now. She had managed to stay out of his way over the past few days. Had she reconsidered and decided to be a true wife in all respects? Or did she have some other more devious reason?

"Good morn to both of you," she said, giving Gouch a brilliant smile. She then turned her false charm toward Darrin. "May I have a word with you, my lord? 'Tis very important."

How dare she interrupt him. He gritted his teeth. How dare she be so bold. "Lady, it will have to wait. My good man Gouch has a problem that must be tended to this moment." Darrin expected her to mumble an apology and leave, but that did not happen.

"Oh, I am so sorry, Master Gouch. I do hope you can find a quick solution."

Gouch shook his head. "Nay, my lady. No one can help me. My heart will stay broke forever. I see it in Darrin's eyes."

"What is this?" She turned an accusatory gaze on Darrin.

"This is none of your affair," he snapped.

She took a step back but did not leave. Instead she looked to Gouch. "Tell me what ails you?"

Gouch poured out his heart and Faith listened patiently.

"Master Gouch, how old are you?" she asked.

Now Darrin found this to be a very odd thing to ask. What did it matter? No woman would want a man who looked more like a hairy goat regardless of his age.

"Well, let's see." Gouch scratched his head as he contemplated the question.

"My mum always got me mixed up with my brother, Liam. So I am thinking thirty summers or mayhap twenty and eight."

"Well, then, you are of an age where you would want a wife," she said.

Gouch smiled and nodded.

Darrin wanted to strangle her. Why was she giving the man hope?

She clasped her hands behind her and began circling Gouch. "Mayhap if we shave the beard...a bath...and a new set of clothes." She stopped in front of him and then smiled. "Aye. You might be pleasing then. What do you say?"

"Huh? My lady, what do you mean?" Gouch rubbed his long beard.

"I mean let's clean you up. Your maid may like what she sees. Of course, you must use proper manners. You can't go running after her. Engage her in polite conversation."

"I'm not sure how to use polite words. I've been living with Darrin and the others a long time. The only one that ever talked fancy was Darrin and sometimes he spoke just like us."

She turned a stern eye toward Darrin. Did she truly think to accuse him for Gouch's lack of education? What haughtiness was this? She was the one who needed a lesson and he planned it give it forthwith.

But she gave him her back. "I see. Let us not worry on this yet. Let's clean you up first and then mayhap a little instruction on how to speak to a maid."

Gouch beamed. "Oh, aye. Can we do it now?"

"Well, if it is all right with Sir Darrin, then aye, we can begin now."

"You don't care, do you, Darrin?" Gouch asked.

"Sir Darrin," Faith corrected.

Gouch nodded. "Right. Proper talk. Sir Darrin."

An angry heat flooded Darrin's body. She had decisively come between him and one of his men. He should say absolutely not, but he could not dash Gouch's hopes. Even if they did remain slim. "'Tis fine. But remember you do have duties to this keep," Darrin quickly added.

A huge smile split across Gouch's face. "I won't forget. I'll get right on my duties after Lady Faith cleans me up."

Without even looking Darrin's way, Faith folded her hands under her chin. Turned and started walking to the battlement steps. "Then come along, Master Gouch. This may take some time. I'll call for a large hot tub of water and—"

"Water. Hot," Gouch said uneasily as he followed her. "Haven't had a bath in months and never in a tub."

"Lady Faith," Darrin called.

She stopped and turned to face him.

"What is it you wished to see me about?"

She hesitated, a look of uncertainty in her eyes. "Oh, it can wait until later."

With that, she left, followed by Gouch, leaving Darrin flummoxed. She had wanted a word with him and now she simply dismissed what had been so important moments ago. Lady Faith had to be closely watched, for certainly she had something evil brewing in her mind.

Mayhap she thought to sway his men against him. To win their loyalty? She would be disappointed, for never would they give up their allegiance to him. Never. Not one. Not ever.

Six

*But above all things, my brethren, swear not, neither by
the heaven, neither by the earth, neither by any other oath:
but let your yea be yea; and your nay, nay;
lest ye fall into condemnation.*
James 5:12

THE WHOLE PROCESS HAD BEEN QUITE AN ORDEAL. A makeshift drape had been placed in a corner of the bailey where a wooden half barrel had been brought in and filled with buckets of warm water. Faith ordered Gouch to step behind the curtain, strip and get into the tub of water. He protested something fierce, complaining the water would scorch his skin off. But in the end, she won out and he complied. Then she ordered a couple of burly servants to give Gouch a good scrubbing and not to let him out of the barrel until every speck of dirt had been removed.

A painful process to be sure, for Gouch screamed and yelled for the better part of an hour, but when he emerged from behind the curtain, he was still very hairy, but also very clean.

"He looks like a wet mongrel," Nun said, shaking her head.

Faith tapped a finger to her lips. "If we cut his hair and give him a shave…"

"We?"

In desperation, Faith turned a pleading eye to Nun. "Oh, please. You do so well with a blade. Sir Adrien always had such a nice, cleanly shaved face."

Nun snorted. "Took many a prayer to keep me from slitting his throat."

"Nun!"

The sister waved off. "Worry not. I never would have taken the blackheart's life. God's word forbids it—love thine enemy. I kept saying it over and over every time I scraped Sir Adrien's face."

There was no proof one way or the other exactly who had slain Darrin's father. But nonetheless, Nun blamed Sir Adrien. Once she found out why Faith implicated Darrin in the murder, Nun became sullen and reserved toward Sir Adrien. To his credit, he did not send her away or harm her, but vowed to leave Nun be as long as Faith did not change her story about that fateful night.

Yet something was off about that eve. Sir Adrien had been just as shaken when he found out about Lord Jean de Longue's death. It had almost been an afterthought when Sir Adrien pressed Faith to incriminate Darrin. Oh, how she wished she had not seen Darrin arguing earlier that day with his father. They had been at odds for some time, and quarreling had become a regular occurrence between the pair.

Nun elbowed Faith in her side. "Let's get this over with. I'll cut and scrape off the beard. You cut his hair."

Faith nodded, taking a long look at the man before her. One task at a time. Clean Gouch up, then think about that fateful night when she had lost Sir Darrin de Longue's friendship forever.

By late afternoon, Faith and Nun, covered in sweat, stepped back and examined the man before them. To be sure, his face was red and swollen, but Nun was indeed a master with the blade. Not one drop of blood graced his cheeks or chin. A miracle since Gouch had been squirming, shaking and blubbering the whole time. His hair was another problem altogether. No matter how hard Faith tried to cut and shape it, Gouch still looked a little shaggy. Mayhap when he calmed down she could coax him into letting her finish the task. Nevertheless, he was by far a much more presentable man.

"Why, would you look at that? His eyes are a babe's blue," Nun commented.

Indeed they were as blue as the sky above them and his hair was not brown at all, but a warm wheat color with shiny specks of red woven throughout. "Why he looks like—"

"A boy of sixteen summers at the most."

Faith would not have made him quite that young, but certainly not the twenty and eight he claimed to be. "Master Gouch, are you sure of your age?"

"Aye, my lady. I had three younger brothers and one younger sister and they all knew how old they were. Liam and I were in the middle. Agatha, Bronwyn, and Johnathan were older than us. I left home because Mum was having another. We were always starving. Figured I could hunt and get food for meself and bring some back for the family. Only, when I returned a few months later, there was nothing there but a burnt-out shell. The plague had come through and might have taken the lot of them." He shrugged. "Guess I'll never know for sure." His cheeks sagged and a darkness clouded his eyes. At that moment, twenty and eight did seem possible.

"I am so sorry, Master Gouch. It is hard losing loved ones."

He dropped his head. "Aye. Hard not having anybody that loves you."

A deep, cold ache settled in the middle of Faith's chest. She understood his words like no other. How often had she wondered about her parents? Her mother died giving birth to her and no one seemed to know anything about her father. Nun said King Richard knew him, but nothing else. When she came to Château du Vent Doux, she thought for sure Lord Jean de Longue was her father. But quickly it became apparent he was not, for he showed little interest in her, and more than once, she suspected he thought of her as a burden.

Tears stung the corners of Faith's eyes. "Well, if all goes as planned, mayhap you will have a new family someday."

The brightness returned to Gouch's face, casting a boyish glow. "Oh, aye, I yearn for Monique something fierce."

Nun frowned and cleared her throat in a most disapproving way. "You will not chase that girl around the bailey anymore. You will hold yourself in a Christian manner."

He dropped his chin again. "Aye, Sister. I'll not force her to do anything. I swear."

"Swearing is a sin," Nun countered.

Gouch scratched his head. "Huh? I wound up in France because Darrin...I mean Sir Darrin swore an oath to King Richard."

A heavy huff left Nun's lips. "Oh, that is different." She then turned to Faith. "Do not ask me to help you educate this one."

Though Nun said her words sternly, Faith knew the older woman couldn't wait for the lessons to begin. "Please, Nun. You are so experienced in doing such things."

Nun harrumphed again, rolling her eyes and folding her arms across her chest. "Oh, all right, if you insist."

Working very hard to hide her knowing smile, Faith focused her attention back on Gouch. "Now for starts, you should work on formally addressing those around you. Mayhap when you see..."

"Monique," Gouch offered.

"Monique. You can call her Mistress Monique. Do give it a try," Faith said.

"What the blazes did you do to him?" The loud voice came from behind her followed by an even louder guffaw. "Wait until Darrin sees this."

Poor Gouch flushed and his red face almost became purple, causing his tormentor more jocularity.

Faith turned to see another hairy goat, Sir Theodore. "Mayhap you would like to be next? What, pray tell, would we find? Perhaps a face like an angel?"

The hilarity instantly fled. He cocked a brow. "No, my lady. You'll find no angel here."

His suggestive tone sent a heat to her cheeks and drew a gasp from Nun.

The sister stormed right up in front of Sir Theodore, an amazing feat since Nun was half Sir Theodore's size. No doubt he could crush her with one blow if he desired. "If you weren't full grown, I'd cut me a stick and throttle you a good one. How dare you say such a thing to Lady Faith?"

The smirk on Sir Theodore's face quickly disappeared. "I mean no disrespect. I am just stating a truth. I am no saint. I left all my good qualities in England."

"And why is that?" Faith asked.

A darkness settled over him. "My lady, you are not my priest."

Nun huffed again.

Faith came to Nun's side and placed a hand on her arm, staying any flow of words that would fuel the situation. If nothing else, he had a sharp mind and his personal life was his own. "Forgive me for prying."

He gave a curt bow and then strode over to where Gouch stood. Sir Theodore paused and ran a hand through his straggly beard. "It is lucky we aren't going into battle. You wouldn't last longer than wind out of my arse. You look more of a babe than Sir Rollin."

Gouch straightened his shoulders and started rolling up the sleeves of his tunic. "I can still fight. Would you care to see?" Sir Theodore spit into his hands, rubbed them together and formed them into fists. The pair began to circle one another.

Without thought, Faith ran between them and Sir Theodore's right fist connected with her jaw. Her head snapped back; the world slowed. Shouts echoed and slid away as her mind began to swim and her vision blurred into darkness.

Screams and cries of anguish greeted Darrin as he descended the battlement steps and entered the bailey. He broke out into a run when he saw Faith lying on the ground with Theo and Nun bending over her.

"You may have broken her jaw, you brute," Nun yelled.

"I-I didn't mean to. She stepped in the way." Theo scraped his fingers through his hair.

Darrin pushed the pair out of the way and knelt down next to Faith. A large red mark marred the left side of her face and something inside him shifted. A bombardment of rage tore through him as he settled his anger in Theo's direction. "What happened here?"

"I was teasing Gouch 'cause with no beard he looks like a smooth babe. We were just going have a fine fight when Lady Faith stepped in the middle. I didn't mean to hit her. Is she going to be all right? Tell me I didn't break anything."

Putting one arm around her shoulders, Darrin raised Lady Faith and slowly began to work her jaw. A moan escaped her lips, but the jaw seemed to be intact. For certain, she would have a fine bruise and might find it a tad hard to eat for a while. But still he wanted her examined.

"Get the barber," Darrin ordered.

Nun pushed in. "I'll see to her. I don't want that butcher touching her. He'd probably put a slice in her cheek, trying to bleed her. That's his answer to every aliment or wound. Bleed them."

As much as Darrin did not care for Faith, he did not want to see her disfigured. She moaned again and her glassy eyes fluttered open. Gently, Darrin put a finger to her moist lips. He bent forward and the soft scent of spring flowers tickled his senses. He briefly wondered how she managed to always smell like a field of flowers before he remembered his place. "Shh. Fear not. All will be fine." He turned his gaze on a few gaping servants. "Take Lady Faith to her chamber. Sister Agnus Bernadette Louise Marie Verna will take care of her."

With the use of Nun's full name, the years of separation were swept away and her head dipped in a moment of recognition to a time when they had seen eye to eye on many matters—when his father ruled this château and Darrin was a dutiful son. Quickly she turned her attention back to Faith and began to order the servants to be careful as they took her up the great hall steps.

When Lady Faith, Nun, and the servants disappeared into the hall, Darrin swept his gaze to Theo and Gouch. "Walk with me."

The trio left the keep without a word. They passed the village, the crops, and went into the forest beyond. Darrin kept his pace until he was certain they were alone. Then he turned on the pair. "What the devil happened?"

Gouch turned pure white, which was a novelty since Darrin had never been able to see anything on the man's face in the past.

"'Tis his fault," he said, pointing to Theo. "He kept pushing, making fun 'cause Lady Faith cleaned me up."

Darrin could not fault Theo there. For Gouch did look more like a milkmaid than a warrior. However, punching Faith in the face could not go unpunished. "Well, Theo, what shall we do about this?"

The knight hung his head. "I've made a muck of things. I think I should leave after I give my apologies to Lady Faith."

"Leave?" Darrin folded his arms and shook his head. "Oh, nay. You'll not leave. Not when I have my uncle sneaking about and not when I have no foreknowledge as to what King John thinks of Richard's decree. Nay, Theo, I need you here. I have another idea."

A wary look entered Theo's eye. "I see no other."

"There is." Darrin smiled; a brilliant plan forming in his mind. "You will be Lady Faith's favored knight. You will be at her call at all hours, day and night. If there is something she wishes to be done, you will do it. You will protect her and honor her. Unless I call for you or need your sword, your duty will be to Lady Faith. Do you understand?"

"Truly you cannot mean this? What do I know of what a lady wants and needs?"

Darrin held up a hand. "You helped Lady Eleanor build her chapel back at Thornwood Keep. You were quite dutiful back then."

A hardness settled in Theo's eyes at the mention of the woman he once fancied to wed. "This is not the same and you know it. Lady Faith is your wife, not mine."

The harsh tone in Theo's voice did not deter Darrin from the plan. Theo would keep an eye on Faith, and if she showed any signs of treachery, Theo, being the loyal sort, would immediately report her actions. "I need you to keep an eye on her. You and no other."

"I be thinking," Gouch broke in. "Why not give me that task? After all, she's going to be teaching me how to act proper. I think I should be the one to look after the lady. Would be an honor to me."

His ire up, Darrin shifted his gaze. "You may think Lady Faith will be in charge of your 'proper education,' but that will quickly change. Nun will be rapping your knuckles with a stick every time you make a wrong move. Besides, what makes you think I'll let this farce continue?"

"Aw, Darrin, I got to have Monique as me wife. I swear, if she'll have me, I'll stay stand by your side forever." Gouch folded his hands like a penitent child.

Darrin wanted to point out that Gouch had said those same words when they left England, but it served no purpose. He was not a knight, only a humble man who could handle an ax like none other. Words of honor and loyalty meant nothing to him and that was precisely why he could not be trusted to keep watch of Faith's actions.

"This is what I am offering. You will do your duties to this keep, and in exchange you will have a small measure of time each afternoon for your education—no more and no less. Is that understood?" Darrin folded his arms across his chest signaling this discussion had ended.

He then turned his gaze on Theo. "And you will be Lady Faith's champion."

Theo folded his own arms across his chest. "She may not want me around."

"And why not?" Darrin asked.

"I don't smell like a flower garden."

Darrin paused. Had Theo, too, noticed that Lady Faith always smelled like bouquet of flowers? Mayhap Theo's heart had not turned to stone as everyone suspected when Lady Eleanor rejected his affections. Whatever the reason, Theo was trustworthy.

Darrin turned his back on them and started to walk toward the edge of the forest. "Take a true bath or not. But you will do as I asked, for you have sworn your allegiance to me until our new king sees fit to take you away."

Theo grumbled beneath his breath but did not say another word, for he knew Darrin spoke the truth.

Seven

*For God is not unrighteous to forget your work and
labour of love, which ye shewed toward his name,
in that ye have ministered to the saints, and do minister.*
Hebrews 6:10

DARRIN MADE HIS WAY BACK TO THE KEEP; HE HAD one more task to complete before he could return to the workings of the château. He must check on Lady Faith's welfare. Not that he wanted to, but not to do so would set tongues wagging across the countryside. It would be prudent if outwardly they seemed to be a tolerable couple. Any friction could easily embolden one of the servants to report the strife to his uncle or King John. He needed time to win the hearts of the people. It would have been easy if the keep had been run-down, but alas his uncle had been a good manager. Darrin couldn't blame the people for being suspicious of him.

A quiet somber held the great hall when he entered. A few servants had lines of concern etched on their faces while others wept in the corners. Some lifted pleading eyes toward him and the bolder ones glared with contempt, clearly blaming him for what had happened to Lady Faith. Darrin ignored them all and headed for the tower stairs. To his surprise, the door to Faith's chamber stood open. Faith lay still on her pallet with a rolled coverlet beneath her feet. Nun stood sentinel, wearing a deep scowl.

Quietly he stepped into the room and toward the bed.

Faith's eyes were closed, her breathing shallow. "Will she be all right?" he whispered to Nun.

"Aye. She's a tough one. Has to be. Always fighting with you when you were a lad." Nun brushed a few strands of hair off of Faith's cheek. "And even more so after you left."

For a moment, Darrin puzzled over her words, but then Faith's eyes fluttered open and his attention changed.

"My lord?" Faith said to him as if his presence were a shock.

"My lady," he answered. "How is the jaw?"

She moved it slightly and then tenderly placed a hand on the red skin. "I fear on the morrow I will have a terrible bruise."

He smiled at her blunt assessment. "Aye. You will and a beautiful one it shall be. I am sorry that Sir Theodore did not have more control."

Her head gave a tiny shake. "Do not blame him, for 'tis I who tried to stop the fight. I should have known better."

"Aye, you should have," Nun piped in.

Her intent listening put Darrin on edge. Though Nun had never been a gossip, he did not know if he could trust her. "Please leave us for a few moments," he said calmly.

Unlike the last time he stood in this room, Nun did not try to stay. She just nodded and left, surprisingly closing the door softly behind her.

Faith put a hand to her brow. "My head hurts something fierce, but I do not want to worry Nun."

"Mayhap you should. As I remember, Nun is a skilled apothecary."

"Aye. Yet she has done little in that area over the last ten years."

He could not believe this. In the past, Nun would spend every free moment concocting some healing potion. "I do not understand. All here should know she has more skill than any barber. What happened to change this?"

When Faith did not answer, Darrin tried to seek out the reason in her gaze. She looked away. Did her head hurt too much to speak or did she not want to tell him?

"Faith," he said gently. "Why did she give up her work in apothecary?"

"You will not believe me."

Her words astonished him. True, he thought of her as a liar, but wondering why Nun gave up something she loved to do was a simple question that begged a simple answer. "Give me the truth and I will believe you."

Faith sighed and placed a hand on her forehead again. "Sir Adrien accused Nun of witchery when he witnessed her helping a man who was injured. He claimed only men could practice the art of healing."

Had his ears deceived him? Darrin sunk down on the foot of the pallet. "He accused one of God's brides of being a witch?"

Faith nodded and grimaced.

"Then why is she not dead?"

"He did not do so publicly. In private he told her to stop or he would burn her before my eyes."

This had to be a lie. Nun never would reveal such a thing to Faith even if it were true. Darrin narrowed his eyes. "Nun told you this?"

"Nay, Sir Adrien."

That could be true. Still he wondered.

The little color she had drained from her face. Darrin edged closer, worried. "Think not more on this." Cautiously he moved until he sat next to her. He raised a few fingers to her temples, lightly brushing back a pale golden curl.

He could see the tension within her ease. She closed her eyes and nestled closer. Her warm body, natural next to his own.

"Mmm...you're right. It is gone from my mind already. I'm safe now."

He paused. What did she mean? Safe from his uncle or safe...with him? Was she playing him false again? His questions scrambled around in his mind. While her anxiety seemed to have fled, his grew and rested between his shoulder blades. *Nonsense. All of it!* Clearing his throat, he stood. Immediately her eyes flew open, filled with questions.

"I will get Nun. I am sure she will have something for your headache."

She did not say a word, but her quizzical gaze followed him to the doorway. Faith was not the only one with questions, for he, too, needed answers, which she would give when she was well again.

Darrin left the grey moodiness that hovered over the keep and walked to the small hamlet that rested near Château du Vent Doux. Dressed in a drab tunic and wearing a brown cap, he hoped most within the village would not give him a second glance. For ten years, no one paid him much heed. Now, ugly glares and stares followed him everywhere and tore at his nerves like a whip tearing tender skin.

In the village, he saw a man struggling with a two-wheel pull cart laden with sacks of grain. A jagged dirt rut held the cart fast. No matter how hard the old man tried to pull or push, the cart would not move. Others walked by him without lending a hand or casting a glance his way. 'Twas as if the man were invisible. Mayhap they knew that even if he did manage to get the cart out, his feeble and weak body would never be able to pull the heavy burden down the dirt road.

"You need an ox or five burly men if you wish to move that cart," Darrin said as he came to the old man's side.

"Mayhap, but I have neither." The old man's clear, almost colorless eyes scanned Darrin's face. "I have only you."

The boldness of the elder's words brought a smile to Darrin's face. "Aye, old man. You have me. Mayhap we should remove these sacks and then try."

"Nay. It has taken me the better part of the day to load it."

Seeing the man's gnarled hands and wrinkled skin,

hanging from muscle-less arms, Darrin did not doubt the aged man's words. "If we do not empty the cart, then we must have help."

The old man reached out and touched Darrin by the shoulder. "Let us give it a try before you seek others."

Such foolishness to be sure, but the old man had such hope in his fathomless eyes, Darrin could not deny him. "All right. I shall push on the back while you pull from the front."

The old man nodded, hobbled to the front and picked up the poles of the cart with surprisingly little effort. Darrin bent his knees and dug in his shoulder.

"Now when I tell you, start to pull," Darrin shouted from the back of the cart. "Pull." With as much strength as he could muster, Darrin gave the cart a mighty push, but nothing happened. 'Twas futile.

"Try once again," the old man called. "I think it moved."

Nay, it did not, but the hopefulness in the old man's voice made Darrin willing to try again. "Once more then. Call when you are ready."

The grey head nodded once again. "Push."

Giving all his might, Darrin pushed until his arms shook and the muscles in his thighs all but screamed at the exertion. The cart rolled forward a little and then settled back in the rut. "'Tis useless. Let me seek help."

Not letting go of the cart handles, the old man shook his head. "Nay. Third time will do it. All good things come in threes."

His heart pounding, Darrin laid a hand on the back of the cart, taking labored breaths. "They do? Name such goodness that comes in threes."

"The Father, the Son and the Holy Ghost."

Now Darrin knew the man was daft and this was probably why others steered away from him in his time of toil. Though most believed in God, not many, if any, ever saw the Almighty come to one's aid in times of trouble. Nonetheless, Darrin lowered his shoulder to the cart again.

"You might try lifting it," the old man said.

Right. Lift it. The man's head was like one of these sacks—filled with grain and naught else. Darrin moved to the side of the cart. "Let me call for help."

Vehemently, the old man shook his head. "No. The power of God is all we need. You'll see. One more time."

Lunacy. Darrin's goodwill had thrown him in the hands of a demented old man. "Once more and then we will seek help or you will sit here alone with your cart."

"Fine. Fine. You'll see. Remember to lift this time."

Aye. Lift. Darrin grabbed the back part of the cart. "I'll need the strength of Samson in order to raise this broken-down heap," he mumbled.

"Did you say something?" the old man called from the front.

"Give the word," Darrin snapped.

"Lift," the man shouted.

Darrin bent his knees, digging his fingernails and the palms of his hands underneath the bed of the cart, and tried to lift. The muscles in his shoulders burned. His arms ached at the strain. Beads of perspiration formed on his forehead and dripped down his face and seeped between his clenched teeth. He closed his eyes and focused on the old man's laughable words—the strength of the Father, the Son and the Holy Ghost.

Just when he had had enough, the weight lightened and it was as if he had the might of ten men. The cart all but floated out of the ditch.

"See? In threes," the old man said as he dropped the handles and came around to the back of the cart, looking at least twenty years younger than he had before. "There, now, that wasn't so bad."

Darrin sat on the ground, huffing and puffing. "Speak for yourself. Exactly what do you have in those bags? Rocks?"

The elder man laughed. "No. Not at all. Just grain and other goods needed by your cook. Will you walk with me to the château?"

Even though the man did look a mite younger, he still had

the thin, spindly arms and legs of an aged man. Wheeling the cart up a steady incline seemed almost impossible alone. "Is the Almighty going to help you maneuver up the hill?"

Cocking his head to the side, the man gave Darrin a speculative look. "He may. If He wishes, or He might want you to help."

This man should have been born a noble, for he was clever as well as entertaining. If he had property and knights of his own, he probably could outwit the kings of France and England. Mayhap even the pope.

With a grunt, Darrin made his way to the front of the cart. "You should have picked a barrel-chested man. But I shall help if you tell me your name."

The old man said nothing, but scampered to take up one of the cart handles.

"You do have a name, don't you?" Darrin asked when the man did not answer.

A seriousness settled on the man's face. "I have many names. Call me what you wish."

This man must have been a villain of some sort, otherwise he would have disclosed his name. Darrin's own past had been riddled with indiscretions, so he could not fault the elder for his disagreeable actions. "Very well, I shall call you Innocent after the pope."

The old man furrowed his brow. "That I have never been called. Nor is it all that pleasant."

Darrin lifted his cart pole. "Nonetheless, you shall be called Innocent as I think you may be far more intelligent than our present spiritual leader."

The newly proclaimed Innocent nodded. "I will not argue with you there."

Darrin chuckled. "Careful, Innocent. Others may not have the same high opinion of you as me."

A melancholy settled on the man's face. "Aye, more than you know."

Darrin looked to the western sun. Though he wondered what caused this man to look like he held the world's burdens, now was not the time to ponder. "Come let us be off. The cart is heavy and the day is short."

"Nay. With good conversation, I believe we shall make it to the keep before the sun hits the yonder trees."

Darrin surmised the sun would set behind the western trees long before they entered the portcullis of the château. But far be it from him to dampen the man's spirits. He tightened his grip on the other pole handle and they began to slowly haul the cart to the keep.

They had not gone far when the old man began to hum a tune Darrin was not familiar with, but that seemed cheerful enough. "What is that song?"

The old man paused and smiled. "It is a mighty tune, is it not? Yet you will not hear it at any court throughout the world."

"And why is that?" Darrin asked.

"Because it has not been written yet."

The clanking of the wheels on the creaky cart must have impaired Darrin's hearing. "Say again?"

"The song has not been written," Innocent answered.

"Are you a musician, composing the music in your head as we work? I have heard of others doing such things."

Innocent smiled. "I am an artist of sorts. I have created many things, but mostly I inspire others. Someone else will complete this tune."

His words were foolish. Age must be warping Innocent's mind. A sadness settled in Darrin's soul. Mayhap he truly didn't remember his own name. Whatever the circumstance, Darrin was determined this man's last days would be spent leisurely in Château du Vent Doux.

"Ah, I can see you do not believe me. You think I am daft in the head. But it will be heard many centuries from now. They shall call it 'The Hallelujah.'"

Did he jest or was he being sly? Darrin could not be sure, but the heaviness that rested on his chest moments ago disappeared. He laughed. "Whatever you say, Innocent. Whatever you say."

They made steady progress toward the keep and did, indeed, make it to the portcullis before the sun drifted behind the trees. Darrin helped the man move the cart near the kitchen wall. Once in place, Innocent leaned against the cart. His face hung with deep, tired lines and his chest heaved with exhaustion. "Good. It is done."

"Wait here. I'll get you some water," Darrin said.

The man reached out, placing a hand on Darrin's arm. "I am fine. We still must discuss your problems."

"Problems?" Darrin's defenses arose. He shrugged in a carefree way. "I have no more problems than any other peasant."

Innocent's gaze did not waver. "But you are not a peasant. You are lord of this keep. You worry about the loyalty within these walls. How to win the people's affections. And the affections of your wife."

So the old man did know Darrin's identity and he knew about his troubles with Faith. Was Faith bragging to the servants about how she denied him? Could she be that low? A stiffness swept up his back. Aye, she would.

He turned a sharp eye on the man. "Many lords have these worries."

"Hmm. Have all lords been accused of murder and have taken over a well-run keep from a respected lord?"

Darrin gritted his teeth. "Just who are you?"

"You dubbed me Innocent. So that is who I am."

"Are you friend or foe? Tell me plainly, for I am tired of these games."

"I wish to be your friend and so much more, but your heart is hard. I wish to help you if you would let me."

"How can an old man help me? What power do you possess that could gain me the allegiance of the people within these walls and my wife's affections?" Darrin turned away, casting his gaze to the servants running to and fro across the bailey, busy at their appointed tasks. "None here will ever care a fig for me."

"Mayhap not if you sit here moping. But if you do for them what you did for me, then they will honor you always."

A bitter laugh hung in Darrin's throat. "And what did I do for you?"

"This cart would still be in stuck in the rut back in the village if it had not been for you. Look about, surely you see how hard all here toil. Help them as you have helped me and then you will have their hearts."

As if his eyes were new, Darrin noticed that one servant struggled with carrying a large bushel heaped with laundry while a young squire dragged heavy axes and swords in his arms. Perhaps the old man did have a worthy idea.

"And as for your lady…"

Darrin's gaze shifted back to Innocent. "I need not your assistance there."

The elder chuckled. "Oh, but you do. You just don't realize it yet. No matter. I will take that water now."

Ignoring Innocent's claim, Darrin made his way to the well in the center of the bailey. He grabbed a small bucket and filled it with water. Before he could make his way back to the old man, Theo waylaid him.

"My lord, I beg you to reconsider. Surely I could serve you better by remaining at your side."

The formal greeting was not lost on Darrin. Theo meant to have his way. "I have not changed my mind. I need you to watch Lady Faith's every move. This is important. Do not ask me to relent again."

Theo lowered his chin. "A terrible thing not to be able to trust your own wife. I'm certain in time she will warm up to you."

"I do not care if she warms up to me or not. I want to be informed of any plan she hatches in her head."

"All right. But once you get her breeding, I am sure she will settle down."

Theo's words made Darrin's insides coil. If Faith's demeanor did not change, then there would be no child. Mayhap the old man did have an answer for his predicament.

Shifting the pail to his other hand, Darrin touched Theo's shoulder. "Come. There is someone I want you to meet."

But when they returned to the cart, the old man was nowhere to be found. Darrin scanned the bailey.

"What are you looking for?" Theo asked.

"The old man. I helped him with this cart. I left him here."

Theo raised a brow. "Darrin, I think you need to rest a mite. For I saw you come into the keep. Alone. In truth, I wondered why you were doing servants' work."

Shaking his head, Darrin chuckled. "You jest." But his friend's face remained serious. "Why would I bring a cart full of grain alone?"

"Aye. Why?" Theo's intense stare spoke volumes.

"I am not daft. There was an old man."

"Boy, come here," Theo called to a young lad who sat on top of a rail fence.

The boy jumped down and came to Theo's side. "Sir?"

"Did you see, Sir Darrin enter the château?"

"Aye, sir." The boy lifted a thumb over his left shoulder. "He was pulling that cart over there."

"And did you see anyone with him?"

Now the lad looked at Theo as if he had received a swift kick in the head. "No, sir. He was alone."

Theo took a coin from his belt and handed it to the boy. "Many thanks."

The lad grabbed the coin and took off without giving either of them a second glance.

Theo pursued his lips. "Well?'

"I swear to you, the man was real."

His friend remained silent. Darrin rubbed his eyes. Could he have imagined the whole thing? Impossible. Yet the boy and Theo stated otherwise. Mayhap he had eaten something that spoiled his stomach and twisted his mind...or he truly was going mad.

Eight

A virtuous woman is a crown to her husband:
but she that maketh ashamed is as rottenness in his bones.
Proverbs 12:4

THERE WAS NO DENYING IT, SHE WAS BEING followed. Faith stepped back up the tower stairs and hid in the shadows when she saw Sir Theodore sitting by one of the trestle tables with a mug of mead in hand. Here he sat, instead of being out on the practice fields with the other knights. At first she thought mayhap he was ill, but quickly negated the idea when he seemed to always be in her view. He followed her to the kitchen, to the brew house, to the livestock pens, to the village and even stood on the edges of her small flower garden. Everywhere she turned, Sir Theodore stood a few steps behind her. It did not take the mind of a scholar to figure out why he was watching her.

With a heavy sigh, she squared her shoulders and stepped out of the shadows. Instantly, Sir Theodore straightened in his seat, his gaze attentively on her. She could ignore him and break her fast as she had done the last couple of days or she could take care of the situation at hand. She chose the latter.

Marching up to where he sat, Faith settled down on the bench across from him. "Tell Sir Darrin that I do not need one of his knights to watch over me."

He put down his mug without taking a drink. "My lady, I am not here for your protection. However, I am sorry for what happened in the bailey. I did not mean to hit you."

Of course. How foolish of her to think otherwise. The man's presence had nothing to do with her safety and everything to do with his guilt. "Please, Sir Theodore. What happened was my fault. I should have let you and Master Gouch pummel one another. Though I will never understand the joy men find in fighting. Your apology is accepted. Now do go about your regular duties."

Sir Theodore fidgeted in his seat as a look of pure dread crossed his face. "That is not why I am...here."

Ah, of course he was not here by his own accord. He did his lord's bidding. "So I must surmise that if I try to contact Sir Adrien de Gascon, you will immediately report the folly to Sir Darrin."

A small smile tugged at the corner of his lips, but he did not confirm or deny her words.

"Well, then, you can report to Sir Darrin that *a wife* owes her faithfulness to her husband."

Sir Theodore picked up his mug and took a long pull of the liquid. A heavy, satisfying sigh left his lips afterward. "Now that is some fine mead. I would thank the brewer, but methinks it is your hand that makes this draught so good."

"Ah, if you believe so, then you must admit to following me?"

"Aye, lady. And in that short time, I have learned much." He smiled and took another healthy swig of his drink.

She stilled. What could he have learned that would be of such great value to Sir Darrin?

As if reading her mind, he continued, "It is you who oversees the making of meals each day. It is you who examines the crops that the peasants have planted. It is you who tells the mead maker how much honey and yeast to add to the drink. This château runs smoothly because of you."

"And you are surprised by this?" She waved a hand. "Who else would?"

"A steward who would take orders from the lord of this keep. In the past, that would have been Sir Adrien."

She wanted to laugh, but Sir Theodore's face remained

void of any mirth. "Sir Adrien spent his days like most men, honing the art of war and hatching who-knows-what in his mind."

Sir Theodore looked at the empty mug and frowned. "Sir Darrin would be happy to learn so. For he has fretted much over this matter."

"What? That Sir Adrien did not care about the workings of the keep? How would this ease my husband's mind?"

He tore his gaze from his mug to look directly at her. "He worried that he could not be as capable a lord as Sir Adrien. Now I can tell him not to agonize over this anymore. 'Tis his wife who the people respect and work for, not Lord de Gascon. Though that may be a bigger problem."

The man talked in riddles. "I do not understand. Why can you not speak plainly?"

He leaned over the table and peered deep into her eyes. "Lady, Sir Darrin does not know for sure if your actions will match your words. And if they do not, then he has a problem indeed."

The statement Sir Theodore referred to bounced around in her mind—*a wife owes her faithfulness to her husband.* "I will not undermine Sir Darrin's authority." The moment the words left her lips, Faith remembered her wedding night when she refused Darrin's affections. A blush quickly heated her skin and was just as quickly misinterpreted.

"If you lie to me, lady…"

She shook her head. "I do not lie. I am glad Sir Adrien is gone."

Sir Theodore's gaze did not waver from hers, as if he were weighing and measuring each of her words. "I believe you," he finally said. "But I am not the one who needs to be convinced, and until you change *your husband's* mind, I will be your companion. And just between you and me, I hope you can convince Sir Darrin quickly. For I do not care for being a lady's maid."

A servant brought Faith a bowl of pottage with hard crust bread on the side. The steamy, thick soup full of vegetables made Faith's mouth water. She picked up a piece of bread and dunked an edge into the soup. "I think I have an idea that may rest Sir Darrin's mind as to my loyalties." Faith popped the bread in her mouth and began to chew.

"Speak, lady, for I am all ears." Sir Theodore's disposition brightened substantially.

She swallowed and looked to repeat the action, but then paused. "It is true I denounced Sir Darrin to the magistrate all those years ago, but Sir Adrien forced me to do so."

"So then Darrin is right. Lord de Gascon did kill his father," he said, taking another swallow of mead.

Faith put the bread down on the table next to her bowl. "I am not sure. I fear that Sir Jean was murdered by another's hand."

"Do you have a thought who that might be?"

"Nay. I cannot say, but I think Sir Jean suspected something was going to happen. The week before his death, he doubled the guard at the gate and had servants check every chamber of the keep before we retired. I cannot say what caused him to act so, but I do know where we may find some answers. Sir Jean was a learned man and scribbled daily on parchment, which he kept in a leather pouch. Every night he locked his writings in a wooden chest."

Sir Theodore placed his mug on the table. The keenness in his hazel eyes became intense. "Where is this chest?"

"In the lower cells, underneath the keep."

He picked up his mug and tapped it against her bowl of pottage. "Eat up, my lady. For we have some hard work ahead of us." He winked.

Her appetite rapidly returning, Faith picked up the hard bread and dipped it in the heavy soup once again. Mayhap, finally, after all these years, the truth would be exposed. A slight chill skidded down her spine. She prayed the answers would exonerate Sir Darrin. For if they did not, then she was yoked to a murderer who could strike again at any time.

On the same morn, Sir Rollin finally returned to the château. Though he and his men were dusty and tired, Darrin held no pity. He expected the knight back days ago and feared Sir Rollin had returned to King John to pledge his allegiance and denounce Darrin's right to Château du Vent Doux.

With crossed arms, Darrin greeted Sir Rollin in the bailey. "Where have you been? I told you to escort Sir Adrien to the river, not to the French court."

Slowly, Sir Rollin dismounted and casually brushed back his chain mail hood. He then turned a sharp eye on Darrin, letting him know even though he might be lord of the château, he was not lord over Sir Rollin de Tosny. "We did. But then I thought it would be prudent to secretly follow to find out in which direction Sir Adrien would go—to King John or King Phillip."

No fault could found for the knight's decision. No wonder King Richard had taken Sir Rollin into his inner circles. The man was quick in the mind as well as quick with the sword. "So what did you discover?" Darrin asked.

"He went toward the French. King Richard was right, Sir Adrien is no friend of England's."

Darrin nodded but still was not satisfied. He followed Sir Rollin and his men to the stables. "Such a discovery should have taken two days at the most. Where have you been the other three?"

A tight grip seemed to take hold of Sir Rollin's mouth. "On our return, we were greeted by a messenger of King John's."

With great control, Darrin resisted the urge to swipe a hand across the back of his neck. He had feared the new king would not let matters rest at Château du Vent Doux. Though he was now the King of England, John had once been an ally of France. Mayhap he wished to seek peace with them now. To show good faith, he might return the château to Sir Adrien. If this was true, then Darrin planned to fight King John to the death instead of becoming an outlaw again.

"And where is this messenger now?" Darrin snapped.

Sir Rollin raised a brow before passing his mount off to a stable boy. Nonchalantly, he pulled a missive out of his tunic, stamped with King John's seal. "His messenger gave me this and returned to King John."

A little too eagerly, Darrin snatched the parchment out of Sir Rollin's hand. "The messenger was willing to give you this missive? Most unusual."

Sir Rollin adjusted his tunic over his mail. "I thought you would be pleased. Better that he give the message to me than for him to see the inside of the château. The last thing we need would be for King John to know our weaknesses."

"We have no weaknesses," Darrin growled as he broke the seal and unrolled the parchment. With swift eyes, he read its contents. It seemed King John was willing to allow Darrin to keep Château du Vent Doux for the time being. A great relief flooded him, but he tried to hold it in check because Sir Rollin watched him intently. Though the knight always acted honorable, the man believed himself superior to most, and any sign of weakness on Darrin's part might cause Sir Rollin to leave. Right now, Darrin needed every knight by his side in case King John changed his mind or Sir Adrien returned with the French.

Darrin rolled up the missive. "King John has honored Richard's request. I can keep the château."

Sir Rollin tucked one stray lock of his dark hair behind his ear. "Marvelous. I'm famished. I do hope the cook has something prepared other than pottage. I am tired of eating that slop." His easy gaze swept the bailey and the livestock pens. "I would so enjoy a nice mutton shank."

It was Darrin's turn to lift a brow. "This is a modest keep. But I am sure something can be found to tempt your appetite."

At that precise moment, Lady Faith descended the great hall steps, she and Theo in lively conversation.

"I am sure you are right," Sir Rollin said, his eyes fixed on Faith.

It did not take a scholar to realize where Rollin's thoughts had gone. When Faith spotted them, she froze and a lovely blush filled her cheeks. Before Darrin could react, Sir Rollin rushed over to her and dropped into a deep bow. Faith's cheeks took on a deeper hue.

"How fairs my lady?" His eyes narrowed as he spotted her black and blue jawline. "Tell me, this was not done by some brut?" Sir Rollin turned a cold gaze on Darrin.

She laughed. "Nay, it was caused by my own folly. It is quite an amusing story. Come inside and I will tell it to you."

"My lady, I would care for nothing more than to sit by your lovely side and listen to your beautiful voice," Sir Rollin said, oozing with charm.

Such horse apples. Darrin wanted to roll his eyes to the heavens, but chose to hold his eyeballs in check. He planned to feign indifference and hoped such an action would spur her to come to him. Yesterday, she had sought him out with a question; still he did not know what she wished to discuss. Mayhap she had thought to correct the error she made on their wedding night and was ready to consummate their marriage. But Gouch and his love-sick heart had turned her thoughts away from her wifely duty.

She did not give Darrin a second glance, but smiled when Sir Rollin placed a small kiss on her hand. Even Theo frowned at that one.

Lady Faith clutched Sir Rollin's hands in hers. "I am so happy you have returned and wondered where you had gone. I meant to ask Sir Darrin about you yesterday but was interrupted by another affair."

What? She wished to speak of Sir Rollin? What tactic was this? She barely spoke a word to him or gazed his way upon his first arrival. Now she acted like they were good friends. Darrin's jaw grew tight. Did she think to bend him to her way of thinking through jealousy? Little did she know that he would gladly hand her over to Sir Rollin if circumstances were different.

Nonetheless, Darrin marched to her side.

Dropping her hands to her sides, she looked up at him.

"Husband, are you all right? You look a mite strained."

Strained. A new tactic—to treat him as some weakling in front of fellow knights? Was that her plan, to sway Sir Rollin and Theo to join forces against him? If so, she would be disappointed, for Theo would never turn on him and Rollin…who knew what was in the man's heart? But King Richard had trusted him. The king had usually been a good judge of character. Darrin looked into Faith's crystal grey eyes…a good judge of character most of the time.

"I am fine. Sir Rollin just informed me that my uncle has gone toward the French lines instead of going to honor our new King John." Darrin watched her intently, yet she hid her thoughts well. Her features and her stance gave nothing away, nor did she fist her hand. Oh, she was a shrewd one. A worthy adversary, indeed.

"I am sure Sir Rollin is tired and hungry from his long journey. Let me get you some decent food," she said, ignoring Darrin's words.

An exuberant smile split across Sir Rollin's lips. "Aye, I am famished. You don't suppose there is any mutton? I have such a strong need for a nice hunk of meat."

Lady Faith laughed and weaved her arm through Rollin's. "I do believe we could find some. Come, rest. Then we can talk about old times when you used to visit Sir Adrien with your father."

What? Sir Rollin had once said he knew of Château du Vent Doux but he never disclosed that he had visited the keep as a guest. Darrin wanted to grab Rollin by the back of the neck and demand some answers, but now was not the time. Not in front of Faith.

Instead he bowed to Faith and feigned indifference. "Aye, Sir Rollin, enjoy a hearty meal and *my wife's* company. We will speak later." He then turned his gaze to Theo. "Let us take a walk." With that, he turned and left his wife and Sir Rollin staring after them.

"Well, you handled that poorly," Theo said, coming up from behind.

Darrin strode to the livestock area without glancing at his friend. "I know not what you mean."

"Don't you now? You looked like a mulish mule in front of your lady. If I did not know better, I would say you are jealous of Blossom."

Theo's snide remark splashed over Darrin like boiling water. "You misunderstood my mood. Sir Rollin knows her, and he never divulged this knowledge to me." Darrin slammed his fist on a fence post and gazed out at the multitude of sheep in the pen.

"Which means he can't be trusted." Theo spit on the dry ground at his feet.

"Mayhap you are right or you could be wrong. However, it does raise many questions for which we have no answers."

"Aye. He's a shifty one. There's something about him...yet I can't figure out what it is."

"Mayhap you met him before he joined King Richard's army."

"Not likely. I came to this country with you. Still, he seems familiar. I have always thought such from the moment I looked into his blossom blue eyes."

"So you have said before. Whatever the case, you are going to find out as much as you can about him from Lady Faith."

Theo's eyes widened. "Me? You're her husband. Why don't you ask her?"

The sheep bleated loudly in the pen as Darrin pondered how to answer. What could he say? His wife had rejected him physically and he refused to go to her until she acquiesced. Theo would howl with laughter.

Darrin looked down and examined the lock on the sheep pen. "If she were close...intimate with Rollin, she would confide in you before me."

"By all that is holy, you truly believe she will discuss such matters with me?" Theo shook his head. "You are her husband. You ask her. Methinks you are afraid of her. She is not the only one I have been watching lately."

"Watch your words," Darrin spat. "It is not my actions you are to judge."

Theo raised his palms. "Calm down. I am still your man and will do what you ask. But as your friend, I think you should spend some time with her. I believe she wants to be a good and dutiful wife."

Darrin leaned over the pen and briefly wondered why all the sheep were still there when they should have been out in the fields. However, the minor distraction could not turn his thoughts away from Theo's words. "She wants naught from me," he muttered.

"Nay, that is not true. Earlier she told me, 'A wife owes her faithfulness to her husband.' She is glad Sir Adrien is gone. She is the one who makes this keep run smoothly. Not Sir Adrien, who went to the practice fields each morn. One thing she did confide, she does not believe he killed your father." Theo looked as if he wished to say more but then thought better of it.

Darrin snorted. "I am not sure I am glad to hear it is a woman's shoes I must fill and not a beloved lord. Still I must be grateful, for the keep is in excellent condition. As far as my uncle, she knows full well Sir Adrien killed my father. Be careful that she does not lead you on a merry chase."

A puzzled look settled over Theo's face as he leaned his back into the fence. "Mayhap you are right or you are just letting her get under your skin."

Under his skin? Aye. Faith had always been able to worm her way through his flesh and bones. As a child, she would tease him until he climbed the highest tree or jumped from the battlements into a cart laden with hay. Luckily, he had only broken an arm with that fall and Nun knew how to bind the injury.

Darrin rubbed his elbow. "She is not under my skin."

Theo grunted. "As you say."

Another flash from the past entered Darrin's mind—of Faith, fourteen summers old. Oh, she had gotten under his skin then, like a hot fire setting him aflame. 'Twas one of the things his father and he had argued about. He wanted to be betrothed to her and his father had vehemently opposed the idea. Now Darrin knew why—she was King Richard's daughter and his father hid the secret.

Darrin straightened and slammed his fists on the fence. "Aye. As I say."

Just then the shepherd came scurrying to the pen. He took off his brown cap and bowed. "My lord, I-I am honored with your presence."

Darrin turned to face the man and folded his arms across his chest. "I am wondering why these sheep are still penned when they should be out in yonder fields, Master…"

"Oddo," Theo supplied.

Darrin nodded his thanks.

Oddo began to twist his cap between his fingers as Darrin noticed a large sheep waddling close behind him. When Oddo realized the sheep had been spotted, he laughed. "My lord, good news. I have found another lost sheep. All have been found."

Quickly Oddo took the key from around his neck, opened the gate and pushed the stray sheep inside with the others. The sheep bleated all the more at another joining their already crowded ranks.

"Ahem," Darrin said. "Should you not be taking the sheep out?"

Oddo chortled nervously. "Oh, aye, my lord." With haste, the shepherd opened the gate and rapidly ushered the sheep toward the château entry, leaving a puff of dirt in their wake.

"There is your sheep thief," Theo confirmed.

"Aye. But as you see, giving him the key has made him an honest man. He returned that which he had taken. I am sure every sheep will be accounted for from this day forth."

Theo slapped Darrin on the back and laughed. "You are a master when it comes to understanding shepherds."

Perhaps. But Darrin wished he were a master at understanding women.

Nine

Now therefore come thou, let us make a covenant, I and thou; and let it be for a witness between me and thee.
Genesis 31:44

LOUD VOICES AND A HEAVY AROMA OF LAMB greeted Darrin's senses when he entered the great hall that eve. Mead and wine flowed as if all were feasting some grand event. What they celebrated baffled him, and what was more, he did not order such a feast. If Theo's claim was true, then Lady Faith was the culprit behind such festivity.

Slowly Darrin meandered through his knights and squires until he found her, sitting leisurely at the head table with Sir Rollin. Her laughter lightened the thick air and tumbled like rocks through Darrin's body. Her bruised cheek did not deter from her beauty. The grey of her eyes shone like a beacon of light every time she cast them Rollin's way. To say the lady was delighted to have Sir Rollin de Tosny at Château du Vent Doux would certainly be an understatement. Every word he uttered brought a sweet smile to her lips, and every move he made, she inched closer to him.

It did not take long for those in the hall to spot Darrin's presence, and the boisterous noise began to fade into a low murmur. But none of this seemed to faze the pair sitting at the head table. Were they a treasonous pair bent on eroding Darrin's position or did she play the enamored lady for Sir Rollin's enormous ego? Either situation did not rest easy with Darrin.

Holding his anger in check, he made his way to the couple. "Good eve to both of you. I hope you are enjoying *my* food and *my* drink."

By the widening of her eyes, Darrin knew his meaning had not been lost. But Rollin, half in his cups, chuckled and motioned with his hand. "Come sit with us. I talked your lovely wife into preparing a small celebration in your honor." Rollin stood and raised his goblet. "To Sir Darrin de Longue. Lord of the finest château on this side of the Loire River."

Immediately every knight in the room rose and gave toast. So did Gouch and the rest of the motley band. Darrin gritted his teeth as he scanned the room at those who did not; the servants hustled to and fro, overworked by the sudden change in the daily routine. Darrin already had the allegiance of his men. He wanted the respect of the château's people. Overworking them would not endear him. This could be a wedge that would widen the gap of the loyalty he so desperately wanted from the peasant class.

A servant girl came to his side and offered him a cup of wine. Instead, Darrin took the pitcher from her hands and filled the cup and handed it to her. He raised the pitcher high. "To the people of Château du Vent Doux. May they know their lord admires their service." He then encouraged the girl to drink. She took a hearty gulp and all within the hall walls cheered. "Give some to the servants," he said as he handed the pitcher back to her.

Sir Rollin clapped his hands. "Bravo, my lord. You take a lesson from the Caesars—win the people."

Without comment, Darrin took the seat on the other side of Faith.

Sir Rollin laughed and gave his attention to a knight sitting next to him.

Another serving maid came forward, poured Darrin a cup of wine and placed a trencher of food in front of him. The heady aroma of cooked lamb and sweet honey set his mouth to water. He dug in, not caring that Faith keenly watched him. With every bite he took, he could feel her intense stare. What thoughts rattled around in her pretty head? What a barbarian she was saddled to? Wishing he were Sir Rollin? Wondering when Sir Adrien would return?

Darrin had cleaned half the trencher when he could take it no longer. "What do you find so interesting, woman?"

His loud, harsh words must have taken her aback, for she jumped a little in her seat and turned her gaze to the hearth on the other side of the room. She fumbled for her own goblet and took a sip but did not answer him.

Somewhere deep within, a sharp…something needled him. "Now that I sit here, you are as quiet as a chapel mouse. Would you feel more at ease if I were to retire so you and Sir Rollin can babble on?"

Like a straight pole, she sat in her chair, her eyes still fixed on the insufferable hearth. "Do whatever pleases you, my lord."

Her cool voice burrowed into him and he almost took her chin in his hands, demanding that she look at him. Rather, he took another drink from his cup to steady his actions. "Aye. Look ahead. 'Tis better than looking back," he mumbled.

She must have heard, for she turned and held his gaze. "My lord?"

Her lower lip glistened with juice from the meat and her cheeks were flushed from the wine. The bruise did not dull her looks one bit. She was a beauty. That had not changed over the years no matter how hard he tried to train his mind into thinking otherwise.

As a child, he had been told that a woman of evil character would soon look the part as well. Why had she not grown a wart on her nose or on her chin? Surely by now her crooked nature should be bursting out. But no, she had to look like an angel with her pale hair glistening like crystal in the muted light.

He shook his head. "'Tis nothing," he said, quickly stuffing his mouth with more food. Only this time the food dropped like a rock to the pit of his stomach. He gave a very uncouth belch. Displeasure settled on her lovely face, confirming she thought him to be a ruffian. He stood, kicked back his chair and gave a curt bow. "Forgive, my lady. I did not mean to disturb your meal with my boorish behavior."

Without looking back, he walked out into the cool spring night. He ignored the soldiers and peasants in the bailey and headed to the armory, planning to polish his sword. In the past, the simple task had always cleared his mind, and if he had no answers after doing so, he would see what other weapons could use a good cleaning. Upon entering, he lit a small lantern, pulled his sword from its scabbard and settled on a wooden stool. After picking up a cloth, he began taking long, even strokes until the metal gleamed in the flickering light.

His mind turned to Faith. How could he make her yield to him without giving up his own authority? He could lie and say he had found God again, even though he had not. Try as he might, he could not warm to the idea. Lying wasn't honorable. Why should he care? She had not been honorable to him. And yet the thought did not sit right within him. He could order her to submit to him…but forcing a woman had never been his wont. He rubbed all the harder until his bent reflection shone in the weapon. What was he to do?

A creak drew his attention to the door and an angel entered—Faith. He rose and let his sword drop to the earth beneath his feet. "My lady, is something wrong?"

She stepped in and shook her head. "Nay. Why would you think so?"

He rubbed his fingers across his calloused palms. "I am just surprised that you would seek me out, that is all." He scanned the small room and spotted an overturned stool not far from where he sat. Quickly, he dusted it off. "Here, my lady, sit."

Faith took the offered seat without a word and folded her hands on her lap. He sat on his own stool but did not attempt to pick up his sword. For a few moments, they sat in silence like a pair of young, tongue-tied lovers.

When she did not speak, he got up the courage to utter a few words of his own. "My lady, is there something you wish to say to me?"

An anguished sigh departed her lips. "Oh, Darrin, must we be so formal? In the past, we did not use titles. Why must we use them now that we are wed?"

Mayhap his acting the indifferent husband had paid off and she was finally willing to submit to him. A puff of pride filled his chest at how rapidly she had come around. "We may be wed, but our marriage has not been consummated. So, I think it is only proper that I address you as any other well-born lady I may encounter. Unless…you wish to finally perform your wifely duties?"

The air in the small structure seemed to grow hot as her gaze burrowed into his. Her clasped hands trembled as if she struggled to keep them together. "Have you decided to turn back to God?" Before he could answer her, she carried on, "Oh, I know faith cannot be rekindled as quickly as a fire, but with prayer and meditation, I know God will touch you again."

He could pray and fix his thoughts on God from now until doomsday and he knew his faith in the Almighty would never become a burning fire within him. She had to give up on such a notion. "My lady, you cannot resurrect the dead and that is what my faith is—dead. I have not the desire praying to a god who does not give a fig about man. Who would rather watch him suffer, daily, than to ease his pain and burdens."

"You do not believe that. You are just angry that your father died and your uncle became lord of Château du Vent Doux."

"And whose fault is that, Lady Faith?"

Her skin flushed, giving him a deep satisfaction. Aye, if she truly wanted them to be close as they used to be, she would not have lied and turned against him. She would have stood by his side—she would have loved him as he had loved her. Pain erupted through him as he remembered how much he had loved her, cherished her and adored her.

He pushed the raw thought from his mind. "So as you see, we are at an impasse. I cannot believe and you will not yield to your husband."

"Mayhap not," she said quietly, looking down at her cupped hands.

Ah, she was breaking. Wonderful!

"I have come to bargain."

He leaned forward. Finally, he had the upper hand. Finally, she would submit to him. Finally, a small piece of revenge would be meted out. "And that bargain is..."

Her hands fell to her sides. Her right palm and fingers twisted in the material of her gown until they became a fist. She dropped her gaze to the ground. "If you show up for morning prayers each day for a month, then upon the completion of that month, we shall become a true husband and wife."

The buzz of elation that filled Darrin's head moments ago fizzled into a low hum. What type of negotiation was this? He expected she'd want coin, goods or her freedom in exchange for her wifely duties...but prayers? He leaned forward until her face was less than a hand from his. "You think to restore my faith through prayers? Your bargain is weak. If I pray every day for a month or for a year, the outcome will remain the same. I'll not take God into my heart. In truth, I hate to take advantage of you. Would you not want jewels, silks or coin instead?"

Her gaze shot to his and her grey eyes glistened in the faint light. "You would pay me like a common whore?"

The urge to curse grew great in Darrin's throat, but he swallowed the profanity, knowing she would take offense. "Lady, I meant no disrespect. I just want you to understand that I will not change. I will never be a man of God again."

She looked away. "Even so, that is my request."

Why would she make such a foolish bargain? In their youth, she had always been shrewd. She knew how to get the upper hand of any deal. But this? This was pure folly.

Mayhap he could push her a little more. "Two weeks," he spat out.

Again she raised her gaze to his and tilted her head. Her right hand still fisted in her gown. She shook her head. "The Holy Spirit needs time to work on hard hearts. A month, nothing less."

Doubt tugged at his innards. Was she buying time for King John to come or Sir Adrien to return? Oh, how he wished he knew what was going on in that comely head. He reached over and covered her fisted hand. "Lady, if you play me false, I can assure you I will exert my husbandly rights and play deaf to your pleas of mercy."

"I do not lie. I speak the truth," she replied without a single flinch.

Darrin released her hand and leaned back, watching, waiting for her to crumple under his glare—she did not. "Very well, my lady. You have a bargain. Prayers for your...wifely compliance. And may your God be a witness in case you should think to break your vow."

Her fist relaxed at her side and a chill swept through Darrin as if he made a terrible bargain, indeed.

Later that eve, he tossed and turned on his pallet, watching the light of the moon stream through his window. First the light illuminated one wall and then floated to another as time waned into the early-morning hours. The mild wind carried in the soft evening sounds—the chirping of crickets, the hoot of an owl, the croaking of frogs and the grunting of pigs. *The grunting of pigs?* Not a usual evening sound. Mayhap a wolf prowled the premises. He thought to rise and check the noise, but then no further sounds were heard. Perhaps his hearing had deceived him or his mind was more unsettled than he thought.

Darrin threw an arm over his face and played the conversation with Faith over in his mind. He cared naught about wasting an hour each morn on his knees in the chapel, but he did worry about the reason for Faith's request. As much as she acted the saint, he knew her soul was as black as his, her piety used as a means to an end. However, whatever she had planned, this time he would be ready. He yawned and rolled over on his side, satisfied he held the upper hand.

Loud shouts from the bailey woke him early the next morn. A knock on his chamber door cleared away any night grogginess.

"My lord, my lord," a guard called. "Come quickly. We have been attacked."

Ten

*Thou shalt not be afraid for the terror by night;
nor for the arrow that flieth by day.*
Psalm 91: 5

DARRIN SHOT OUT OF HIS BED, DONNED HIS breeches, grabbed a tunic, his sword, and then raced down the tower stairs. Near the pigpen, he spied the shepherd, Rollin, and Theo standing on the edge of bloody pig guts and body parts.

"What happened here?" Darrin asked.

Master Oddo, who was given charge of the livestock, wailed and fell to his knees. "I swear, lord, I had nothing to do with this. When I checked last night, all was well. The swine were fine. Even ask the lad who slops the pigs."

"Get up, man." Darrin held out a hand and helped Oddo to his feet. "No one is blaming you. Go get this lad and then get others to help clean up this mess."

The shepherd nodded and wiped his tear-streaked face. "Thank you, sir. I told my missus that you were a fair man, I did. I told others too."

Darrin waved off. "Yes, yes. Now go get the lad."

After a little more groveling and a nodding, Oddo left in search of the boy. Darrin took count as to what had happened. At least ten pigs, if not more, had been slaughtered.

"Whomever did this did so quickly." Theo pointed to the side of the pen which was streaked in blood. "They picked up the young pigs and one by one slit their throats and ran a sharp knife down their bellies."

"Aye, and this side of the pen is farthest away from the other livestock," Rollin added, kicking his boot against a bloody rope. "My guess is they napped one, muzzled it posthaste and then did the deed. This was a well-planned attack by someone who knows this keep."

"Agreed." Darrin examined the appearance of his closest knights. Sir Rollin still looked spotless, his boots shiny and his tunic a pristine white. His hair glistened with water. Clearly he had just washed, but that revealed nothing. Rollin was always clean and spotless. Darrin's gaze then swiveled to Theo. Dirty and matted as ever; however, not a drop of blood could be seen through his filth. Except Theo's hands did look a mite cleaner.

Then Darrin surveyed the entire area. The pen was on the edge of the bailey and shadowed by the château walls. Anyone could slip along the edges without being noticed. "The attack was meant to scare us but has instead revealed one of our weaknesses. We'll double the guard along this section." Darrin spied a few more possible spots where invaders might choose to enter the keep. "Sir Rollin, take a few men and check every corner of the bailey. Report anything that looks suspicious."

"Aye, my lord." Rollin took one more look at the pig entrails and wrinkled his nose. "Only a monster would do this." The knight turned and left, calling to a few of his men.

At almost the same moment, Oddo returned with the lad who had slopped the pigs last eve. "Here he is." Oddo pushed the trembling lad forward.

"I swear, sir, I know naught what happed. I gave the feed and called for Master Oddo to lock the gate."

Oddo reddened and cuffed the boy on the back of the head. "That isn't what his lordship asked you."

"Stop." Darrin raised a hand and let his gaze drop over the lad. Dirty and crusted with mud like most peasants, but again, not a smattering of blood on his person. "You sleep close by, do you not?"

The boy nodded his head.

"Then, pray tell, did you hear or see anything last night?"

Fearing another bash on the back of the head, the lad looked at Oddo. "I'm sorry, my lord. But I slept like the dead last night on account of the celebratin'. One of the servin' wenches brought me a cup of honeyed mead from the hall. Best I ever had. I couldn't keep me eyes open after that. I slept until Master Oddo woke me."

If the boy was bleary-eyed this morn, the only person Darrin could admonish was himself. After all, he gave the servants permission to participate in the merriment last eve. Or the mead might have been tampered with. "Very well then…What is your name?"

"Ancel, sir." The boy bowed his head as if he still expected to be punished for what happened here.

"Well, Master Ancel, then I do not believe you can be held accountable for what has happened. And I believe you should break your fast immediately. Go tell the cook to give you a plate of leftover hearty meats. By the way, do you remember who brought you the mead?"

Ancel shrugged. "Never saw her before."

Which meant she could have come soon after Darrin arrived. New knights to a keep always drew fresh whores looking for a protector. No doubt, she was long gone with coin. "Thank you, Ancel. You may go."

But the lad did not move. "Beggin' your pardon, but I doubt the cook will listen to me."

Darrin smiled. Had the bold lad been born under different circumstances, he would have made a fine squire. With a motion of his hand, Darrin beckoned one of his knights. "Take Master Ancel to the cook and make sure he gets a fine plate of food."

"My thanks, sir," Ancel said before striding after the knight like a proud page.

"Master Oddo," Darrien bellowed, his charity gone. "If

you wish to keep your position as keeper of my pens, then you will never hit another lad nor anyone else under your authority again. Do I make myself clear?"

Oddo slid his cap off his head and crushed the material between his fingers. "Aye, my lord. It will never happen again."

"Good. I want you personally to oversee the cleaning up of this mess," Darrin ordered.

Oddo's face drooped, but he did not utter a word. Instead he took small steps backward, bowing as he went.

Darrin scanned the disarray at his feet one more time, then looked at Theo. "Come."

Quickly the pair strode away from the pens and up the battlement stairs. There, Darrin stopped and surveyed the wall above the pens. "These walls are secure."

Theo casually leaned against the stone barrage. "They did not come over this wall. Our problem lies within."

"Aye, I know every stone and corner of this keep from my youth."

His friend raised a brow. "If you know every corner, then why did you send Blossom to inspect every cranny?"

Why indeed? Darrin rolled the thought around in his mind. "He's been here after my uncle took control. If changes have been made, he might know of them or find things I have overlooked."

"And you trust him to do this?" The wariness in Theo's eye said it all.

"You do not trust him? Even after you have fought side by side with him in battle?"

Theo laughed and shook his head. "You have been at this game as long as I. It takes more than a few battles to trust a man. You should have sent me to check the keep."

Could Theo be jealous of Sir Rollin? A certain amount of rivalry between knights was good. It kept the men sharp and ready, but if not held in check, it could erode the workings of the keep. On the other hand, Darrin had never known Theo to be jealous of anyone… Nay, that was not true. Theo had been quite upset when Sir Hugh de Maury challenged him at an archery competition for Lady Eleanor's hand. Theo's loss had spurred him to follow King Richard to France. Still, looking at the mangy man, no one could ever think him to be full of zealous pride. He also had more experience in battle and at being a knight. Hence another reason Darrin trusted him.

"I have already given you a task. You are to watch my lady... Oh, no." Darrin looked to the rising sun. "I must go." He turned toward the battlement stairs. "I'm late."

"Late for what?" Theo asked.

"Morning prayers," Darrin shouted over his shoulder.

Theo's laughter followed Darrin down the steps. "You praying. The chapel might fall down around you."

Faith had heard the ruckus in the bailey, but Nun refused to let her see what was going on until after their morning prayers. "There is nothing that is so important that cannot wait until after we have spent time with God."

Of course, she was right, but nevertheless, Faith could not curb her curiosity. When she entered the chapel and only found Father Chabot, her spirits fell. Darrin had promised. Surely whatever happened in the bailey had taken precedent, and he had just forgotten about his pledge. Yet she could not be sure of the truth.

She kneeled with Nun in the front of the chapel. Father Chabot began with a morning Psalm. Faith tried to remain focused as the priest droned on, but her thoughts kept swaying to Darrin and where he could be. A nudge in her ribs and a stern look on Nun's face returned Faith to her prayers.

The good father paused midsentence when the chapel door creaked open and heavy footfalls made their way to the front of the sanctuary. Faith was tempted to look up but knew such an action would be met with another of Nun's jabs. Whoever entered must have taken to their knees a half a hand behind her.

When Father Chabot resumed the Psalm, his voice seemed much lighter, as if he, too, was pleased with the new arrival. When he finished, the chapel door squeaked on its hinges again. A shuffle of feet sounded behind Faith. Oh, the temptation was great just to take one peek.

Before she could, Father Chabot began another prayer and then another. Finally, he announced, "Let us all say the prayer our Lord taught us."

More than one male voice joined Faith as she said, "Our Father, who art in Heaven…"

When morning prayers were done, Faith looked up to see Darrin, but also Sir Rollin and a few of his men. "How wonderful that you all came," Faith said, looking only at Darrin.

But he did not seem as pleased as she, for he immediately turned to Sir Rollin. "I gave you a task to complete. Are you finished already?"

One would expect Sir Rollin to cower at his lord's inquiry, but he did not. He turned his blue-hazel gaze to her, bowed and then casually looked to Darrin. "I began and then I remembered my obligation to God. I immediately ordered those with me to come to the chapel. God must always come first in our lives, above all other commands."

The comment brought a visible stiffness to Darrin's body, but he did not reprimand Sir Rollin further.

"How nice to know that your faith has grown since the last time you were at Château du Vent Doux," Nun said, coming to Sir Rollin's side with Father Chabot.

The revelation brought a tight smile to Sir Rollin's face and a noticeable ease to Darrin's shoulders. Neither man moved, but stood almost toe to toe and eye to eye. 'Twas the first time Faith noticed that both men were almost the same height, though Darrin seemed to have a little more muscle. However, if it ever came to a game of sport, Faith would not want to wager the outcome.

"I suggest you return to your duty," Darrin said in a low voice.

This time Sir Rollin seemed eager to comply. He bowed towards her again. "My lady." Then he gave a curt nod to Nun. Without acknowledging Darrin or the priest, Sir Rollin departed but left a chill in the chapel air.

Faith reached out when Darrin planned to follow. "A word with you, my lord."

He stared at the hand on his arm as if it were a strange object that he had never beheld before. "My lady, I have pressing duties."

"Please," she begged.

Nun cleared her throat. "We are so glad that you joined us this day, are we not, Father Chabot?"

The priest clasped his hands in front of him. "My prayers have been answered. I do hope some of my words have given you enlightenment this day."

The blank stare of Darrin's face gave proof that the priest's Psalms had fallen on deaf ears.

"I am sure we all were spiritually uplifted today," Nun answered, coming to Darrin's defense. She wrapped her arm through Father Chabot's and started walking him to the chapel entry. "I was hoping we could discuss Psalm forty-three? It's meaning is a little perplexing to me."

"Nun is as crafty as ever, changing the priest's thoughts." Darrin said, turning toward Faith. "What do you wish to speak of?"

Her heart kicked up a beat at the intensity of his gaze. Her tongue seemed to grow wide and her throat grew tight.

He took the fingers that still rested on his arm and held them tight in his. "Faith? Are you ill?" His gaze rested on her bruised cheek. "You look a mite better today."

Her given name freely spoken loosened her lips. "I want to give you my thanks for coming this morn."

He smiled. "In truth, I did not hear a word, so fixed was I on being late."

She laughed and shook her head. "I must confess, nor did I. My thoughts fixed on your presence." The smile fled his face, replaced by a stony stare. She should have kept her thoughts private. "I-I am sorry for my boldness. But I am happy you plan to keep our bargain."

A pause lingered between them. Then he raised his hand and softly touched her bruised cheek. "Are you, now?"

A warmth sped through her and just as quickly disappeared when he dropped his hand to his side.

"Forgive me," he whispered.

A thought to grab his hand and put his fingers back on her cheek seized her. If he asked her to fulfill her marriage vows now, she would gladly comply. Her gaze caught the cross above the altar. Loathing and contrition filled her soul. How could she think of such things here?

He then stepped back and bowed. "Until later."

Later. What did he mean? Later in the bailey? Later in the hall? Later in her chamber? A warm blush heated her cheeks. His footsteps took him closer to the chapel door. She should let him go. But she could not...not yet. "Sir Darrin. I heard a commotion in the bailey this morn. Is everything all right?"

A heaviness settled on his features and his shoulders slumped. "Nay. At least ten young piglets were slaughtered last eve and their remains left. I fear we have intruders who wish to bring harm and fear to Château du Vent Doux."

She rushed to his side. "Do you have any idea who would do this?"

Again he shook his head. "I sent Sir Rollin out earlier to check every corner of this keep in search of clues. I fear his presence at prayers this morn may have spoiled any chance of finding the culprits. They could be anywhere by now."

Faith put a hand to her heart. "I pray not. Mayhap there is something I can do?"

A stiffness swept down his body, chilling her heart. "Nay, my lady. You have done quite enough."

On that, he left the chapel. Faith leaned against the cold wall, a lone tear slipping down her cheek. He spoke of the past, of her betrayal of him. Why could he not see the truth? Why could he not hear? Why would he not believe she only wished to help and heal him?

Eleven

*Faithful are the wounds of a friend;
but the kisses of an enemy are deceitful.*
Proverbs 27:6

GRABBING A FEW TALLOWS FROM HER CHAMBER, FAITH found Sir Theodore sitting on a bale of hay next to the stables, wiping his blade clean of blood. He stood the moment he saw her and placed the knife into a sheath.

"Lady Faith, how are you this fine morn?"

"Quite well, thank you." She paused, debating if she should ask about the bloody blade or not. Had it not been for the incident this morn, she would have thought nothing of a knight cleaning his blade. When he looked expectant, she decided to continue. "I have been looking for you. When I did not see you breaking your fast, I thought perhaps Sir Darrin gave you another task considering what transpired last night."

She followed Sir Theodore's gaze as he glanced around the keep. What he looked for she could not fathom. The smithy hammered, the servants delivered grains and vegetables to the kitchen, the sound of clanging weapons could be heard from the practice yards and the pigpen had been emptied while peasants scrubbed the fence rails. Except for the pen nothing seemed out of the ordinary.

"Nay, I have no other task, my lady, than to be your servant." His tone was flat and devoid of any joy. Obviously, he wished to be anywhere other than with her, but Darrin did not deem to give him another duty.

She folded her hands in front of her. "I am sorry, Sir Theodore. I know you are as much a prisoner to Sir Darrin's decisions as I. But let us make the best of it. I wish to unearth Sir Jean de Longue's trunk. For I am certain it holds the key to his murder and mayhap even to what is happening at the château now."

An eager look entered his eyes. "Ah, perhaps you are right, my lady. Though do not be surprised if Sir Adrien is behind all of this."

"You know I do not believe so, but whatever the outcome, I will be happy as long as it clears Sir Darrin's name." She turned and headed toward the great hall. "Come, we must go to the dungeon." She took off with the knight in tow and did not stop until they were at the door which would take them to the bowels of the keep.

The iron door did not budge when Sir Theodore gave a healthy tug. Nor did it move much when he used both hands and all his strength. "I take it there are no inhabitants below?"

Faith took out a two tallows she had placed in the skirt of her gown and them while Sir Theodore fought with the creaking and stubborn door. "Nay, not for some time. Sir Adrien was always swift with his punishments—either you followed the rules of the keep or you would die. As you can see, it seemed to be a good deterrent."

Finally, with a few more hefty pulls, the hinges wailed as they gave way. The heavy door scraped the floor. Excitement fluttered in Faith's chest as a glint of danger flashed upon Sir Theodore's face. A putrid smell of sweat, bile, and waste greeted them as they peered down the dark stairs.

"Mayhap my lady would care to remain here as I search below?" Sir Theodore offered.

"Nay, I will not. There may be more than one chest below and only I would be able to identify Sir Jean's. Proceed. For I am anxious for the adventure to begin."

Once she became used to the rancid smells and the squealing rats, the escapade took on a thrill she had never known. Pushing away stray cobwebs and stepping cautiously on moist stones held far more appeal than doing needlework or overseeing Cook's meals.

Sir Theodore took the lead and held out his arm as if the simple action would protect her. Each held their tallow high and took caution as they descended the winding stairs. Once at the bottom, they spotted two cells, both with their doors wide open. Both were dark and dank.

"My lady, do you have a preference which one we should examine first?" Sir Theodore asked.

She looked left and then right, but neither held more appeal over the other. Finally she shrugged. "Your choice, Sir Theodore."

Without a word, he stepped into the left cell. Faith followed and raised a hand to her nose as a foul stench assailed her senses. "I did not think it could get worse, but I was wrong."

Sir Theodore raised his tallow to the corners of the cell. Rat droppings and bits of spoiling food strewed the floor. He raised the light to a ledge where the mortar had been broken down, leaving a large hole. "I wager the kitchens are right above us. The rats have made quite a home for themselves here."

Faith gagged. "This will have to be fixed. We do not need rats in the château's food supply."

"Agreed. This needs repair and the cell will be burnt out." Slowly, he held out the light to every corner of the cell. "There is naught else here."

Satisfied, both of them stepped out into the narrow hallway. They hesitated before they entered the next cell, fearing it could be worse than the last. Sir Theodore pulled a heavy breath of damp air, held it and stepped into the other cell. With careful steps, Faith followed.

This cell did not have the stench of the other, but it smelled musty and ancient. Piled high against the walls were at least five trunks and old furniture. In the dim light, it was hard to tell one from another.

"We should show all this to Darrin," Sir Theodore said.

Faith held her tallow to each trunk, looking for Sir Jean's seal. "I agree, but let us find Sir Jean's trunk first. I fear if he finds it, he will store it away and we will never find out the truth."

"If you tell him what you search for, surely he will understand."

"Nay, he will not. He does not trust me. If I do not examine Sir Jean's trunk now, I will never get a chance again." She rubbed her hand over every chest, yet she could not find Sir Jean's. "It must be here."

"My lady, it will be easier to examine them once they are brought above. Come. I will get some hearty men."

She fell to her knees, searching the lower chests. Once a gaggle of servants hauled these trunks to the surface, Darrin would learn of their existence. "Please. I only look for one. When it is found and retrieved, I do not care what you do."

He knelt down next to her. "It may not be here. Sir Adrien could have easily burned all of Sir Jean's things."

Her heart sunk. He could be right. Mayhap the trunk she saw taken all those years ago was not Sir Jean's. She stood, ready to give up when she spotted a gold gilded chair. Her memory snapped back. "That is Sir Jean's dressing chair. I saw it often enough when Darrin and I would go to his chamber each eve to say a night prayer." She rubbed her hands over the back of the chair. "See here? These are his initials." Immediately she fell to her knees again, and behind the chair sat a large chest, with Sir Jean's initials etched in gold leaf. "Here!"

Swiftly, Sir Theodore handed her his tallow, moved the chair out of the way and pulled the trunk to the middle of the cell. "Are you sure, my lady?"

"Aye. This is his." Elation filled Faith's soul. "We must get this chest above before the others. We can put it somewhere safe, where we can go through it without prying eyes."

Sir Theodore paused. "My lady, you should tell Sir

Darrin. He will not be pleased when he finds out you have withheld this from him."

She shook her head. "Nay. I cannot tell him. Not now. Only after, when I have found the proof to clear his name."

Still, Sir Theodore hesitated, doubt firmly resting on his face.

She placed one of the tallows on another trunk, taking his hand in hers. "Please. I beg you."

He did not move, nor seem to be swayed by her distress.

Letting his hand fall from hers, Faith squared her shoulders and lifted her chin. "Sir Darrin said you are to be my knight. My champion. Did he not?"

A weariness settled on Sir Theodore's features. "Aye."

"Then you will move this chest to…" She could not move it to her chamber. Tongues would wag and Darrin would discover its presence quickly enough. Where? Where could she hide the trunk? As if given by God, a vision of a small shack, near the forest, abandoned years ago when most of the peasants moved closer to the keep, entered her mind. 'Twould be the perfect place. "There is an old hut near the forest's edge. It is far from prying eyes. We will take the trunk there, and you will remain silent of its whereabouts. Do you understand, Sir Theodore?"

"My lady—"

"Do you understand?" She knew she had him when his gaze dropped to the floor of the cell. But she still needed him to voice the words. "Sir Theodore?"

His gaze shot to hers. "Aye, my lady. I understand. But I fear this deception will come back and bite us both in our…"

Even though he did not finish his words, his meaning was clear. Sir Darrin does not handle deceit well, no matter what the outcome. However, she saw no other choice. If he hated her forever, so be it. But once she found the truth—he would have his honor back and be truly noble again. And that alone would make her rejoice.

"We have found nothing, my lord." The words from Sir Rollin did not surprise Darrin, only irritated him.

"No wayward weapons, no strange tracks, no blood?" Darrin stood next to the now clean pigpen and wondered why he had been so hasty to remove any trace of this morning's events. His own actions might have made the situation worse.

"We checked every knight's sword, we went through the armory, and nothing was out of place or seemed odd. No spot of pig's blood other than what we saw this morn could be found. And as far as tracks..." Rollin waved around the keep. "With all these peasants milling about, we could not discern the villains from the good."

Sir Rollin's words were sound. This act was done deliberately in plain sight. The villain could be among them this very second or could be far, far away. "We must keep looking. Go check the village outside the gate. Mayhap the people there know something."

"Or maybe harboring a stranger or two," Rollin said.

A thought tripped in Darrin's mind—the old man who Darrin had dubbed Pope Innocent. Could he be part of this? He had conveniently disappeared once inside the keep. As much as Darrin wanted to deny, it could be true. Innocent could be part of a group of ruffians loyal to Sir Adrien. Darrin took a deep breath of balmy bailey air. Mayhap he should ask his own questions of the villagers.

His decision made, Darrin headed to the stables. There he found Theo hitching a horse to a cart. "What do you do here? Why are you not watching Lady Faith?"

Surprise traveled across Theo's face as he spun about. "My lord, Darrin." Theo's eyes seemed to bulge in his head as if he were caught in some dastardly deed. "I... The lady needs a cart..."

When no further explanation was given, Darrin prompted, "For what?"

"Ah, she seems to have some items that need to be thrown away." Theo shifted his feet back and forth and then flashed his gaze around the bailey as if searching for something.

Darrin tried to follow his gaze. "Do you see something out of the ordinary?"

Theo pinned Darrin with a glare. "I think you need to talk to your wife," he snapped, turning his attention back to the horse and cart.

With a light touch, Darrin put his hand on Theo's shoulder. "I am sorry. I know this task is not to your liking. But she will open up to you long before me. She may hold the key to solving who is disrupting the workings of this keep. I know you can help unravel this mystery."

Theo's hands paused on the horse's reins, but he did not turn around. "What if you don't like the discovery? Mayhap you are wrong about Lady Faith. Mayhap she holds your welfare close to her heart."

What was this? Was Theo being twisted into Faith's deceitful web? A sharp pang cut into Darrin's midsection. "Hold to your wits, man. And remember whose wife she is."

Theo turned, a flash of menace in his eye. He poked a finger into Darrin's chest. "I remember." Quickly Theo turned back to the cart and hoisted himself up on the seat. "But do you?" With a slap of the reins on the horse's rump, Theo maneuvered the cart toward the great hall entrance, not waiting for an answer.

Someday, hopefully Theo would understand. Darrin scrubbed the back of his neck. He could not get too close to Faith until he was certain she could not steal his heart again.

Twelve

*Whoso keepeth his mouth and his tongue
keepeth his soul from trouble.*
Proverbs 21:23

HIS TIME IN THE VILLAGE PROVED NAUGHT. WITH SIR Rollin, they went from home to home, into the fields and questioned every man and woman. They even talked to the older children. Yet none had any answers. No one had seen anything out of the ordinary, no one had ever seen nor heard of an old man that matched Darrin's description. Finally, the knights returned to the château with no more knowledge than they had that morn.

The sun had already set and Darrin expected to find Faith at the hearth or already sitting at the head table, but she was nowhere to be seen…and neither was Theo. At first, relief flooded Darrin, but then as time passed and he sat alone with a goblet of wine, a prickle of annoyance niggled at him. Where could they be? He thought to send a servant to check Lady Faith's chamber, but then thought it would be too presumptuous. Plus, Theo would not be lingering in Lady Faith's chamber…

The tallows on the table had dwindled to stubs before the pair sauntered in, covered in dirt, laughing. Darrin took another hefty swig of wine, letting the warm burgundy liquid slide down his throat and burn in the pit of his stomach. Faith tried to tuck wayward strands of hair under her crooked veil when she spotted him, as if doing so would hide the folly that happened this day.

Immediately she sped to the head table and curtsied. "My lord, I do so hope you had a fine day?"

Darrin nodded, placing his goblet on the table. "But not as fine as yours, I imagine."

A bright pink hue flooded her cheeks before she dropped her chin to her chest. "Excuse me, my lord. I wish to tidy up a bit before I sup." She did not wait for an answer, but scurried up the tower steps as if a hot poker were jabbing her in the back.

Rollin sauntered up from behind with a pitcher of wine and filled Darrin's goblet. He dropped into the chair to Darrin's left. "My lady looks a little distressed. Mayhap it could be from an invigorating day."

"Hold your tongue, Sir Rollin. Things are not always as they seem." Darrin shifted his gaze to Theo, who stood near a basin of water splashing his face and hands. Aye, things were not as they seemed, for Darrin could not remember the last time he had seen Theo wash up before he ate.

The knight in question made his way over to the table. "What are you looking at, Blossom?" Theo asked.

Sir Rollin chuckled and poured Theo a cup of wine. "Come sit with us and tell us about your afternoon with our lovely lady."

Theo frowned, took the offered drink and sat on Darrin's other side as if he had the rights to do so. "Do not make more of something where there is naught. All day long, Lady Faith instructed me and a few servants to bring up old trunks that were forgotten in the dungeon."

That was not what Theo said earlier. He said Lady Faith wanted to get rid of some things. Darrin narrowed his eyes. "Did she dispose of these chests?"

"Nay, they sit outside the kitchen." Theo took a gulp of wine and wiped his mouth. "There are at least five of them. Very old. I think we should burn the lot. We also found an infestation of rats. Seems they have found an easy path to the kitchen."

The thought of plague sobered Darrin's mind. Keeping

his hold on Château du Vent Doux would be a moot point if disease ravaged the keep. Nonetheless, his curiosity was piqued. "I would like to take a look at these trunks first."

Theo seemed to brighten and grabbed a trencher of food from one of the servants. "Then I shall leave them where they are until morn. I have already posted a guard, so there should be no stealing."

"I have yet another question. Why did Lady Faith want to go to the dungeon in the first place? Was she looking for something special?"

Theo paused mid-chew. He gazed at Darrin and took a hard swallow. He reached for his cup and took another healthy swig of wine. As if by divine intervention, Lady Faith descended the stairs. Theo motioned to her. "Why don't you ask the lady yourself?" Without waiting for Darrin to respond, Theo vacated the seat and went to join another group of knights near the hearth.

Darrin frowned. This did not bode well. Theo purposely didn't want to answer him. Had Faith turned Theo's heart to her way of thinking already? Darrin eyed his wife, who had changed her overgown and veil. Dressed in purple and holding her head high, she looked every bit a royal. More and more he was beginning to see the resemblance between her and King Richard.

Gently, Darrin rubbed his chest, where Richard's letter still resided. A brief flash of guilt slashed through him, but he quickly pushed it aside. In due time, he would tell her all. In due time.

Faith greeted Rollin first with a warm smile, at which he raised his cup. "My lady, your bruise begins to fade, or is it, your beauty cannot be hidden? Come sit next to me."

For a moment, Faith hesitated, as if she thought to do so, but then she remembered her place and came to sit next to Darrin without saying a word.

The observance of proper decorum was not lost on Sir Rollin, for he guffawed and leaned toward Darrin. "You are a lucky man. What I would do to be you."

Darrin gripped the arms of his chair. "Watch what you say, *Sir Rollin*. She is my wife."

"Oh, oh. Forgive me, *my lord.* I meant no offense. I just speak what every man in this room is thinking. There are many that would be willing to trade places."

A scan of the hall confirmed Sir Rollin had spoken the truth, for almost every knight who had rotated his gaze to Faith had envy in his eyes. Out if his periphery, Darrin caught Theo staring at Faith also. Though his eyes held a different look, but Darrin could not interpret it. From time to time, Faith returned his gaze—a silent communication. Aye, there was a secret here and Darrin would not rest this eve until he found out what the pair were trying to hide.

He leaned toward her and caught a scent of roses. "My lady, tell me how can you possibly smell like a rose garden when you have been dwelling in dungeon stench all day?"

A tinkle of laughter filled the air. "I have changed my gown and washed my hands, arms and face in water laced with rose oil. Perhaps we could find a scent for you as well."

Darrin sat back in his chair. Did she mean to say that he smelled badly?

Another gentle laugh left her lips and a glint of merriment filled her eyes.

"You jest," he said.

"Aye, you do not offend my nose, my lord. I wish I could say the same for all your knights." She gazed at Theo.

"Theo is his own man. If he splashes water on his person at least once a week, consider it a gift from God."

She fixed a skeptical gaze on Darrin. "So you still do have some faith in God?"

"I never said I did not believe God exists. I am just not willing to give praise to a God who allows the innocent to die and the guilty to go free."

Her face became a frosty mask as he could see his real meaning take form in her mind. "Excuse me." She made to stand, but he quickly dropped his hand on hers, staying her exit.

"Nay, my lady. You will not leave until you explain to me what happened this day. Why were in you my dungeon? Unless you were checking out the accommodations, just in case..." His words hovered in the air, but she gave no response. Then a sadness settled into her eyes and Darrin wished he had chosen his words more carefully.

"After your father died, I remembered there were many possessions that were taken to the dungeon. I thought perhaps some of your things were sent there and you would like them returned. So Sir Theodore and I went in search and we found several trunks."

How had she gotten Theo to be an accomplice in the matter? "And were any of these trunks mine?"

She refused to look at him, keeping her gaze fixed on nothing in particular. "I do not know. It took us most of the day to get them above ground."

Darrin stood and held out his hand. "Then I suggest we go look at them now."

She stared at his hand as if it were filled with plague boils. "Now, my lord?"

"Aye. I am excited to see what you have found. We will take a couple of torches—"

"The cells below were filthy and infested with rats. If we open those trunks in the bailey, I fear what infestations we will find within."

Now she looked at him, her eyes murky and guarded. Oh, she found something, all right. But he wagered it had nothing to do with him. "A wise thought. Then we shall move them outside the keep walls in the morning, after prayers, and we will open them there—together. However, I would like to see them now. Even without opening, I might recognize one of the chests." He held out his hand again. This time she put her shaking fingers in his palm.

Darrin called for a couple of servants to follow him with torches. She said not a word as they left the great hall and headed toward a stone wall behind the kitchens. Cool spring air swirled around them, and Faith trembled all the more.

"You are cold, my lady." Darrin put his arm around her, meaning to intimidate her, but his tactic failed when her soft body, so close, sent a ripple of pleasure through him.

Instead of pulling away as he expected her to do, she snuggled closer. Her trembling ceased. "My thanks."

He shuddered, but he did not let her go. Clearing his throat, he picked up his pace. *She might just kill me without raising a sword.* When he spotted the trunks, an exhilaration sped through him. Aye, she had been right, he should have waited until morn to take a look, for now he wanted to open them.

Darrin took a torch from one of the servants and squatted next to the trunks. Some were eloquently marked with gold and ornate seals, while others were plain. He pointed to one of the impressive chests. "This one, I think, belonged to my grandfather." He moved to another. "And this one, I think, is Lady Rochelle's. You remember her, don't you? My father's cousin, who came to stay with us."

Faith knelt next to him. Her veil fluttered in the cool wind, the smell of roses assaulting his senses once again. "Of course I do. She was very old. We used to call her—"

"Old hook nose," they said in unison.

Faith's laughter ripped at his heart. How he had loved her. First as a friend and then... With a clench of his jaw, Darrin hardened his heart. He stood. "That is enough for now."

The merriment left her face as she rose to her feet. The askance look in her eye caused him to turn away. The gentle touch of the hand stayed him like a tight vice. "Darrin," she said softly.

Quickly he pulled away and turned to the servants. "Please escort Lady Faith back to the hall." He then bowed. "Good evening, my lady." Darrin stormed away before she could capture him again with a simple touch, a tender glance or an old memory. Nay, he would not let her back into his heart for as long as he drew breath.

Another foul night of tossing and turning did not improve Darrin's mood. In the morn, he rose as he always did and was sorely tempted to skip morning prayers. Kneeling on a cold stone floor while Father Chabot droned on held less appeal than going into battle with the French. Nevertheless, it was a small sacrifice when the prize would be so deeply rewarding.

Darrin rolled to his feet and made his way to a cistern of fresh water. Quickly he splashed his face and upper body before he donned a dark tunic and breeches. After stamping his feet into his boots, he headed for the chapel, and like yesterday, everyone was assembled in their appointed spots—Father Chabot before the humble altar, Nun and Lady Faith on their knees in front of him. A little farther back knelt Rollin and a few other knights, and to the rear was the smithy's daughter, Monique, with Gouch? *By the holy cross. Gouch—saying prayers?* He winked and was quickly reprimanded when Monique jabbed her elbow into his rib cage. Darrin shook his head, strode to his spot next to Faith and knelt on the cold stones, making the sign of the cross upon his chest.

"My children, I thought this morn we could begin with some words from Hosea. *'O Israel, return unto the Lord your God; for thou hast fallen by thine iniquity.'*"

Since Father Chabot was looking directly at Darrin, there was no doubt to whom he was speaking. But there were other sinners here as well, though none of them seemed to be fazed by the priest's words.

"'Take with you words, and turn to the Lord...'"

Could not the priest find some more comforting words? Darrin tried to fix his mind on some of the Holy Scripture Nun had taught him and Faith years ago. *Whoso findeth a wife findeth a good thing, and obtaineth favour of the Lord.* The words jarred Darrin back to the present. Of all the scripture that he had learned, these words entered his mind?

Out of the corner of his eye, he saw Faith, head bowed, eyes shut and her soft hands clasped against her chest. Oh, had not the past been so destructive, then he would have indeed glorified in the thought that she was his wife. He would have adored her and given her anything. But alas, that was impossible. A present chill swept into him and he welcomed the hard stones beneath his knees. Though unseen by the eye, her heart was bent and cruel. She sought power and possessions which were not her own. The priest should be casting his reprimand toward her.

"'...for the ways of the Lord are right, and the just shall walk in them: but the transgressors shall fall therein.'"

If he must be on his knees every morn, perhaps he should pray. A cynical smile lodged on his lips. *Vengeance, Lord. Give me vengeance on those who seek to harm me. Protect the wicked no longer.* Anger and hatred warmed his cold joints and blocked out any further prayers that Father Chabot uttered.

Thirteen

*A talebearer revealeth secrets: but he that is
of a faithful spirit concealeth the matter.*
Proverbs 11:13

SOON AFTER PRAYERS AND AFTER BREAKING THEIR fast, Darrin escorted Faith, who was followed by Nun, to the wall behind the kitchen. A cart laden with large barrels stood where the trunks had been placed. A boy, dressed in rags, not more than ten summers, sat on top with a large stick in hand and a fierce look upon his face.

"Unless, ye have me shillin's for these barrels, I suggest ye stand back." The boy slapped the stick in his palm.

"Where are the trunks that were placed here last night?" Darrin called to the lad.

"Eh? Trunks? Know Nothin' about them. I've come to drop off these barrels ordered by Lord Adrien de Gascon."

Clearly the boy was not from around here or he would have known that Sir Adrien was no longer lord here. "I am Sir Darrin de Longue. I am the lord here now."

The boy's shoulders slumped. His face crumpled, tears glistening in his once determined eyes. He dropped the stick to his lap. "The rumors I heard are then true. Me father will strip me skin if I come home without coin." He brightened some. "Surely ye'd be needin' these fine barrels. Ye can stuff them with just about everythin'—grain, wine, salted meats, mead—anythin'."

Though the boy could be blown over with a gentle wind,

he had a lot of grit. Faith cleared her throat and stepped forward. "Good morn, Devon. Do you remember me?"

A quirk of a smile slipped across the boy's lips. "Aye, me lady. I remember ye. Ye talked Sir Adrien into gettin' these barrels."

Even though Faith was the reason the château was in excellent condition. She didn't have controlled the purse strings, but she obviously had enough influence to sway Sir Adrien's thinking.

She turned a pleading gaze in Darrin's direction. "We have many resources here. We use these barrels to store grain for the winter months, house the little bit of wine we make and, as the boy said, for salted meats."

"Seems to me, my lady, we have plenty of carpenters of our own. Why order these from a different village?"

Her sad gaze lingered on the dirty, bone-thin boy, then she removed a small jeweled brooch that held her cloak in place. "Because Master Devon and his father are fine craftsmen."

Faith moved closer to the cart, but Darrin stayed her hand as she held out the jewel to the boy. This had nothing to do with carpentry, but the boy's and his father's empty bellies. Darrin pulled a small leather pouch from his tunic and handed over a handful of shillings to Devon. "Keep your jewels, my lady. You are right these are fine barrels."

With ease, the boy jumped down, jingling the coins in his hand. "Could ye have the same knights that hauled away those trunks help move these barrels?"

Darrin narrowed his gaze. "I though you knew naught about the trunks?"

The boy shrugged. "Had to make sure I got me coin first."

"So could you identify these knights?" Darrin asked.

"Aye." The boy pointed. "One of them is standin' right behind ye."

Darrin turned and there in all his mangy glory stood Theo. "And who ordered you to move the trunks?"

Theo motioned to Faith. "Your lady. She said you wanted them outside the keep walls before they were opened. I took the liberty to do so right away."

The pair exchanged a look of allegiance that was not lost on Darrin. "And just when was this order given?" he asked Faith.

She blinked several times, clearly trying to come up with an acceptable answer. However, 'twas Theo who came to her rescue. "Lady Faith found me in the hall early this morn, before going to chapel. She asked me to move the trunks when I got the chance."

"Aye, that is true," chimed in Nun. "I was with her."

Darrin raised a cold gaze to Theo. "You should have spoken to me before you moved them."

Theo cocked a brow and put his hands on his hips. "Why? The reason for moving them was sound. One that was suggested to you last night. What does it matter? The deed is done. Would you like to see what is inside them or would you rather I bring them back to the château?"

"Nay. But you will stay here and help this lad empty his cart," Darrin said through thin lips.

The heavy tension between them did not dissipate as Darrin made for the keep gate. Something was amiss. Later, when alone, he would confront Theo and, if necessary, beat the truth out of him.

Outside the portcullis, Darrin had another surprise. There stood Sir Rollin and a handful of his men, plus another guard. "Are you that bored with the duties I gave you that you must stand around with a gaggle of your men to keep you company?"

A forced laugh split Sir Rollin's lips. "I searched for the pig butchers all day yesterday and nothing out of the ordinary was discovered." He gestured to the trunks. "Perhaps these chests will shed some light into the mysteries that swirl around this château."

A poor excuse. "These trunks are years old and have naught to do with the pig slaughter."

Caught in a lie, Sir Rollin casually lifted one shoulder. "True. But there may still be something of value within these chests that we can all benefit from."

Ah, the truth. Sir Rollin was in it for the profit...or for the knowledge which could be as useful as coin. The warrior inside Darrin rose to the surface. Sir Rollin and all his men wore swords and some even had mail on over their padded tunics.

Was there not one knight he could trust? Darrin's hand slid down his thigh. He had foolishly left the keep without a weapon.

An ally came from the strangest place. Nun stumbled forward, coughing and grabbing at her wimple. "Goodness, I feel so warm." She fell right into Sir Rollin's arms. "Mayhap I shouldn't have spent last night washing the gown Lady Faith wore yesterday in the dungeon. The dirt and muck was thick. I haven't seen that much rat waste since the plague ravaged the Abbey of Sainte-Marie-des-Dames years ago."

Turning a shade between white and grey, Rollin quickly handed her off to one of his knights. "Sir Gentry and Sir Keaton will see you safely to your chamber."

"My thanks. It may be nothing. Lady Faith was a little ill last night, but now today she is quite fit."

Faith coughed slightly and Sir Rollin's skin almost became translucent. The knights reluctantly followed his orders and quickly carried away Nun, who moaned about those fateful days at the abbey.

She had never spoken about such a terrifying time all the years Darrin had known her. He suspected she sympathized with his predicament and came to his aid. Later, he would have to thank her. For now, Sir Rollin stood with only one other knight while Darrin had but the one guard. The odds were still not perfect, but they had improved.

Faith came forward and placed her hand on Sir Rollin's arm. "Mayhap we should have a cloth to cover our noses and mouths. I would feel so much better if we had some protection from what could lie within." She glanced over her shoulder at Sir Rollin's other knight. "Would you mind finding one of the weavers and see if some coarse cloth can be given?"

The knight looked to Sir Rollin, who nodded. Without a word, the young knight tore off to the château.

She helped him. Why? There was naught but questions rattling around in Darrin's head, and if the courage to speak to Faith would not elude him, he would have answers.

"Hand me your sword," Darrin said to his guard. The man hesitated. "I need it to break these locks." The guard nodded and handed over his weapon. "Go to the armory and get an ax. Some of these locks may be stubborn."

However, the guard did not have to carry out the order, because marching out of the keep with a sword in one hand and an ax in the other came Theo, huffing and puffing like a warhorse in the heat of battle. He held out the sword. "Thought you might need this."

Again Darrin had to weigh out the situation. Was Theo friend or foe? The familiar glint in his eye would say friend, but still…

"What?" Theo asked. "You're looking at me like I got pottage all over my face." Which he did, well, in his beard. "I helped the lad. All the barrels are in the cellar." He handed Darrin the sword.

It would seem the odds had improved greatly. Darrin returned the guards sword, then smiled at Faith. "Which one first, my lady?"

"Hold. Should we not wait for the cloths?" Sir Rollin said, removing Faith's hand from his arm.

Faith swayed and then placed her hands on Sir Rollin's chest. "I'm feeling a little woozy again."

A mixture of horror and duress flooded his features as he tried to pull away from her. "Perhaps you should return to the keep, my lady."

She shook her head. "Nay, but perhaps you could get me a stool to sit on."

Sir Rollin looked to the guard and then to Theo, but neither offered to help. And Rollin knew better than to ask since the guard took his orders from Darrin, and Theo would do whatever he pleased. "All right. I shall return shortly." He handed Faith over to the guard and stomped away, muttering.

The moment Sir Rollin was out of sight, Faith pushed away from the guard. "Quick. Let us open one of the chests before he returns. Which one are you most interested in, my lord?"

Again, she sided with him.

"Which one?" she shouted at his inaction.

Darrin did a fast survey of the trunks. "My grandfather's."

They removed the chests that stood on top of his grandfather's trunk and Theo hefted the ax above his head and gave the padlock a hearty whack. The lock did not budge. Again he lifted the ax and this time the padlock split in two. When Theo flipped open the lid, dust and the smell of mold and must assailed Darrin's senses. Plus a familiar odor. He coughed and sneezed.

The guard next to Darrin gagged. "Ack. What's reeks?"

A smell from Darrin's childhood—pig fat. With his sword, Darrin poked around the trunk until he found a few jars with cracking seals. "I suspect those jars are filled with boiled pig fat, onion, garlic and leeks. My grandfather believed rubbing such a poultice on his elbows and knees would take away the aches. If I remember correctly, it mostly just drew flies. No one wanted to sit by him very long. The poultice has not improved with age."

"You may return to the keep. Your services are no longer needed," Darrin said to the guard.

The man did not say another word but took off to the château in a run.

Faith pulled the sleeve of her gown over her hand and held it up to her nose. "Is there anything else of worth inside?" she said, her voice a muffle through fabric.

"Let's see…" Theo dropped the ax, came forward and started to rummage through the items, the smell did not seem to bothering him at all. "Clothes, three jars of this stuff…"

He put the jar to his nose and took a sniff, then shrugged. "Not that bad." He then hauled out a smaller chest. "We better hurry and open this one before Blossom comes back."

Darrin dropped his sword and picked up the ax and gave the chest a whack. The smaller lock fell to the ground.

A sigh flew out of Theo's mouth. "Nothing in here but old parchments." He turned his attention back to the larger trunk. "No gold, silver or jewels. Just garments and strips of cloth, probably used to hold that poultice in place."

Darrin knelt down by the smaller chest and looked at a few of the letters. One missive was neatly wrapped in leather. Carefully he unfolded it. "I am not sure, but I think this is an agreement between my grandfather and Lord Edmond de...Tosny."

"What?" Theo dropped the fabrics in his hands.

Faith rushed behind Darrin and bent low to read over his shoulder. "I give Lord Edmond de Tosny my son, Jean de Longue, into knight's training. Did you know about this?"

Darrin shook his head. "Nay. He never told me he had been sent away. I just assumed he had been trained here. Grandfather trained many a knight."

"Most are sent away," Theo said. "I was."

"Aye, but my father was so adamant I stay here, I just assumed my father—"

"Perhaps it was not a pleasant experience for him and he wanted to save you the same unpleasantness," Faith offered.

"Training to be a knight is supposed to be a torture," Theo huffed.

"Agreed. My father and others who trained me were not kind in the least." Darrin shook his head. "There has to be another reason."

Theo stood and glanced at the château. "Look lively. Blossom is returning."

Darrin jammed the missive in his tunic and closed the small chest. He would examine the rest of the contents in private. He stood and waved to Sir Rollin. "Hold. You may not want to come closer."

The moment the stench reached Rollin's nose, the knight stopped as if a hedgerow lay between them. "By all that is holy, what is that…"

Theo reached into the chest and held up a jar of poultice. "I think it might be rat guts. You want some, Blossom?"

Immediately Sir Rollin covered his nose with a cloth. "Nay, I think I shall remain here."

"Go get the other cloths," Darrin whispered to Faith. "And try to get him to leave."

Faith nodded and ran toward Sir Rollin. The pair exchanged a few words. Then suddenly he handed Faith the remaining cloths and started heading back to the château at a rapid pace. She ran back to where Darrin and Theo stood. "I told him your grandfather was interested in finding a way to cure the plague and often he kept plague body parts in jars to study and these jars looked to be filled with decomposing plague parts."

Darrin again marveled at Faith's quick thinking. Once again she hid the truth. He peered into her eyes, hoping to find unspoken answers. The grey pools were dark and would not give up their secrets. *Oh, what was going on in her mind? Could he trust her?* There was a time…the past rolled forward of Faith a child becoming a maid…his heart aching with love and want. Back then, he would have done anything for her, and she for him. Then his mind turned to her betrayal and crushed the kernel of trust within him. Nay. He would not be fooled again. He turned away from her without a word.

Theo guffawed and grabbed a tunic from the larger trunk. "Can I have this?"

"What for? 'Tis filled with holes and it reeks of the poultice," Darrin said.

"Aye." Theo grinned. "I can't wait to don this and sit right next to Blossom as we sup. The man might just choke to death."

Darrin shook his head. "Take it, but burn the rest."

Theo pulled the red filthy tunic over his head. "How do I look?" he asked, moving his eyebrows up and down.

Faith laughed and Darrin's thoughts twirled to the past once again—her soft laughter when they used to pick wildflowers in the spring or when they waded through the river in the summer. The light, soft timbre of her laughter weaved its way back into his heart. He pointed to the trunks. "Which one next, my lady?"

She laughed again, smiled and clapped her hands.

"Old hook nose's," they said, again in unison.

Fourteen

*Seeing then that these things cannot be spoken against,
ye ought to be quiet, and to do nothing rashly.*
Acts 19:36

THE NEXT MORN, FAITH ROSE EARLY, DID HER TOILET and then found Theo in the hall sleeping in a lone corner, wearing that vile tunic. She covered her nose and nudged him lightly in the thigh with her foot. "Sir Theodore, get up," she whispered.

He moved his leg and mumbled something, but he did not awake. She kicked him hard in the shin.

"Huh?" His eyes fluttered open briefly and he belched. A heavy odor of stale wine drifted on the air.

Faith bent down and punched him in the shoulder. "Wake up, you oaf."

This time he raised his hand and blinked. "What the devil? What, are your prayers over already?"

Cuffing him in the head seemed like an excellent idea. Instead, she put her hands on her hips. "Nay. But I want you to go to the old shack. Now."

No recognition registered on his face. "Where the trunk is," she said through clenched teeth.

Finally, the cobwebs seemed to clear from his brain. "Why are we going there so early?"

She glanced around the hall. Most were still sleeping and those who had risen could not see them in the predawn shadows. "Not we. You. I don't want to raise Sir Darrin's suspicions, which might happen if he sees us leaving the keep together."

Sir Theodore washed a hand over his face. "You should just tell him the truth."

"Nay. We don't know what is in the chest and if we find something that might—"

He gave her a pointed look. "Darrin's not guilty. And lady, when he does find out…now that is something to fear."

A chance she was willing to take, but she had to know for certain if he was guilty or not before turning the trunk over to him. Because if he did kill his father…what would she do? She shook her head. "Nevertheless, I want you to leave before I am finished with prayers. And do take that filthy tunic off."

Sir Theodore wiped a hand over the shirt and then smiled. "Every time I touched Blossom, he washed himself. Must have been at least five times last night." He stood and stretched. "But if it offends you, then I shall burn it." A mischievous look entered his eye. "Or I could tuck it under Blossom's head while he sleeps."

"You'll do no such thing. Try not to bring any attention to yourself until we find out the truth."

He shrugged. "All right, my lady. Anything else you might want me to do this morn?"

Faith thought about it for a moment and then an idea sprang in her head. "Aye, I wish you to pray as you journey to the hut. I wish to see you pray more and drink less."

He gave her a sour look but did not answer.

Satisfied that he would carry out her orders, she hurried to the chapel. Father Chabot and Nun were already there.

"You rose quite early this morn. Where have you been?" Nun asked.

To avoid Nun's penetrating gaze, Faith folded her hands and looked at her toes. "I kept thinking about the trunks we opened yesterday." Her words weren't a lie, but it was not the trunks they opened that pricked her mind, but the one she planned to open today.

"I thought nothing of importance was found," Nun said.

"Nay, naught much worth keeping, but my mind ran wild with wonder about the owners." Guilt stabbed Faith. She had not given a second thought to the other chests.

They only found a set of pearls in Lady Rochelle's trunk and gowns and leather shoes so old they fell to pieces when touched. The other chests were even older and had nothing worth keeping. In the end, Darrin had ordered everything burned except for the pearls, which he placed in the small chest retrieved from his grandfather's belongings.

The chapel door swung open and Darrin walked in.

"My lord, how wonderful for you to be here on time," Nun said. "Were you, too, up all night thinking about the trunks like Lady Faith?"

Darrin raised a brow as his gaze slid to Faith's. "Nay. I slept well. The only thing that disappoints me is I did not find my father's or mother's things among the trunks. But perhaps Sir Adrien had everything destroyed."

Nun tapped a finger to her lips, looking perplexed. "I am trying to remember…I could have sworn Sir Adrien ordered—"

"Is it now time to begin?" Faith asked rapidly, looking at Father Chabot. The last thing she needed was Nun remembering where Sir Jean's trunk had been stored.

All three stared at her as if she were some termagant. This was not going well. She had wanted Darrin to come to chapel in hopes that his faith would be rekindled. She hoped to be an example of a good Christian. Instead, she had lied and covered up the truth, adding more distance and suspicion between them. Oh, she should give confession right now, but she held her tongue, fostering the divide between them.

Heavy feet pounding on the stones in the hallway drew their attention and saved Faith from any more scrutiny. Sir Rollin entered with his small group of knights, followed by a well-groomed Gouch and Monique.

"For the love of…" Darrin mumbled when he saw Gouch. "How long will this go on?"

Nun jabbed Darrin in the ribs. "Shh. This could be God's doing."

Father Chabot cleared his throat and asked for everyone to kneel. When all were ready, he began, "Lord God Almighty, blessed is the one who trusts in you."

Trust. The loss of trust had separated Darrin and her all those years ago. She should have stepped forward to protect Darrin when his father died, but she feared Sir Adrien would kill Nun. Would the reason make a difference to Darrin now? Probably not. That's why she needed to come to him with the proof that would clear his name forever. Then maybe he would trust her again.

And if he was guilty?

Faith tried to turn her attention back to Father Chabot's chants. "Woe unto them that call evil good and good evil..."

Was she doing that? Lying about the existence of Sir Jean's trunk to gain...what? Her husband's trust? Perhaps Sir Theodore was right. It would be better to tell the truth now than to try to explain her deception later. But how would that gain her husband's trust? She had already hidden the other trunk. To change course now before she had proof would not strengthen their relation.

Nay. Right or wrong, she would have to stay the course. A tear slipped down her cheek. *God forgive her.*

When Father Chabot finished the last prayer, the weight of her guilt hung heavy on her shoulders—lying to Darrin, hiding the truth and planning more deception in front of God's altar. *Could her soul be lost already?*

"Lady Faith?" Darrin's concerned face hovered above her as he held out his hand and helped her to her feet. "Are you well?"

She nodded and looked away, only to catch Nun's steady glare. *They both know.* A hard, large lump lodged in Faith's throat and almost choked the truth out of her. She coughed. "I am fine. Sometimes the dampness lays heavy on my chest."

Darrin nodded but did not leave as he usually did. He

clasped his hands behind him but did not offer a word. *Any moment now, he will call you out for the liar you are and throw you into one of the cells below.*

She could take it no longer. "My Lord, is there something you wish to say?"

"I-I am wondering"—he paused until they were alone, though Nun and Father Chabot were hovering near the entry—"if you would like to go through my grandfather's missives with me. Perhaps together, we could find something important."

The force of her deception slammed hard in her chest. He was reaching out to her. He wanted her help. This was the first time since his arrival he wanted to spend time with her, sharing confidences—like a true husband and wife.

The aye fluttered close to her lips. But then she thought of Sir Theodore waiting at the shed near the forest. *Don't be a fool. Darrin wants to spend time with you.*

"All right, should we take a look after we break our fast?" She held out her hand and he took it in his warm one.

A tenderness filled his eyes. "Aye, my lady." His smooth voice sent a quiver down her spine.

A commotion in the hall paused their exit. "My lord, my lord. You must come quickly. There's a fight in the village and I fear it might lead to death."

The fine lines on Darrin's forehead deepened; a hardness cloaked his eyes. "Forgive me, my lady. Perhaps later."

He strode from the chapel without a look back. Faith's knees became weak. An emotion between relief and disappointment washed over her. She crumpled to the floor and gazed up at the chapel cross, wondering if God's will had been done.

"Well, it's about time you got here," Sir Theodore huffed. "After I prayed all the way here because my lady asked, I used this ax to cut wood." He motioned to the chest with the ax in hand. "I should have been smashing that lock. I was beginning to think you changed your mind."

Her chilled cheeks from the brisk spring wind began to thaw in the warm, cozy hut. Though modest, she thought it was a lovely place—an old straw pallet, a few stools and a table. If she added a few blankets and a good, sturdy pot for cooking, then this would be a fine home, indeed. She sighed and turned her attention to Sir Theodore. "I almost did. Darrin wanted me to go read through his grandfather's letters."

Sir Theodore leaned the ax against a wall and threw some wood onto the hearth fire. "And you turned him down? Not a wise decision, my lady."

"Nay, I said I would help him, but then a commotion in the village pulled him away." Faith dragged a stool close to Darrin's father's trunk and then she noticed how tightly Sir Theodore gripped the ax. Visions of him cleaning a bloody knife the day at the pigpens pricked her fear. Mayhap coming here alone had been a terrible mistake.

"Is there something wrong?" he asked.

She licked her dry lips. "I-I am wondering..."

"Wondering what?"

She stood and edged her way to the door. She should run, but... "Sir Theodore, when the pigs were slaughtered, I saw you cleaning blood from your dagger."

He scratched his head. "Aye, pig's blood. What of it?"

"You admit it? You killed those pigs?"

He pulled his chin in and eyed her like she was the crazy one in the hut. "Nay. They were dead already. I only sawed off a leg or two so the parts would be easier for the peasants to lift and remove." Then he started laughing. "You think I am the culprit who has been causing all the trouble at the château? Oh, lady, you have much to learn about fighting and intrigue. If I were guilty, I sure wouldn't be cleaning my blade in plain sight."

The fear within her dissolved. How could she believe Sir Theodore the villain? If Darrin trusted him, then so should she. Faith returned to her stool and smiled. "Let's get started. For I am certain we will find answers to Sir Jean's death within."

Sir Theodore nodded, raised the ax, but paused. "What kind of a commotion?"

"What?" she asked, not following his train of thought.

"You said there was a commotion in the village."

"A fight. Some of the villagers were arguing about something." A war of emotions raced across Sir Theodore's face as he processed her words. "If you wish to go help Sir Darrin please do."

Sir Theodore combed a hand through his dirty beard. "Nay. A fight would do him good. If he gets in the middle, it might knock some sense into him."

"Sense about what?" Faith asked.

Sir Theodore snorted. "I think you two are a fine pair. Both as naïve as newborn babes." He raised the ax again and whacked the lock, which tumbled to the ground. "Well, my lady..." He winked. "Let us see what treasures are within."

Faith held her cloak over her nose and waited for whatever rank smell would seep out. But none came forth other than a mild musty scent from lack of attention. Tunics, breeches, cloaks and hose were neatly piled. Two pairs of boots, chain mail, a helm and Sir Jean's sword were all placed with care.

"I doubt this was packed by Sir Adrien." Sir Theodore pulled the sword from its scabbard. "He wouldn't have left this behind."

Faith ran her fingers along the edges of the trunk. "I remember. Nun packed this chest and ordered a few servants to take it to the dungeon. She threw in dried orris root mixed with roses and lavender."

"Yet yesterday, she said naught about it not being with the others."

"Nay. She didn't. Which means she knows we took it." Faith dug deeper in the trunk and pulled out a leather pouch with fine parchment within.

"Perhaps she hides a few secrets of her own and wants Sir Adrien to return." Sir Theodore knelt on one knee and pulled out the chain mail, examining it for holes.

Faith shook her head. "She and Sir Adrien argued all the time. They did not see eye to eye. He threatened often to send her away." Faith unfolded and scanned the parchments.

Sir Theodore dropped the chain mail back into the trunk and peered over her shoulder. "Do you see anything that would give us some answers?"

"I am not sure. These are accounts. Look here. This is the price Sir Jean received for the sale of a destrier and here is the amount received for an ox." She peeled through page after page. "This is interesting. Every month Sir Jean received an income from the Abbey of Sainte-Marie des Dames."

Sir Theodore leaned in closer. "This makes little sense. Why would Sir Jean receive money from an abbey? Usually it is the other way around. The Church demands money from the lords."

Indeed. Why was Sir Jean getting an income from the very abbey where she had been born? Her heart lurched. Nun must have known about this, but for years she had said nothing. Even though the room was warm, a chill gripped Faith's fingers and toes. Did the abbey give the money to Sir Jean to raise her? But why would they? She was but a child of some poor woman who stumbled on the abbey steps, heavy with child.

Unless that wasn't the truth. Had Nun lied? A sharp twist in Faith's stomach caused her body to sway on the stool. She grabbed the side of the trunk. The parchment slipped through her fingers and fell to the floor.

Sir Theodore caught her before she tumbled backward. "My lady?"

His features danced above her and then her foggy mind cleared. She wrinkled her nose. "Sir Theodore, you truly need a bath."

Perplexity etched the lines on his face and then suddenly he guffawed. "My lady, if my odor might cause you to faint, then by all means, I shall bathe." His mood then swung and became sober. "Will you be all right if I go to the yonder river? I shan't be long."

She eased away from him and leaned her back against the trunk. "You do not have to go now. You...your...dirtiness did not cause me to become light-headed. I fear it was the letter and what it means."

Sir Theodore picked it up and handed it back to her. "My lady, there must be something special about you indeed. For why else would King Richard order you to marry Darrin? Are you sure you are a peasant's daughter? Mayhap you are some grander lady's child."

His words sent her head to spinning again. Her lips and throat grew dry. "I... Nun would have told me if my circumstances were different."

His concerned brows drew upward. "My lady, you look pale. Here, let me help you to yonder pallet. You rest and I will take a bath."

With the letter still in her hand, he helped her to the pallet. Before leaving, he stoked the fire one more time. Faith closed her eyes. The crackle of the fire calmed her pounding head and eased her racing thoughts. Could she truly be a real lady? Sir Jean had raised her as such, but that was an act of compassion, not because she had any noble blood.

Her mind fluttered in a dream state. When she was little...before coming to the château, she remembered a man with eyes as grey as hers standing above her... What did he say...? *"Look at that fist."* Faith's eyes flew open as the man's laughter floated away. Was it a dream or was it truth? Could that have been a relative of hers?

Slowly she sat up. There might be other secrets with Sir Jean's things. She inched back to the trunk, returned the ledger page, and then dug to the bottom. Her fingers grazed on another small leather pouch. Inside she found a ruby ring and a small piece of parchment, worn as if it had been read and reread often. There were only a few words written. *Sorry. My love wasn't strong enough. A.*

The ring glistened in the firelight. The gold band was braided—a symbol of strength, a strong union. Could these have belonged to Darrin's mother? She had died when Darrin was young. Was that what this note meant? Unable to fight off illness, she wrote this quick note to Darrin's father? Were these the last words she gave to a scribe?

Faith glanced down at the worn wooden chest with its rusty hinges. A prick of shame filled her body. Sir Theodore had been right. Darrin should be searching through these belongings, not her. Instead of returning the note and ring to the chest, she jammed them into the pocket of her cloak. Nun might know who these belonged to as well. She closed the trunk. If there was more to learn, then it would be discovered by Darrin. Not by her and Sir Theodore.

She had barely returned to the pallet when Sir Theodore entered, soaking wet. "You did not remove your clothes?" she asked.

"Aye, but they stank worse than me so I dunked them in the stream as well, though I think they could use a good boiling."

"We can take care of that later." She stood and brushed some of the straw from her gown. "I have decided. This trunk is not for us to look through. Let us get a cart and take the chest back to Sir Darrin."

Sir Theodore wrung out his long hair and then gave it a shake, sending water droplets in every direction. "Aye, we should have left it with the others. He's not going to be happy about this. You might want to come up with a good explanation why you took it in the first place."

"I'll tell him the truth." Faith clasped her sweaty palms as she thought about Darrin's reaction.

Wadding his tunic in his hand, Sir Theodore squeezed out some excess water. "I think you should make something up. He doesn't trust you to begin with."

His words were a sharp blade. *He doesn't trust you.* She knew that, but hearing it from another only made the divide between her and Darrin grow. The broken lock, lying carelessly on the floor, taunted her. How would she explain her intrusion into Sir Jean's personal things? What reason could she give that would not heighten suspicion against her? The ring and note burned against her thigh. Why did she take the ring? If she gave it to Darrin, might he not wonder what else she had taken? She should return them to the trunk, but then Sir Theodore would know what she had done. Later, when he returned the cart to the stable, she would try to slip the ring and note back into the trunk. Hopefully, no one would be the wiser.

She brushed by him toward the door. "Come. Let us not tarry. For I want this off my conscience before nightfall."

They both mounted their horses. "My lady, a conscience is never satisfied and can never be cleared. The best we can do is live with it."

She pulled the reins of her horse toward the château. Then all she could do was pray for mercy, and that God would soften Darrin's heart. For if the Almighty did not, then very possibly she might be the first tenant in the dungeon in decades.

Fifteen

*And the prayer of faith shall save the sick, and the Lord
shall raise him up; and if he have committed sins,
they shall be forgiven him.*
James 5:15

IN THE DISTANCE, THEY SAW SMOKE COMING FROM the village. Sir Theodore pushed his horse into a gallop and Faith followed. The bellow of grey rose above the town. Injured men coughed and staggered, leaning on others, and the wailing of women could be heard before they were seen. In the midst of it all stood Sir Rollin with his sword drawn, barking out orders to his knights. Nausea squeezed Faith's stomach as she looked from one bloody farmer to the next. A few knights and peasants lay dead.

Sir Theodore quickly dismounted his horse and rushed to where Sir Rollin stood. "What happened here?"

Sir Rollin pointed his bloody sword to a pile of burning carts and then to a pile of broken hoes, ploughs and harrows. "A dispute broke out. One farmer accused another of breaking his plough, while another complained of a smashed harrow and cracked hoes. Yet another joined in the fight saying the wheels on his cart had been shattered. By the time Sir Darrin and I arrived, one of the carts was blazing and the villagers were charging each other with fists and pitchforks."

Faith dismounted and came to Sir Rollin's side. "Where is Sir Darrin?"

The color drained from his face. "My lady, we are not sure how it happened, but his lordship stepped into the middle of the fray and tried to restore peace diplomatically. At first it looked to be successful, then out of nowhere, blood started to flow from his back. He'd been stabbed. And that set the whole town aflame again."

"So you butchered these people to gain control?" Sir Theodore stood less than a finger from Sir Rollin and barked, "You're a knight. Surely you could have regained the peace and disarmed them without shedding more blood. They have pitchforks, not swords or spears."

Sir Rollin pushed Sir Theodore away. "Mayhap if you were here, things could have been handled differently. But Lord de Longue was down and clearly the wound was not caused by a pitchfork or spear, but a dagger. A very lethal weapon."

Remorse and anger flickered across Sir Theodore's face and guilt curled up Faith's spine. Part of this was her fault. Had she not asked for Sir Theodore's assistance earlier, he might have been with Darrin. A sudden chill of fear chased away the guilt. Her eyes quickly scanned the pile of dead. Where was Darrin? Her throat closed and she could not answer the question that seized her voice.

As if knowing her distress, Sir Theodore's gaze became cold. "Where's Darrin?"

Sir Rollin motioned with his head. "Back at the château."

Faith's heart quickened; she did not wait to hear more. She ran to her mount, but Sir Theodore's hand on her arm stalled her retreat. "I'll go with you," he said, his face packed with concern. She did not answer him right away, her mind a whirl of conflicts—guilt, remorse, caring and love flooded her body at the same time. *Oh, God, please do not take my husband.* The prayer shattered her. He was her husband and she had denied him because she questioned his faith.

The last few days' events rushed through her racing mind. Had she been any better? Had she acted like a Christian? She demanded he attend chapel and pray, yet her own thoughts during those prayers had been just as wayward and far from God. If he lived, she would take away the ultimatum. She could not, would not force him to attend chapel if his heart was not soft enough to accept Christ.

"Lady?" Sir Theodore's word came gently.

She nodded. The knight helped her mount the horse, but she did not wait for him to do the same. She needed to see Darrin, to tell him, he did indeed have a true wife.

Upon entering the hall, Faith was filled with a wave of relief when she saw Darrin, sitting in the lord's chair with Nun hovering over him. The smell of vinegar and myrrh greeted Faith as she knelt beside him. His bare chest was caked with dry blood except where a white cloth crisscrossed his shoulder, creating a wide bandage. A greyness painted his face and his breathing was ragged. Yet his hazel eyes rimmed with bright blue held recognition.

"Lady Faith," he rasped. "Come to see if you are a widow? I am sorry, but not yet."

She picked up his hand, placed it to her cheek. "My lord, I want no such thing. I pray you will survive this day and many more. I just wonder why you are not in your bed, where you could heal more swiftly." She looked up at Nun in question.

"He refused to go farther. Said he wanted all to see their lord was strong. Ridiculous. So I cleaned the wound as best I could and applied a poultice of yarrow and another herb I acquired from an old crusader awhile back—opium. He said it would help with the pain."

Before she finished her words, Darrin's eyes began to glaze. "Wine," he said. "I want some wine," he slurred.

"He'll be out soon," Nun whispered.

The hall door flew up and Sir Theodore strode in. "How is he?" he thundered from across the hall.

"What's this...Theo clean?" Darrin's glazed gaze rested on hers. "Faith..." He raised his good hand and thumped it on his chest. "Losing his heart...all lose their hearts." His hand slid to his side and his eyelids fluttered, then closed.

"He's delirious," Sir Theodore said.

Faith stood. "Aye. From the wound and the poultice." She went to the back of the chair, trying to get a better look at Darrin's wound. "I understand one of the peasants stabbed him."

Nun shook her head. "Who told you that?"

"Sir Rollin. He said that a skirmish broke out between the peasants and Sir Darrin got wounded trying to stop it," Sir Theodore piped in.

Nun laughed. "Sir Darrin may have been trying to stop it, but he wasn't stabbed by a peasant." She lifted the bandage. "Take a look. The wound goes straight through the shoulder. No dagger did this. This was done by a sword. Had the blade gone a little higher, I would have had to saw off his arm. As it stands now, I am not sure he will ever be able to hold a sword, let alone wield one again."

A soft cry left Faith's lips as Nun's words took meaning. A knight would rather die than not be able to wield his sword. The takeover of the château had not been easy. Many servants and peasants still believed Darrin murdered his father, and others were still loyal to Sir Adrien. "We must make sure the wound heals as clean as possible." If he could at least hold a sword, then mayhap he could still maintain control of the château.

Sir Theodore put his arm around Faith's shoulder. "Fear not, my lady. He is tough. He'll come out of this stronger."

A loud snore rattled and seeped out of Darrin's mouth as his head fell forward.

"Good. He finally is asleep." Nun motioned to a few servants standing close by. "Take Lord de Longue to his chamber. Make sure you are careful with his shoulder."

Three servants and Sir Theodore struggled to get Darrin out of the chair and up the stairs without waking him. He grumbled when they stumbled and when Sir Theodore banged into a wall sconce, but Darrin did not rouse from his deep sleep. Once in his room, Faith discarded her cloak, then ordered a fire to be built in the small hearth. She called for more linens and water for the cistern and pushed Sir Theodore out of the room. Nun entered with her herb sack and together they sat and watched Darrin's erratic breathing. They changed his dressing once and bathed his skin with cool water when he felt too hot.

When the noonday sun waned, Nun stretched and rubbed her back. "His breathing is even. He should rest easy for a while. I think you should go and rest. I will keep watch."

Faith shook her head. "Nay. It is a wife's duty. You go and rest first."

Nun placed a hand on Darrin's forehead. "He still is warm. Time will tell if the poultice can draw the poison from his body." She picked up the soiled linens. "I'll get some fresh ones and then I shall go rest for a few hours. If something changes, come and get me."

Once Nun left, Faith settled back in her vigil. Hope rose as she noticed the ashen color had left his cheeks. She folded her hands and prayed. *Dear Heavenly Father, thank you for your everlasting blessings and for the gift of your son to die for our sins. I humbly come before you to ask you to spare the life of Sir Darrin. He does not know it, but he is still your servant. Heal him and return his strength so that he may give service to you once again.*

A ragged cough tore through Darrin's chest and postponed the end of Faith's prayer. Spittle and sweat spewed from his mouth, but she could not find any linens to wipe his face. Then she remembered the cloth in her cloak. With haste, she retrieved the cloth, ignoring the tiny clink she heard as she made her way to Darrin's bedside.

Carefully she wiped his face. "You're going to be fine. God will heal you."

His eyes fluttered open and he stared at her as if she were a stranger. "Faith, what do you here? Father will be angry."

His lids slid shut, his mind still fogged and living in the past.

She folded the cloth over and dabbed his forehead. "Better sometimes to stay in the past, where our biggest worries were to be caught playing in each other's chambers."

Again he opened his eyes, thrashing on the bed. "Faith, kiss me. Just once. For I shall die without one kiss." His grip relaxed and his ghostly eyes closed.

Her heart flipped as she remembered when...the night his father had died. He had come home drunk and bawdy. He had been stumbling up the tower stairs as she was descending them. It had been a long time since they had played like children. He was a man of eighteen now and her a maid of fourteen. Their interest in each other had changed. Cornering her, he pinned her to the wall with his muscular body and begged for a kiss. She turned away from the foul odor of wine on his breath. He laughed and she squirmed to gain her release. She loved him and wanted him, but not like this. She wanted to kiss him in the daylight, when his breath was fresh and his mind was filled with pure thoughts.

His father shouted and immediately Darrin released her. She raced back up into her room as the shouts continued between father and son. The argument had ended with Darrin storming away. She remembered hearing him take to his horse and fleeing the keep as the winter wind howled. All night long she had tossed and turned as sleet pelted her window. Where had he gone on such a cold, shivering night? She had prayed he would return safely.

In the predawn hours, she heard a commotion outside her door. She grabbed a shawl and lit a tallow and made her way out in the hall. There, on the stair landing, she saw Darrin with a dagger in hand and his father lying in a pool of blood. His words rang in her ears. "'Tis not what you think...I found him thus."

She never doubted his words, but her uncle did and threatened to kill Nun if she did not tell the magistrate what she saw. The anger and hate that filled Darrin's eyes at her betrayal chilled her soul and never went away. Sometimes late at night, when she would close her eyes, she could still see his accusing and unbearable glare. She killed his love for her that day. Another murder, only this one was of the heart.

A tear slid down her cheek, which she quickly wiped away when Nun waltzed back into the room with fresh linens, placing them on the table.

The change in atmosphere was not lost on the older woman. "Has something happened?"

Faith moved back to her chair. "Nay, he is just speaking gibberish."

Again Nun looked at her patient and placed a palm on his head. "His body is still fighting the poison. Let us pray he wins the battle."

If he lived, Faith hoped someday he would forgive her. For she desperately wanted to win his heart again.

"Child? Where is your mind?"

Where, indeed? Faith shook her head. "I am just concerned. I hope he will be well."

Nun gave a slow, unbelieving nod. "Are you sure you wish to stay?"

Faith cast her gaze to Darrin. "Aye. There is nowhere else I wish to be."

Sixteen

*Her princes in the midst thereof are like wolves ravening
the prey, to shed blood, and to destroy souls,
to get dishonest gain.*
Ezekiel 22:27

THE NEXT MORNING, FAITH FOUND SIR THEODORE milling around Darrin's door. "How is he?" he asked.

Seeing the worry in his eyes, Faith placed a gentle hand on his chest. "He fights. The fever still rages within."

Sir Theodore raked a hand through his wild hair. "Is there naught I can do?"

"Aye. You can pray."

He stepped back and gave a look of disbelief. "You ask again for prayer. I know not if God listens. In truth, before the other day, I do not think I have spoken to the Lord since leaving England."

Shock coursed through her. "Not even before a battle?"

He shrugged. "I figured if God wanted to take me, then so be it. I have not much to live for."

His story was known by many. Jilted by Lady Eleanor de Maury for another. But could such a rejection kill his desire to live? Then she thought of Darrin struggling to live. If he would die, would she care for her own life? The last ten years had been a torture not knowing where he was or if he lived or died. Yet she had hope that one day he would return. But what if he died today or on the morrow?

Would she be able to survive without him?

The horrible thought pressed heavier than a sack of grain on her chest—living without Darrin day after day, month after month, year after year. She had already done so and it had been torture. She understood Sir Theodore's actions. She took his hands in hers. "I am certain that God has a very special plan for you and for Sir Darrin. Go and pray. And when you are tired, pray some more."

His head fell to his chest. "All right, my lady. I will. For you and for him."

"And for yourself," she said, giving his hands a gentle squeeze.

He nodded and turned away, but not before she saw the tears in his eyes.

Nun and Faith rotated their duties for the next two days. Each morn before taking her place next to Darrin's bed, Faith would go to the chapel and pray. Often she would find Gouch and Monique there, praying for Darrin too. Once, upon leaving, Sir Theodore stood in the doorway. Neither of them said a word, but communicated their concern with a simple nod.

On the night of the third day, Faith refused to leave Darrin's chamber when Nun came in to give relief. "I will stay here until he wakes, for he has slept long enough."

Nun plopped the clean linens down on the table, which had become her new habit. "Do you think your diligence will wake him?" She laughed and shook her head. "He may sleep another month." She went over and felt Darrin's brow, another daily habit. "He is cool. A good thing." She turned back to Faith. "If you do not wish to sleep, mayhap you should bathe. Unless you wish to assault his senses when he does awakes."

Faith looked down at her crushed gown. What was Nun speaking about? Each morn she changed her garments. A heavy sniff gave clear meaning—she had not bathed since the day Darrin had been injured.

"Perhaps you are right. I shall take a quick bath. But do not get too comfortable; I shall return." Faith rushed out of Darrin's chamber, caught a servant in the hall and called for a tub and hot water to be brought to her room as soon as possible. Once inside her chamber, she stripped out of her clothes and placed a cloak around her shoulders and waited. The efficiency of the servants surprised her when she heard a swift knock. But when she opened the door, she did not find the servants, but Sir Rollin.

Seeing her present...state, he uncomfortably cleared his throat. "My lady, I-I am sorry." His gaze swept around the room and came to rest on the pile of clothes on the floor.

Faith clutched the top of her cloak and expected him to back into the hallway, but that was not the case. Instead he stepped closer. Immediately she retreated backwards. Not wanting to look fearful, she straightened her shoulders and lifted her head, giving him a sharp eye. "What do you want, Sir Rollin?"

"I, we, all the knights, have been concerned. No word has come to us about how Sir Darrin fares?" Those may have been his words, but his eyes bespoke of other thoughts as he came closer still.

She took another step back and bumped into a chair that went crashing to the floor. Before she could move, Sir Rollin swept farther into the room, righting the chair. "You must be careful, my lady," he said, his voice low and sultry. He reached out and took a lock of her hair and wrapped it around his finger.

She tried to step away, but her back was met by the cold stone wall. Her throat constricted. "Remember yourself, Sir Rollin." Her words came out like a tiny squeak from a trapped mouse.

He leaned into her. "I remember much from our past, Faith. Surely, you remember how close we were?" he whispered in her ear.

"I remember I am a married woman and you have overstepped your boundary." She slammed her bare foot on top of his boots.

He laughed and pushed in even closer. "Lady, there is naught you can do to me that could cause me harm." A loud ruckus from the hallway drew his attention and he immediately stepped away.

"Blossom!" Sir Theodore called from the doorway, a bucket of hot water in hand. A gaggle of servants followed him into the small chamber, carrying an iron tub and more hot water. To make room, Sir Theodore inched over to stand in front of Sir Rollin. A large amount of hot water sloshed onto the knight's clothing. "Oh, sorry, Blossom. I guess you get another bath today," Sir Theodore guffawed. "What's that make, five or six? Pretty soon you will be like those shriveled dates from the Holy Land."

Sir Rollin's lips thinned as he wiped a hand on his wet tunic. "At least I do not stink as you."

"Hey? I took a bath two days ago and changed my tunic too. But if you think I need another bath, so be it." With his free arm, Sir Theodore grabbed Sir Rollin around the shoulder and dumped the remaining water from the bucket on both their heads.

Sir Rollin gasped, wiped his face with both his hands and stepped away. "You're mad," he shouted.

"Aye." Sir Theodore grinned, crazy-eyed.

Even Faith could not hold back her laughter. Pretty soon the servants chuckled as they filled the tub with the remaining tepid water. With a huff, Sir Rollin exited the room. The servants followed after him with their empty buckets, laughing and jeering.

When they were alone, Sir Theodore became instantly serious. "My lady, you must learn to be prudent while Darrin is ill. Some may try to take advantage of you. I shall have a guard posted outside your door."

She clutched the cloak around her even more so. "I had not thought that would be necessary, but I guess I was wrong." Her thoughts immediately drifted to the village skirmish. "Have you been able to uncover what happened in the village…who started the trouble?"

His eyes became hooded. "Nay, my lady, but… I shall not rest until all is solved."

Even though she knew he held something back, she did not press him. The time would come when Darrin would be strong again. "Thank you, Sir Theodore."

He bowed and made his way to the door.

Then her mind took a switch. "One more thing. The trunk…"

He turned. "Aye?"

"Where is it?"

"In the hut. With all that has happened, I thought it would be best to leave it there."

"Could you bring it to Darrin's chamber? I would have it there for him when he awakes."

A slight smile set on his lips. "Aye, my lady. I shall fetch it now if thieves have not taken it already."

Faith's heart lurched. "You do not think—"

"Nay. No one has been there in years and none would think anything of value would remain within. I am sure the chest is safe."

She nodded. He bowed and made his way to the door.

"Sir Theodore, one more thing. Since your hair and beard are wet, perhaps you might want to clean them up a bit."

He tilted his head. "If it pleases you, then I shall." He tipped his head and left, closing the door behind him.

Had she known it would have been so simple, she would have asked him to do so the first night they met. Sir Theodore was indeed an odd mystery.

Though the water was warm and comforting, after a short time, Faith exited the bath and smoothed her fingers through her wet, tangled hair. She dried her body, put on a clean, pale blue gown and wrapped a silver-threaded girdle around her waist. She plaited her hair but left it plain; after all, she had no plans of going into the great hall or anywhere in the château other than Darrin's chamber. She'd watch and wait for Darrin to awake from his deep sleep.

Wouldn't that be wonderful if today was the day? Nun said he was getting stronger. Faith rubbed her hands over her gown. Oh, she hoped there was some way to close the gap between them. A streak of sunlight filtered in through the narrow window and danced off the wall behind her. Certainly, the birds chipped loudly in the trees because of the cheery day. Soon there would be more flowers in the meadow. This would be a fine day for Darrin to wake. Like this new spring day, she would try to start anew with him. She would be a loving wife. Together they could conquer the past, and maybe, just maybe, they could learn to love again.

"My lady, my lady." Her soft musings were interrupted by a servant at her chamber door. "Come quick. Sir Darrin is awake!"

Seventeen

*And the man said, The woman whom thou gavest
to be with me, she gave me of the tree, and I did eat it.*
Genesis 3:12

THE ACHE IN THE BACK OF HIS HEAD GREW AS IT spread forward around his ears and eye sockets to spike up to his forehead. His vision wobbled in and out along with his hearing. Darrin tried to focus his mind on where he was and what had happened. Slowly, his memory returned. He had been wounded in the shoulder, but he wouldn't be surprised if his head had been split open as well.

Two shadowy figures stood above him, whispering. One of the spirits gently took his cool hand, cocooning it in warmth. The other leaned over him. "Wake up, Sir Darrin. You cannot sleep the day away," the voice thundered.

He knew the owner of that voice. "Nun," he muttered. "Not so loud."

"Mmm. He will be fine," she said to the spirit holding his hand.

The tender, quiet spirit sat down next to him and kissed his hand. "Darrin, Darrin," she said gently. "Do wake up. It is such a glorious day. Listen, do you hear the birds?"

He forced his mind to concentrate on the soft twitters that drifted into his chamber on a mild breeze. Now he remembered it was spring and every day more and more songbirds returned from their winter homes. Yet, when he opened his eyes, an angel held his hand. Her pale blonde hair sparkled gold and silver in the bright light.

"I am dead," he said. "Has God sent an angel to pass judgment on me?"

A heavy pressure came down on his forehead and then touched each of his cheeks. "He's cool, yet he raves like a lunatic."

Why was Nun here? Had she passed on with him? If so, then mayhap his sentence had been given and Nun would deal out his punishment. "Nun, are you dead too?"

"Nay. You and I are still among the living."

Her voice throbbed through his head and grew until he could hear his beating heart. "I feel dead. My head...feels like a split-open pomegranate." He raised a hand and touched his forehead to make sure it still was intact.

"'Tis the opium. In a few days, you will be fine."

He did not believe her, but said nothing. Soft fingers traveled from his other hand and up his arm, sending a peace through his whole being. With great effort, he opened his eyes and looked at the angel sitting next to him, her body and face taking form—a pale blue angel, come to give him comfort. Slowly her features bent and swayed until his vision returned.

Faith? The racing of his heart grew louder in his ears. Faith sat next to him, stroking his arm like the dutiful, loving wife. Could she not just come to him as she truly was, a viper waiting to fill him with poison? Nay, she came to him as an angel pretending to be full of love and trust.

His body shuddered as he fought to regain his anger toward her, but instead his rage sent his wounded shoulder pulsing. "Why? Why do you torture me?"

Perplexity filled her eyes and wrinkled her brow. She leaned forward and put her cool, soft palm on his cheek. "I have not come to torture you. From this day forth, there shall be no grief between us. This I promise. You are my husband and I am your wife."

Her words swept away the fury and the pain, leaving only

exhaustion. His eyelids grew heavy and once again he drifted into a dream world filled with angels that all looked like his wife, Faith.

Loud snoring brought him out of his sleep and it took him a few moments to realize it was his own. His eyes adjusted to the fading afternoon light. A path of dancing dust particles glimmered within the rays and ended at the foot of his pallet. There, he saw Faith, sitting in a chair, her head pillowed in her hands, resting on a small table. White-hot pain pierced his shoulder when he tried to sit up. 'Twas then he noticed the cumbersome bandage. Ah, the wound from the village. He tried to flex his fingers. A river of pain sluiced up his arm. A loud groan escaped his lips and woke Faith. Unknowingly she ran a few fingers across her lips and set his insides afire. If she knew the power she held over him, he would be destroyed before a nightingale could sing.

She smiled and stood, stretching her lithe form before him. "How are you this eve?" she asked.

If he told her he was as weak as a lamb and his shoulder hurt like the whole French army marched through it, would she come and caress his brow with her tender touch and gentle, healing words or would she laugh and mock him in his weakened state? He tried to push himself farther up, ignoring the shards of agony shooting up his arm. "I am fine."

She raised a skeptical eyebrow and came to sit next to him. "I think you are putting on a brave front. Nun has taken away the herb which shielded the pain. She fears you may grow too fond of it. Perhaps I should tell her to give you a little more."

Even though the pain was indeed great, he shook his head. "Nay. She is right. Better to suffer through than to be seized by a new devil."

"Do you speak of this plant or another demon?"

He wanted to say both. The demon of hate and revenge had helped him to survive when he left his home all those years ago and had kept him from loving her. But instead of saying thus he chose the safe route. "I fought with many returning Crusaders. They came back with many things an apothecary might use. I have had worse pain in the past from other injuries. I can endure this."

She became quiet and looked away. "I am sorry," she said softly.

He gave a mirthless laugh. "Not as much as I, my lady." Silence and sorrow of a life long lost sat between them. Uncertain how it happened, he found her hand in his and gave it a slight squeeze. "I suppose I will have these days added to my chapel time before you will fulfill your vow?"

Her eyes glistened with tears, for now or for the past, he wasn't sure. She shook her head. "Nay. You do not have to come anymore. I will become a true wife as soon as you are able."

A new pain filled the middle of his chest and chiseled at the ice in his heart. This ache scared him more than any other wound he had received before. "You will give of yourself freely with no conditions, even though I do not love you?"

Sadness swept into her eyes and was quickly covered with the drop of her gaze. "I am your wife."

Torment dug deep in his chest and split it in two. He had won. He had broken her. Where was the joy? The relief? She would give him all he wanted for nothing in return. A selfless act. Why? This was not her true nature. He tried to rekindle old hates that had protected him in the past and found they were harder to summon. A film of unshed tears hung at the corners of his eyes. He threw his head back to stop their spilling. "Leave me. I am tired."

She leaned over the bed. "Are you in pain? How can I help you?"

He turned his face away from her and closed his eyes, willing the tears to remain where they were. "Nay. Just tired. Go."

But she did not leave. She sat back down and folded her hands like a patient wife.

He gritted his teeth. If she did not leave now, he would break down like a young child wailing for his mother. He cleared his throat, struggling to hold the flood at bay. "I think I am hungry."

He heard her rise. "I-I will see what I can find." She paused at the door. "Are you certain you will be all right?"

"Aye," he croaked out.

The door closed with a click. He waited…then wept for what was and what might be.

As Faith was running down the stairs, she encountered Sir Theodore and a few servants huffing as they carried Darrin's father's trunk upward. "Where are you going with that?" Faith asked, trying to hide the horror in her voice.

Cleanly shaved, Sir Theodore ordered the servants to lower the trunk, cautiously balancing it between two steps. "Where you told me to take it. To Sir Darrin's chamber."

Faith put a hand on her throat. "Oh, dear. I do not think that is wise to do so now."

"Come again?" Sir Theodore asked, placing his hands on his hips.

She bit her lower lip. "I think we should wait. He has just woken up and I don't think we should upset him just yet," Faith said, barely above a whisper.

Sir Theodore narrowed his eyes and looked at the servants, who were quietly taking in the whole conversation. "Then where should we go?"

Where? The trunk couldn't sit in the great hall. Without a lock, it would be looted. Not to mention, the questions the trunk would raise if it were left in such a public place. Her gaze went up and down the stairs. "Take it to my chamber."

The servants did not move, but looked to Sir Theodore, who stared at her. "Are you sure?"

Unable to give voice to her uncertain decision, she nodded.

"To Lady Faith's chamber. I shall follow you shortly." With the wave of his hand, the servants lifted the trunk and continued up the stairs. When they were safely out of hearing, he turned back to Faith. "You are making a mistake."

Those weren't the words she wished to hear. "Sir Darrin has just awakened and he is...acting odd. This might cause more harm than good right now."

"If he finds the chest in your room, there will be hell to pay. My lady, reconsider. Put it back in the dungeon. It has been burnt out and scrubbed clean. I'll find a sturdy lock for it. No one will be the wiser. Then later, we can say it was found in another part of the dungeon."

"No one will be the wiser? Surely you jest? The servants know, and what about the cooks in the kitchen and anyone else you may have encountered while dragging the trunk about? And as far as putting a new lock on an old trunk, don't you think Sir Darrin would notice? And let us not forget Sir Rollin. What would he do if he saw you hauling that trunk around?"

Sir Theodore rubbed his smooth chin. "Aye. We do not know his loyalties."

She put a hand on his elbow. "Then please. Put it in my room for now. We can move it later, at night, when Darrin sleeps. We will tuck it under the table. He will not see it until he is well enough to get out of bed, which I am certain wouldn't be for a few more days. He'll have more strength to deal with what the trunk holds." *And she would have time to return the ring.*

"Nay, the plan is bad." Sir Theodore glanced over his shoulder to make sure they were alone. "Darrin has spent many nights on the battlefield. Now that he is feeling better, even the slightest noise will wake him. You'll not be able to dupe him."

There has to be a way. The smell of fowl and leeks wafted up the château steps. *The food, of course.* "Sir Darrin has asked for a meal. I will add some of Nun's herbs to make him sleep. Then we should be able to sneak the trunk into his room. None will be the wiser."

Sir Theodore's eyes clouded with doubt. "My lady, I don't know—"

"It has to work. It is the only way. Please."

He dropped his chin to his chest. "All right. But methinks this is foolery. Nothing good ever comes from deception, my lady. Nothing."

His words hit her hard. She didn't want to deceive Darrin; she just wanted to protect him until he was strong enough to hear the truth—all of it. "Aye you are right, but let us pray this is not one of those times. One more thing, Sir Theodore."

"Aye?" He lifted a wary brow.

"I would have never guessed, but you are quite handsome."

His face turned as pink as a spring rose.

Darrin lay in the dark staring at a candle. The tiny flame fought for its life until the wax became a watery soup and snuffed out the struggling embers. Faith had brought him a plate of food, and at first, he craved it, but then his appetite eased until he could not take more than a few bites. She had become overly stressed at his lack of enthusiasm toward the meal, and to ease her nerves, he told her to leave the trencher, promising he would eat later. He then sent her on a mission to find some wine. After she was gone, he spied a boot close to the bed. He reached over and dumped the contents of the trencher into the boot. When she returned the empty trencher brought a smile to her face. He took a few sips of wine and surprisingly enjoyed her endless chatter.

Nun came in to change his dressing, and pronounced him well on the way to a full recovery. He had some doubts since his arm remained stiff. As the eve wore on, he grew more and more tired and both women left, vowing to check on him later. But sleep did not come. He wondered about the damage in his shoulder, but mostly, he thought about Faith and her desire to be a true wife. Perhaps he had been wrong about her all along. Perhaps her words to the magistrate, when his father died, had been innocently given with no malice. Perhaps she really wanted to be a true wife because she cared for him.

He wanted to trust her, but then what? A rush of fear entered his chest and spread like wildfire through his body. If he trusted her, he might fall under her spell again. When he was a young man of eighteen summers, his heart burst with love for her.

Just as the flames of the past started thawing his frozen heart, he heard latch on the door click open. He closed his eyes, feigning sleep, not wanting Nun or Faith to waste their evening watching over him.

"Good, he sleeps," he heard Faith whisper.

He kept his eyes shut as he heard her make her way down the hall, forgetting to close the door. Should he call after her? Nay, he was sure he could hobble over and close it. But then he heard her again and the grunts and mumbles of others. With perked ears, he could sense a man standing over him.

"Are you sure he is out?" Theo nudged Darrin in his good shoulder.

"Aye. Nun's herbs were in the food and I added more to the wine. It took a while, but he finally fell asleep," Faith said.

There was a commotion in the room. Darrin cracked open his eyelids and peeked through his lashes. Even in the darkness, he was pretty sure two servants lumbered in with a trunk, placing it under a small table.

Theo ordered the servants out and then turned to Faith. "I hope you know what you are doing."

"Don't worry. He will understand. Now go and make

sure the servants say nothing about this to anyone. I'll come along shortly. I just want to sit a bit with him."

Theo grunted, glanced briefly toward the bed and then left, closing the door quietly behind him. But Faith did not sit down. From what Darrin could see in the dark, she began to rummage through her cloak. A little gasp left her lips when she did not find what she was looking for. Again she patted herself down, then removed the cloak, searching for something. When the item was not found, she opened the door but again did not close it.

As the serpent of distrust grew anew within him, Darrin waited. He listened to her knocking around down the hall, perhaps in her chamber. Finally, she returned with a fresh tallow in hand. She placed it on the table and began looking around the room. He feared she would find the food in his boot and prayed her search would not take her near the bed. While she looked in the hearth, a glitter of gold caught his eye, lodged between two wooden floorboards near the table.

Was this what she looked for? He could not be sure. But whatever she sought and could not find was causing her great distress. A ripple of fresh betrayal coursed through his body. If he had been strong enough, he would have gotten up and wrung her neck. How stupid he had been. He was ready to believe her, trust her and love her.

When her search failed, she picked up the candle and quit the room, closing the door behind her. Darrin waited until he heard her steps retreat down the tower stairs. *Blast her to hell.* Rage and fury pulsed through him and gave him the strength to rise from his bed and stumble over to the table. He knelt down and dug out the golden object. Once in his hand, the object felt rough and then smooth. A large hole gaped in the middle. *A ring.*

Darrin leaned on the table and struggled to his feet. He held the ring up to the moonlight. The braided band stretched up to a red ruby. A woman's ring. A ring he remembered when he was a young boy. A ring he had not seen for a very long time.

A cold, icy chill rushed up Darrin's spine and sent a hard layer of frost around his frozen heart. This was his mother's ring.

The next morn, the spring air disappeared and the frigid winds of the winter past returned. No birds were heard in the courtyard below, nor were there sunny rays beaming down into Darrin's chamber. The greyness of the day suited him just fine, for it fit his mood perfectly. He pushed himself to a sitting position and waited. The fury of last night's betrayal had ebbed into a low simmer of malice and resentment.

Faith's arrival should have been a lovely distraction. Dressed in a radiant blue gown, her hair unadorned, a braid of spun silver and gold drifted down her slender back. What word could be used to describe her? More than exquisite, more than magnificent, angelic and yet bewitching. Aye, she had the look of an angel and the heart of a witch who could tear the soul from one's body.

She gave a faint smile and pleasant, "Good morning," but her gaze never lit upon his. Her eyes kept scanning the room, searching for the object that now sat in his father's chest. After dumping the contents of his boot out the window, Darrin had spent part of the night looking through his father's things. The broken lock had not gone unnoticed. For some reason, Faith and Theo had concealed his father's trunk, until now. What were they looking for? What else might she have stolen?

He had been rash in the past, wanting to trust her, but once again, she showed who she really was—a person who could turn even the best of men with her wiles. Never would he have thought Theo would be taken in by her. And yet he snuck around with Faith. Darrin wondered what other games the two played.

She placed another trencher of food on his lap and then

her nose wrinkled as she spotted his boot with last night's food drippings on the side. "Have you been ill?" she asked.

He shrugged and continued to stare at her. "I slept fitfully. Either the food had gone sour or my innards were not ready to accept it."

Her hands began to shake and he could see the wheels in her mind turn. She wondered if he heard them bring in the trunk last night. Oh, how wonderful to see her squirm. Faith held out a cup of honeyed mead and he took a sip, keeping his gaze steady on hers.

"But fear not, my lady. I think by week's end I will be strong enough to fulfill my duties to you as a husband." The cup slipped from her grip, but he quickly caught the vessel and her hand. Her fingers were icy when he slipped his hand upward to graze her wrist. Her pulse was rapid, dancing a fine tune. "I am the one lying in bed, but you are colder than me. Are you feeling well this day…Faith?"

The reaction of using her given name in a sensual way made Faith jerk her hand, yet he held on tight, enjoying her discomfort. Again, she gave her hand a tug, and this time, slowly, he let it go.

Before either could say a word, she was on her feet and across the room, gazing out the window. "I-I am fine. I, too, did not sleep well last night."

"Is it a trouble I could help you with? The look of worry is deep in your eyes."

The corner of her mouth twitched, but she only shook her head. Darrin's inquisition was interrupted when Nun swept into the room with fresh linens.

"Good morning, Sir Darrin. How fare you this morn?" She stopped when she saw the trencher of food on his lap. "Are you eating?" Nun gazed down at the pieces of meat in a thick sauce and then turned a sharp eye on Faith. "What are you thinking? He should be eating a watery pottage, not heavy meats." Nun took the trencher from Darrin's lap and handed it to Faith.

Darrin rejoiced as her face turned as pale as her hair.

Suffer, my dear. Suffer as I have. Where, oh, where is that precious ring?

But the torment should come from him, not another. "Do not blame her. Last night, I was extremely hungry and *my wife*"—he paused and smiled—"wanting to please me, gave me a fine meal. This morn, she wished to please me again."

Nun twisted her head from him to Faith and then back to him. "Well, aren't the two of you a loving pair." Nun narrowed her gaze on Faith. "Get the pottage."

His spirits fell when Faith did not hesitate; she was out of the door with the trencher of food faster than a fox shags up a tree in a hunt. Darrin took a deep breath. The game would have to wait until later.

"What is going on?" Nun asked as she took the old linen off his wound.

"I don't know what you are talking about." He winced as she raised his arm a mite.

"You don't? You're a simpering sod and she's as frightened as a child caught stealing a loaf of sweet bread. What goes on here?"

Darrin motioned with his head to the trunk under the table. "See there."

A gasp left Nun's lips as she paused while changing his dressing. She went to the table and bent down. "Why, that's your father's chest. Where was it found?"

"Where indeed," Darrin said dryly.

Nun rose and came back to the bed and resumed fixing his wound. "I don't like the tone of your voice. I know what you are thinking."

He looked up at her and raised a brow. "And what am I thinking?"

"That Faith hid that trunk from you until now. If she did, she had a good reason." Nun tugged hard on the dressing.

Darrin gritted his teeth until the pain subsided. "And, pray tell, what would be that reason? Look at the hacks and grooves on the latch. The lock has been cut off."

She frowned. "There has to be a good reason for her actions."

"A reason, aye. Good, nay. She meant to hide this from me until she had examined what lay inside."

Nun dumped the soiled linen into a basket. "Mayhap she feared you wouldn't share the contents with her."

A cynical laugh left Darrin's lips. "Truly you believe that? Did I not open all the other trunks in her presence and did I not ask her to go through my grandfather's letters with me? Nay. She knew whose trunk this was and she feared the contents would incriminate her."

Nun dropped the basket on the floor and put her hands on her hips. "She had nothing to do with your father's death. Your mind has been spoiled to the point I don't think you would see the truth staring you in the face. If she meant to hide this, why did she return it?"

To cover her evil deeds. But he kept his thoughts to himself. He wanted to worm the truth out of Faith's beautiful lips with slow torture. He wanted her confession and he wanted her to hang for the complicity in his father's death and for the destruction of his heart.

The friction had only begun when the door opened again and Faith entered with the pottage. He took the bowl and smiled up at her. "My thanks, my dear." He let his gaze travel to Nun. "I wish to be alone with my wife," he said calmly.

Nun's lips formed a hard line and an array of emotions passed over her face before she roughly picked up the basket and made her way to the door. "Don't do anything you're going to regret," she huffed before leaving the room, slamming the door behind her.

With bewilderment, Faith turned to Darrin. "What was that all about?"

Now. Her punishment would begin.

Darrin took a slurp of his soup and then, with his spoon, he pointed to the trunk. "Look. Someone has brought me a gift in the middle of the night."

The paleness of her skin became almost translucent. She bit her lower lip to stop its tremble. Blue swirled with the grey in her eyes, creating a stormy appearance. Her spine snapped stiff.

"Do you think we should open it?" he asked.

The fingers on both her hands curled until all that was visible was two white-knuckled fists.

Perfect!

Eighteen

*I will open my mouth in a parable: I will utter
dark sayings of old: Which we have heard and known,
and our fathers have told us.*
Psalm 78: 2 & 3

A SWIFT, IRRITATING KNOCK AT THE DOOR DIVERTED Darrin's plan for a moment. It better not be Nun returning to interfere.

"Enter," Darrin snapped.

Theo popped his head into the room, looking more than a little worried. "I have just dropped by to see how you are doing." Though those were his words, his gaze darted around the chamber and came to rest on Faith with a look of relief. Probably Nun had found him in the hall and sent him up, thinking Lady Faith might need an ally.

"Theo, you have removed your whiskers and smell a mite better. What brings about this great change?"

"Lady Faith asked me to take them off," Theo said, rubbing his chin as if the beard remained intact.

Darrin slid his gaze to Faith. "Of course. It is hard to say no to our lady." The ache in his arm traveled to his heart. Had they cuckolded him—his friend and his wife?

Bright blotches of color began to form on her skin as she tried to hide her fists within the folds of her gown.

With a heavy sigh, Darrin hid the hurt deep within. He held out the bowl to Faith. "Can you put this on the table? I am not hungry anymore."

She unfolded her hands and Darrin noticed the cruel red marks where her nails had dug into the palms of her hands. But he said nothing as she took the bowl from him and placed it on the table.

"Look, Theo. My father's trunk has been returned. Isn't that interesting?" Darrin gestured to where the chest sat.

The pleading look Theo gave Faith filled Darrin's gut with resentment. *Theo looks to her? His loyalty should be to him.*

"I ordered the trunk to be brought here," Faith said, the color now high in her cheeks. "With you being ill, I did not know if you were strong enough to have knowledge of the trunk and its contents, so I ordered it to be delivered while you slept. I believed once you were well enough to notice, you'd be strong enough to explore your father's things."

When he moved and stared over the edge of the bed, Darrin clenched his teeth to hide the pain from his injury and the mutilation of his heart. "Was this trunk with the others? Why did you not bring it to me then?"

"I did not want others to see it. Such as Sir Rollin," she said, her voice almost a whisper.

Liar! She could not even look at him as she spoke... Yet he held his control. The time would come to take both to task for their treachery. "Ah, good thinking. Bring the trunk over, as I am excited to see what lies within." *And watch her actions betray her.*

His friend, Sir Theodore de Born, stood like a piece of petrified wood with large, knotty saucer eyes while Faith twisted and wound her hands in her blue gown until it resembled a ripple of waves in a turbulent sea. Even her skin seemed to be taking on a blue hue as the redness seeped away from her cheeks.

"My lord, are you sure you are up to this? Mayhap later, after you have had a little more of your pottage," she said, still staring at the boards beneath her feet.

Whatever was inside or wasn't inside they both truly feared. Did they think to put off the truth forever or was there another plan afoot? "Aye. I am filled with excited energy. Come. Let us have a look."

Faith nodded to Theo. And as if the roots beneath his feet had been whacked away, he stumbled forward and hauled it over to the bedside.

Once again, the mangled latch void of a lock sent a fire of fury to Darrin's gut. But he tamped it down by patting the bed and pulling his lips back into a smile. "Come here, my dear. Let us look together."

She hesitated, then smoothed her hand on her wrinkled gown and came to sit next to him. Spirals of pain shot up his arm when he tried to lift his forearm to her lap. She must have noticed his discomfort, for she tenderly placed it there for him. The coolness of her hand seeped into his warm, throbbing skin. In another time, he would have relished such a simple act of kindness.

He steeled his mind from such a thought and turned his gaze to Theo. "Open it. Let us see what secrets my father has."

Darrin felt Faith's body stiffen, and she held her breath as Theo flipped open the latch and lifted the lid. Everything was as he had found it last night—his father's tunics neatly folded on top. He reached over and grabbed a green brocade tunic. "I remember this, don't you, Faith?"

When he looked at her, the blue tint of her skin faded away, being replaced by a green almost the same color as his father's brocade tunic. A laugh stuck in Darrin's throat. Since she had come to his chamber this morn, her face had gone from white to red to blue and now to green. What would be next? Yellow or orange? Mayhap she could produce all the colors of the rainbow if she stayed here long enough.

Again she tilted her head in acknowledgement but remained quiet. So did her loyal knight, Sir Theodore. He knelt down next to the chest as if it were a sepulcher. Darrin almost called the pair out for the scoundrels they were, but instead he focused on his hate that would soon give him justice.

Theo handed Darrin the green tunic and also his father's sword. Carefully, he pulled it from its scabbard. It was as he remembered. The grip made of iron and braided with a heavy leather. The pommel a simple circle engraved with a cross. The *chappe* smoothly carved with a dove to represent the Holy Spirit. His father, a religious man, not only in speech but in action as well. A pang of shame and despair crept into Darrin's heart. *How he had failed his father.* With care, Darrin ran his fingers along the blade as his throat clogged with unshed tears. "'Tis beautiful."

"Aye," Theo answered without even looking up. Confirming Darrin's suspicions all the more—Theo had seen this sword before when he helped Faith open the chest.

Darrin returned the sword to its scabbard. "What else is there?" he asked quietly.

"There is more clothing, and this." As if knowing where to go, Theo moved his hand under the garments and pulled out a leather pouch.

"What?" Darrin opened the pouch. "Parchments?"

Neither conspirator gave comment.

Though he had briefly looked at the ledgers last night, he feigned ignorance. He flipped through the pages. "Why, these are my father's ledgers."

Without much thought, he flipped to the last entry. The day of his father's death. He wondered why his uncle would not have kept these with his accounts, the same with his father's sword. The sword carried value and the ledgers carried knowledge of the château. Yet both had been stowed away.

Darrin handed them to Faith. "Perhaps you and I could go through these later."

Her neck gave another wobbly nod. Her silence continued. Perhaps the trunk had swallowed up her voice. He almost laughed at the thought, but instead, to keep his composure, he glanced inside once again.

"Is there anything else?" Darrin asked.

"Besides clothing, there is your father's chain mail and

padded tunics, boots and gauntlets," Theo pronounced without even glancing in the chest.

"Lift everything out. For I swear I saw something glitter in the corner." Darrin pointed to the right side of the trunk.

Dutifully Theo lifted out all the clothes, the mail, boots and sword. And indeed, there was Darrin's mother's ring, but Darrin did not stare at it as the others did. Instead he watched the pair's reactions.

Theo picked up the ring and examined it in the light. Puzzlement and perplexity rode across his face, along with a fair amount of honesty. "This looks like a woman's ring." Right then and there, Darrin knew Theo had never cast his eyes on the ring before this moment.

Darrin took the ring and held it high. Even in the gloomy morning light, the ruby stone shone bright and rich. "Why, this was my mother's. Obviously my father could not part with it when she died." He held the ring out to Faith. "What do you think of it?"

She blanched. A yellow tinge invaded the green of her skin as a startled recognition filled her eyes. This was indeed what she had been searching for the other night. Yet she hid this prize from Theo. Why?

"Since you are my wife, I think you should have this. It would have pleased my father and my mother." Darrin placed the ring in Faith's hand.

Color flooded her cheeks until her skin did indeed take on an orange quality. Truly, her skin had taken on almost every color of the rainbow. He wondered what would turn her skin indigo and violet.

The next day brought those shades to Faith's skin. Lack of sleep had made the skin beneath her puffy eyes appear to be a bright indigo that faded into a lighter violet. Yesterday she had taken the ring without a thank you. Not long thereafter, she made an excuse to flee the room and Theo quickly followed. Where they went or what they did, Darrin did not care. He had his jealousy and hate to keep him company.

Yet here she stood, the next morn, all blurry-eyed and compliant. "How fare you this day, my lord?" she asked, holding a fresh bowl of pottage.

He stretched and winced. "Fine enough, but my arm is still stiff and it is difficult to move. I wonder how I will ever be able to hold and survey my father's ledgers."

"Mayhap you need a little nourishment to give you strength." She came over to the bed with the bowl. "Eat first, and then, if you wish, we can look at those ledgers together."

Darrin's eyebrows shot upward as he could not hold back his shock. Why would she wish to examine something she had seen before? Aye, he had suggested they should do so together yesterday, but that she brought it up today did put a wariness in his soul. "May I ask why you wish to help?"

She sat on the edge of the bed with the bowl still in hand. "I have a confession to make. Sir Theodore and I went through the trunk before I brought it to you. I am sorry. We— I thought I might find something within to prove you innocent of your father's death. We really only glanced at the contents and we were going to bring it to you, but then you were injured. Please do not blame Sir Theodore, for the guilt is all mine. He wanted you to have it right away."

What turn was this? He had not expected a confession, yet he could not shake the feeling that she didn't have another dubious plan in her head. "And did you find anything?" he asked cautiously, wondering again what else she had taken besides his mother's ring.

"Nay. But I did find something peculiar." She rose and placed the bowl on the table. Then she picked up a few pages of the ledger and brought them back to Darrin. "See here. Each month your father received money from the Abbey of Sainte-Marie des Dames, where I was born. What do you make of that?"

Her face showed no cunning lines or deceptive creases. Still, his own gut rolled and ebbed, for he knew the answer she sought. Who was the fiend in this case? Him or her? How could he accuse her of deceit when he held on to a very deep and dark secret?

Her brow winkled and her tongue peeked out between her lips as she tried to search out the answer. "I thought to ask Nun about it. For I am certain she would know."

Nun! Of course. It had never occurred to him that she might know of Faith's birthright. No matter how hard the woman tried to act impartial, she had always favored Faith above him and any other child within the château. Was that because she knew of Faith's heritage? And yet what were the chances of a mother superior and this monk, Klein, bringing a humble nun into their confidences? The ledger showed that his father did know about Faith's birthright. It would also explain the ugly argument they had on the night of his father's death.

His father had smacked Darrin hard across the face after catching him on the tower stairs with Faith. An ugly argument ensued later in the lord's chamber.

"Father, I love her. I want to marry her," Darrin proclaimed.

Like a whip, his father slapped him in the face, twice. "You will never look or think of Lady Faith in that manner again. Do you hear me?"

Darrin took his fingers and dabbed them to his throbbing split lip. "I hear you, but I will ask her, with or without your blessing."

His father reached out and struck him again, his eyes wild and his body shaking. Never had he seen his father so angry. "You fool. Has she ever said a word of love to you?"

When Darrin did not answer, his father gave him a knowing glare. White-hot fury pulsed inside Darrin. He raised his fist to his father. "Just because she has not said the words, it does not mean she has no affection for me." He tapped his heart. "I feel it, in here. I know she loves me and I plan to make her my wife."

With great strength, his father rushed forward and

pinned Darrin against a chamber wall. "You speak like a young, rash boy. What do you know of love? You trust women so easily. Let me give you a clear lesson on a woman's heart. They are fickle. One day they will shower you with words of loving adoration and then the next day they will turn on you and slither away like the snakes they are."

At the time, Darrin thought his father spoke such words to ease his grief of losing his wife. Many would remark that Sir Jean remained loyal to his wife even after she had died. His father had never taken another wife. But now Darrin realized his father truly did know a woman's heart and only tried to protect his son.

However, that was neither here nor there. The past could not be changed. But the questions remained. What did Nun know, and could Darrin find out without giving up his own secrets? He put a hand on his chest. The missive from King Richard was gone. Did he lose it in the village fight or did someone take it? His pulse quickened. Nun had taken off his tunic. Perhaps she had taken the note.

He gazed at Faith. "Go find Nun and bring her here."

Faith sprung up from the bed and rushed away. But as quickly as she had left, she returned and handed him his pottage.

"Here," she said, with the breathtaking smile of an innocent. "You may need your strength for whatever Nun may say." With that, she left once more.

Darrin could not eat. What if Nun did know and she revealed all? What would Faith do with that knowledge? He was not strong enough to protect her if she decided to make her paternity public. Did he want to protect her? Since their marriage had never been consummated, they could easily have it annulled. That thought did not sit easy with him either.

By the time Faith had returned with Nun, the bowl in his hands had cooled. Faith took the pottage away as Nun picked up the ledgers.

She squinted, examining each sheet. When finished, Nun placed them on the foot of the bed but did not offer any comment, though her tight expression and rigid body spoke volumes. She was not at all surprised by these findings.

"You have nothing to say, Nun?" Darrin asked.

She folded her hands. "It is obvious. The abbess paid for Lady Faith's and my keep."

Darrin leaned forward, hoping doing so would encourage her to speak more. "And this does not surprise you?"

"Nay. Why should it? Her father, whoever he may be, harbored guilt and did not want his daughter raised in a convent. So he found a way to pay for her keep."

The words were spoken coldly and their meaning sent a sadness in Faith's face. Darrin had to quell the urge to console her.

Instead he pressed the situation all the more. "And yet, from viewing my uncle's records, these payments stopped when my father died. Does that not seem odd?"

Nun shrugged. "Mayhap, unless Sir Jean was blackmailing Lady Faith's father."

Faith gasped and stumbled to sit on the bed. "Why would Sir Jean do such a thing?"

Blackmail! His father was not blackmailing the king. But Darrin could see how Nun had come up with this conclusion.

"It could very well explain his death," Nun added nonchalantly.

Slowly the shock left Faith's face and was replaced with an eagerness he had not seen since their youth. "Then all we have to do is find out who my real father is. He must be the killer." She turned to Darrin, her eyes aglow. "If we expose him, then your name will be cleared."

Did she not understand what she had just said? She wanted to find her father not because she sought his love, but because she wanted to free her husband from guilt. Darrin's heart lurched. Once again she had managed to send his emotions into a tumble. Only a loving wife would sacrifice her father for her husband. Granted, she did not know who had sired her, so no love could grow. Still, their marriage was not based on love nor even a mild affection, so why would she wish to help him?

Unless she really cares for you. Nay, nay, nay. He gave his mind a mental shake. *Be careful or she will steal your heart again.*

Faith jumped up and raised a finger into the air. "I have it! Sir Adrien must be my father."

"What? I thought you said he was innocent?" Darrin croaked out. How had her mind raced to such an outcome?

"Aye, I did. For he seemed surprised when he found out about the murder. But now, it makes perfect sense. The money stopped coming after Sir Jean's death. Not to mention his threats against Nun that night."

"Threats against me?" Nun spoke sharply. "What are you talking about?"

Faith gave Nun a woeful look. "If I did not say publicly that I saw Darrin leaving from Sir Jean's chamber that night, then Sir Adrien would have killed you. I never believed Darrin killed his father. Never."

"Good heavens." Nun plunked down on a stool near the table.

Threats against Nun. Was this the truth or was Faith trying to cover her own sinful role that night? If she spoke the truth, then she was innocent of any wrongdoing. His head swam with doubts and wants. He wanted to believe her, but he could not help but doubt her words.

Faith shook her head. "It makes perfect sense. He would have sent me back to the convent if he were not." She sighed. "Now I understand his odd behavior. At times he would be sweet and ever so kind, then again he would be cruel and sharp. He could not come to terms with having a bastard daughter."

Nun rose quickly, toppling the stool. "I think we should go to the chapel and pray on this." She picked up the pottage bowl and handed it to Faith. "Here, take this to the kitchens and then I will meet you there."

The moment Faith's footsteps faded from hearing, Nun faced Darrin. "This is all rot. Sir Adrien is not Faith's father. We must stir her mind from such a foolish notion."

"What do you know? Did you take the note I had on my person?" Darrin asked.

Nun pulled the parchment from her habit. "Aye, but I did not read it." She handed it to Darrin and then stormed out of the room without another word.

She might or might not have read the missive. But one thing was certain, she knew King Richard was Faith's father.

Nineteen

*He that trusteth in his own heart is a fool:
but whoso walketh wisely, he shall be delivered.*
Proverbs 28: 26

THE DAY WAS NAUGHT BUT PITIFUL, POURING RAIN pounded the roof and howling winds brought a deathly chill to Darrin's chamber. Faith returned later that afternoon like a cheery bird chirping away.

"Sir Theodore and I had a long discussion about Sir Adrien and what we discovered this morning and he agrees with me. Sir Adrien probably is my father and he probably killed Sir Jean."

Once again, the pair were plotting or were they just trying to discover the truth? Either way, Darrin could not come to terms with the pangs of jealousy that brewed within him. Better to think Faith fancied someone else than to be caught under her spell. However, Theo had been his friend and closest ally. The loss of his allegiance would be great. Darrin kicked the coverlet from his feet and swung his legs over the side of the bed.

"What are you doing?" Faith asked, racing to the side of the bed.

"I am getting up. I have been lying around long enough. I have a château to run."

She placed her hands on his chest, upon his beating heart. "You are not going anywhere. The air is chilly and you are weaker than a young child. You are far from well to go prancing around the château."

"My lady, I do not intend to prance," he snapped as he tried to stand, sending shards of pain ricocheting through his shoulder.

"Oh, you are such a stubborn man. Here, I will help you to the chair by the hearth."

Throwing his arm over her shoulder, he hobbled to the chair and sat. The warmth from the close fire seemed to soothe the aches from his weary bones and ease his troubled mind.

Faith brought a coverlet and threw it over his legs. "Are you still in pain?"

"Only when I try to move my arm," he muttered sourly.

"I am not surprised. But you must move it or the stiffness will settle in permanently." Gently she took his elbow in her hands, slowly raising it. Hot pain shot up to his injured shoulder. She raised and lowered his arm several times. He could feel the pull in his dormant muscles.

The fire cast a sparkling shine on her pale hair. A beautiful face set in a veil of gold. He reached out with his other hand and let his fingers flow freely through the soft tendrils. Startled, she stopped and gazed at him with those blue-grey eyes glittering boldly. He wagered the Virgin Mother had not looked as lovely.

His heart squeezed. She was his wife. Not Theo's, not Rollin's nor any other fool who wished to claim her. Slowly, he leaned forward, and when she did not retreat, he kissed her, reveling in her sweet, warm lips. When he pulled away, her eyes were smoky. He wondered what went through her mind, but he did not ask and she did not comment. Both knew, soon, be it in love or hate, she would be his completely.

She took his fingers in hers and began working the stiffness from each joint. His eyelids closed and he let out a sigh. Undeniably, he could get used to this. When she stopped the massaging, he opened his eyes and caught her looking at the smaller chest in the corner that held his grandfather's papers.

"Go and bring it here. We shall look for clues together," he said, unable to deny her curiosity.

She placed the small gilded chest on the floor in front of him and opened it. They combed through the letters. Most were from Darrin's father, describing his knight's training at Lord de Tosny's keep. But the last one they read was a letter of betrothal between his mother, Lady Angelina, and his father.

A dark shadow settled over Faith's features as she carefully refolded the letter and placed it back in the trunk. "Your father loved her very much?"

"Aye, from what I can remember. I can still hear them laughing together—hers soft and airy and his loud and energetic."

"How did she die?"

The memories were thick, heavy clouds with only a few spots of light. "One day she was here and the next she was not. I remember waking up one morning to find my father sitting next to me. He simply said, 'Your mother is gone. Mourn a little, but then we must carry on.'"

Faith's eyes held pity. "We buried your father next to her in the chapel."

He looked into the hearth; the flames jumped and swayed. What did he remember of his mother's death and burial? Almost nothing. He couldn't remember a mass or what her coffin had looked like. As if by magic, a stone appeared on the chapel floor bearing her name. His father took him to see it once and then no one visited the chapel unless a priest showed up to give Mass. But all that changed when Faith and Nun arrived. He remembered spending every morn on his knees, staring at the worn stone that bore his mother's name.

He turned his gaze back to Faith. "Tomorrow I shall come to morning prayers with you."

Faith walked out of the great hall and into the sunshine of the beautiful spring day. The lingering winter winds had disappeared and the promise of summer drifted on a warm, fragrant breeze. For a fortnight, Darrin had dutifully showed up for prayers. Faith could not tell if he was finding God again or if he was just going through the motions. Whatever the reason, she could not hide her joy. She thanked God over and over for bringing Darrin each morn to the small chapel, proving what she had known all along, that God could make good out of bad.

As the days wore on, an easy routine settled over them—after they prayed, they would break their fast together, then she would help him stretch and work his arm. Through it all, their conversations dealt mostly with talk of the weather, the meals and how the crops were planted and how they were growing. Not once had he come to her chamber at night. They acted like acquaintances instead of husband and wife, which was better than acting like enemies.

However, every time she brought up Sir Adrien as possibly being her father, Darrin would become quiet or he would quickly turn the conversation elsewhere. Why he avoided the issue, she could not understand. When Darrin had arrived at the keep, he had accused Sir Adrien of killing his father. Why he shied away from the discussion now, she did not know.

Maybe his thoughts were elsewhere. They had never found the man who had wounded Darrin. Theo believed it was a knight who did the deed and not some peasant. Yet their searches and interrogations had produced nothing.

A flash of sunlight danced off her finger and drew Faith's gaze—Lady Angelina's ring. The ring with the pretentious ruby almost made Faith gag. She would have happily left it in Sir Jean's trunk had not Darrin insisted she wear it. Often she wondered how the ring managed to get back into the trunk. The moment she realized the ring had fallen out of her cloak, she had retraced her steps, certain she must have lost it in Darrin's chamber. But who placed it back in the trunk?

There wasn't a soul Faith could ask without confessing she had taken it in the first place.

All would be fine, but she had one more secret. *The note she had found with the ring.* After losing the ring, Faith kept the note wrapped in a fine piece of cloth, which was tied securely to her shift. She should give it to Darrin, but then he would know she had taken the ring. She feared such a confession might upset their fragile truce. However, she could not put off the truth forever. A relationship based on lies and deceit would not last.

She made her way to the château gate and spotted Nun in her small herb garden, examining the growing plants. "Will you have a good garden this year?" Faith asked.

Nun cut away some of last year's growth from a sage plant. "All depends on the weather and God's will. But the plants all look healthy and strong. But I do not think it was the interest in my garden that has brought you here."

A small honey bee lit on a newly bloomed clary sage flower. Nun claimed it was the scent of the bloom which attracted the honey bees, but Faith believed the pleasant blue-purple color might be the attraction. "I worry about Sir Darrin."

"Why? His shoulder is healing nicely. He no longer needs comfrey for healing. I just give him chamomile to ease his sleeping."

"Mayhap I could use some chamomile."

Nun stopped her pruning and placed a hand on her lower back. "It will not stop a mind from racing; only God can do that. What are your worries?"

"Sir Darrin is not the same. He seems...indifferent." Faith feigned great interest in a fledgling dill plant to avoid Nun's scrutiny.

"Indifferent how?"

"He does not seem interested in talking about Sir Adrien and he does not seem interested in...other things."

Nun folded her arms. "He is coming to chapel every day."

"Aye," Faith said softly, still intently looking at the herbs.

"Is that not what you wanted? For him to find God?"

"Aye. Though I am not sure that is the reason he is coming to the chapel."

"He seems ardent in his prayers. God will do the rest."

"Rest of what?" Faith asked, kicking the moist soil.

"Bringing him back to his faith. Only God can fill a man with the spirit. But this is not your concern, is it?"

Nonchalantly, Faith bent down and let her fingers glide over the young plants. "Is he well enough?"

Nun resumed her pruning. "The arm needs time to strengthen. If he does not overly use it, I think, in time, he will regain most of his strength."

Faith tried to curb her annoyance. "Nay. That is not what I mean. Is there anything in this garden that could give…heighten…a man's desires?"

Though she could not see, Faith felt Nun's intent glare. "What is this? We no longer want him to find God first?"

Faith stood and sighed. "Aye. But I had a change of heart and gave him permission to…"

Nun raised a knowing brow. "To consummate your marriage. And he has not done so."

Faith shook her head. "He has not come to my chambers once, though he seems fit enough to walk about."

"Mayhap he has other things on his mind."

"Such as?"

Nun turned back to her plants. "It could be anything. Only a man knows his own heart. Mayhap he harbors a secret or it could be something else that weighs on his mind."

A queasiness overcame Faith. 'Twas not Darrin who held a secret, but her. "Then there is naught I can do."

"I did not say that. Continue with your kindness. Be patient. He will come around." Nun dug around a dill plant. "They all do," she mumbled.

Making sure his sword was firmly in its scabbard, Darrin made his way to the practice yard, flexing his hand and rotating his arm. He had been lying about for several weeks with naught but his dark thoughts to keep him company. None of those weighed heavier than his fear of keeping the château safe. The time had come to see what he could do.

Theo waved when he saw Darrin approaching. "Come to watch a master and his skill?" Theo teased as he dropped his sword to his side.

Darrin pulled his weapon from its scabbard and took a firm grip on the hilt. His breath came short as a piercing pain shot up his arm. Pure determination made him ignore the constant throb. "I have not come to watch, but to practice."

The subtle wince that crossed Darrin's face was not lost to Theo. "Are you sure you are ready for this?" he whispered. "Mayhap you need more time to heal."

Darrin clenched his teeth, bent his knees and raised his weapon to be level with Theo's chest. "I do not need to sit in a chair and stiffen up like an old woman. Let's begin."

Theo tipped his head, took his stance and began to move slowly inward. With lightning swiftness, he struck the edge of Darrin's sword, who quickly countered with a hit against Theo's flat. Theo stepped backward and began circling Darrin, thrusting and cutting whenever possible.

Beads of sweat formed on Darrin's brow and trickled down his face. Each strike shot white-hot agony up his arm. His thoughts turned from disarming his opponent to keeping his sword in hand as he tried to fend off the assault. A small group of knights formed around them, goading and cheering them on. Theo thrust his sword forward to make his signature lethal blow—taking the edge of his sword and ripping upward, gutting his opponent, or in this case, disarming him. But instead of ending the fight, he backed off. His strikes became less enthusiastic and he feigned that Darrin's whacks and cuts were hard hits. The sparring became weaker and weaker and the knights slowly stopped their cheers.

Frustration and humiliation poured through Darrin and hurt him more than the excruciating pain pulsing through his arm and shoulder. He threw down his weapon and thinned his lips against the pity he saw in Theo's eyes.

"I expected a fair fight. How dare you treat me as a lad, learning how to use the sword." Darrin stormed away, rage flowing out of every pore in his body. Those in his path quickly stepped aside without offering a greeting. His anger pushed him onward until he found himself at the edge of the village among the damaged wheels and cart parts that still had not been repaired since the village unrest.

He kicked some of the shattered wood, sending the fragments flying in the air. One landed with a thud into the bed of a broken cart. A grey head popped up on the other side of the cart followed by a low whistle.

"You mean to kill someone with that missile?"

'Twas the old man who Darrin had duped Innocent. "What is that? I know nothing of a missile. Speak plainly. I merely sent some fragments of wood in the air and they landed near you." Darrin started walking toward the man.

Innocent came to stand next to the cart, holding a mallet. "That is what the word means. To launch things in the air. The word will be known well enough in the future. Give it a few hundred years."

The man was as odd and peculiar as ever and could quite possibly be the instigator behind many of the troubles that had befallen the château and village. Darrin eyed the mallet in Innocent's hand and approached him cautiously. "I am unarmed."

"Surely you don't think I would use this on you?" Innocent tossed the tool in the bed of the cart.

"I know naught what you have in mind as you disappeared as suddenly as you have reappeared."

Innocent snorted and rolled a mended wheel from the side of the cart until it rested next to the axle. "I have been here and there, but I am not the one who has caused all your woes. Come help me get this wheel in place. Raise the cart, just a little."

"I cannot. I am injured." Darrin tapped his shoulder and stayed his distance from the old man.

Innocent blinked. "Then use your other shoulder. That one is not injured, is it?"

"Nay, it might strain—"

"Are you making excuses to get out of working?"

The twist of anger started to brew within Darrin again. "Nay. I wish I were strong to help you with the cart and to keep those in this village and the château safe."

"Ah, then you do not trust or believe me."

Darrin did not answer as he did not understand the man's meaning.

"There is the worry. You have no faith or trust in anyone. Therefore you rely on yourself. But you are not strong, and you fear your enemies will attack you."

Darrin leaned against the cart and did not deny Innocent's words. "I am surprised Sir Adrien has not returned already. I am certain, by now, word of my injury has reached him."

Innocent brushed some mud off the wheel. "So what of it? You have knights to defend the château."

"But as you said, I know not who to trust. They are not a unit, but a group of men who fight for themselves."

"Is that truth or your perception?"

Darrin shrugged and thought of Gouch and the rest of his motley band. "I believe the men that came with me from England would stand with me." His mind began ticking through all the other men. His thoughts stalled when he came to Theo and Rollin. "Well, most of them."

"Then your answer is simple. Trust those you are certain about and be wary of those you are not." Innocent held up a finger. "But make sure you know the difference."

"There is the problem. Those I thought to be most faithful could be conspiring against me. My mind is a muddled mess." With a heavy sigh, Darrin gestured toward Innocent. "Look here, I am pouring out confidences to a man I have met twice and I may not be able to trust. Perhaps it was God's will that I should lose the château."

Innocent chuckled. "You are no longer angry at God. This is good, but you do not trust Him to help you."

Darrin weighed the idea in his mind. Truth be told, he was indeed finding peace in the morning prayers, but the moment he stepped out of the chapel, his old fears and worries returned—he had lost the heart and mind of a warrior knight.

"I am not one of God's favorites. Therefore, I don't believe His divine intervention will be given when Sir Adrien marches on Château du Vent Doux."

"Mmm, you are indeed a weak man."

Darrin straightened and bristled. "Keep your opinions to yourself, old man."

Innocent chuckled again and smiled. "You are a proud man and that is your biggest downfall. Come now, let us not quarrel. Put your good shoulder to the wheel. Show me your strength."

Still fuming from Innocent's words, Darrin made his way to the rear of the cart and put his healthy shoulder under the bed and levered upward. The cart rose and Innocent quickly put the wheel in place.

"Hand me the mallet and the hub of wood in the bed of the cart."

Darrin complied, and with a few whacks, Innocent secured the wheel.

He then stepped back. "There, almost as good as new."

Definitely, the old man was a good craftsman, for never had Darrin seen a finer cart, new or repaired. "I wish I were as good a château lord as you are a carpenter."

Stepping back, Innocent pointed to the château and then to the cart. "Look at the size of the cart and the size of the château. A single man can build a cart and drive it down the road. But a single man cannot build a château, nor can a single man take care of its upkeep. You have been given a big responsibility, but it is not yours alone. There are many who will help you if you ask them."

"But who? Who can I ask if I don't know who to trust?"

Innocent made his way to the front of the cart and lifted the handles. He looked over his shoulder. "Pay attention as you say your morning prayers. I think you will find the answer there."

Before Darrin could comment on Innocent's vague words, a loud band of knights came galloping toward him. Even though he knew the leader, Darrin wished he had his sword.

Sir Rollin in the lead, without a greeting, leaped from his horse. "Sir Darrin, you need to come with me now."

The authoritative tone of the younger knight irritated Darrin. He folded his arms across his chest. "And why should I?"

"It is Sir Adrien," he said, trying to catch his breath.

"He has returned? How many men are with him? We need to get everyone into the château."

Sir Rollin vehemently shook his head. "Nay. He has not returned. He has never left."

His bizarre words raised Darrin's suspicions. He turned to see Innocent's reaction, but the older man had once again disappeared. Darrin looked in every direction, yet there was no sign that Innocent was ever there.

"My lord, fear not. There is no army coming. Sir Adrien is dead. His remains are in yonder forest."

Twenty

*Then shall ye call upon me, and ye shall go
and pray unto me, and I will hearken unto you.*
Jeremiah 29:12

THE BODY LAY IN A SHALLOW GRAVE, BEHIND HEAVY vegetation, not far from the river. Garbed in the same clothing he had worn the day he left, Sir Adrien's bloated, decaying face stared up to the heavens, the identity of his killer going with him. With a coarse cloth to cover his nose and mouth, Darrin knelt next to the body. A deep gash had struck Sir Adrien just below the ribs, cutting upward to ensure lethal damage. The fatal wound was one he had seen often before.

"Give me your knife," he said. Without comment, Sir Rollin handed over the weapon and Darrin cut a piece of Sir Adrien's tunic. Then Darrin stood, his gaze still on the corpse. "I thought you followed him toward France."

"Aye, I did," Sir Rollin answered, staring at the same remains. "He must have known and circled back after we stopped our tracking."

"If that be the case, where are the rest of his men?"

Sir Rollin shrugged as if it were nothing, when in fact, it was everything. Sir Adrien had left with at least twenty men, yet there were no other graves. No signs of a struggle. No hoofprints, ripped clothing, broken weapons—nothing. Granted, it had been weeks since Sir Adrien had left; still, the whole sight seemed planned—the placement of the grave, the lack of evidence.

Darrin made for his horse. "Bring the body back to the château."

"Why? It is apparent who did this carnage." Rollin pointed to the gaping wound. "The edge of the sword twisted upward, ripping through the chest. You know this is Theo's deadly mark."

Indeed it was. Darrin turned the mount toward the château. "All the more reason to bring the body back. Sir Rollin, you come with me. Your men can see to the body."

Reluctantly, Rollin followed. The usually arrogant knight brooded all the way back to the château. Every so often, he cast a glance over his shoulders, as if expecting Sir Adrien to rise from the dead. Clearly he wanted to stay with the body. Why? Darrin wondered if there was something he had missed.

The warm, sunny day should be as cold as ice. His thoughts were sharper when the air was fresh and clean. The spring winds had turned to summer, Darrin's mind grew sluggish. He schooled his feelings. This was not the time to think of May days and running barefoot through the fields. He needed to remain focused and sift out who was his friend and who was his enemy.

Upon entering the bailey, Darrin spotted Theo and Faith. The pair sat on the great hall steps chattering and laughing as if they didn't have a care in the world. Darrin's sword lay across Faith's thighs.

Theo lifted a lazy hand in greeting when Darrin and Rollin dismounted. "My lord and Blossom. Where have you been? You missed Gouch's grand announcement." Theo rose to his feet. "He plans to wed the smithy's daughter." The somber attitude of the two knights made Theo pause. "I told him he should ask you first."

Darrin ascended the steps, holding the piece of Sir Adrien's tunic in his hand. He held the object before Theo. "Do you know who this belongs to?"

Faith gasped and rose to her feet, the sword clattering down a few steps, her eyes wide with surprise. "Why, that is a piece of Sir Adrien's favorite tunic."

Darrin reached over and picked up his sword. "Correct, my lady." Was her shock and astonishment an act or truth? Oh, how he wished the old man, Innocent, were here to give insight.

Theo took the offered cloth. "Where did you find this?"

The tip of Darrin's sword rested upon the stone step. "Where you left the body."

Puzzlement traveled across Theo's face, and in another time, Darrin would have thought the reaction to be honest. But not now. The man was so different than the one he had fought alongside. Clean and shaved and ever so attentive to his wife. Did he have designs on becoming lord of the château? Theo had come to Normandy in search of a fiefdom of his own. Had that been his plan the day they left King Richard's bedside? To take what Darrin owned?

Faith leaned over and put her arm through Theo's. "Surely you do not think Sir Theodore had anything to do with his death?"

At that moment, several of Sir Rollin's knights brought Sir Adrien's body and laid it at the foot of the stairs. Faith covered her mouth and Theo stood like stone, staring at the blood-caked hole in Sir Adrien's chest.

Finally, as if he had just realized he had legs, Theo raced down the stairs and knelt next to the body, intently examining the wound. He shook his head several times and then rose to his feet. "Truly, you do not think I did this? I was with you while Sir Rollin tracked Sir Adrien."

Slowly, Darrin descended the stairs, never taking his eyes off Theo. "You, too, were gone for a while, making sure Sir Rollin was indeed on the mission I had sent him." Darrin pointed to the body. "How often have I seen you kill a man just so?"

The bewilderment in Theo's eyes turned to hurt and disillusionment. "Anyone could have killed him so to lay the blame at my feet. If I had done this, I would have told you. We all knew it would be better if he were dead. But I did not kill him. How can you think otherwise?" Theo stood and placed a hand across his heart. "You cut me here."

Uncertainty crept up Darrin's spine, he knew nothing of truth and loyalty anymore? "Take Sir Theodore to the dungeon."

Faith rushed down the steps and grabbed Darrin's injured arm. "You're making a mistake. Don't do this." Her high, shrill plea tore through the air.

Darrin's insides frosted at her desperation. "It is a good thing you had the dungeon cleaned out, my lady. At least your champion will have a tolerable stay." With that, Darrin stormed up the great hall stairs. "Take the body to the stables and someone find me Nun!"

Nun stood over the body clicking her tongue while Darrin sat on a barrel waiting what seemed like ten lifetimes for her to come up with a conclusion. After throwing Theo in the dungeon, Darrin ordered the guard to escort Lady Faith to her chamber. He feared she might do something rash, such as trying to free Theo. Tongues were already wagging and wagering just what her relationship with the knight might be.

Unclear as to who he could trust, Darrin summoned Nun to examine the body. Though she was loyal to Faith above all things, the older woman was wise enough to know Faith would never have a future with Theo and would not lie if he were the guilty murderer.

All groomsmen and the stable master were relieved from their duties to give Nun the privacy she needed to examine Sir Adrien.

"Well, what do you think?" Darrin asked.

Nun wrinkled her brow, never turning her attention from the body. "These things take time. But I can tell you one thing for sure. Look here."

Darrin jumped off the barrel and dropped to one knee next to Nun. She raised one of Sir Adrien's hands, pulling a piece of hemp from the hair about his wrist. "His hands were bound." She then pointed to his mouth. "The skin is broken around his lips. Methinks he must have been gagged too."

"Then he did not die by a surprise attack."

She shook her head. "Nay. He was tied up for a while. Where did you say you found him?"

"By the river in a shallow grave. But there were no signs of a struggle. Could he have died elsewhere?"

"Possibly. However, I am certain he died bound and gagged, sitting in a chair. See how his legs are slightly bent? He was left in that chair for a while after his death."

"Are you sure? The grave was narrow and short. Could his legs have been bent then?"

Nun laid her hands across Sir Adrien's knees. "See how even these are? This means his legs were bent over something like the edge of a chair. If his legs had been moved after his death, they would be uneven. I doubt our killer would have taken the time to bend them perfectly. You did say the grave looked like it was dug with haste?"

"Aye. The ground around the body had been hacked and chopped out. The body carelessly thrown in the grave. Sir Rollin spotted a piece of Sir Adrien's tunic sticking out of the ground."

"Mmm." Nun frowned and ran her fingers over Sir Adrien's chest. "Roll him over," she commanded.

Darrin slowly rolled Sir Adrien on his stomach and again Nun examined his tunic.

"Roll him back." Nun ran her fingers along Sir Adrien's sides and then leaned forward to sniff his body. "Was the body protected from sunlight? Were there heavy trees about?"

Closing his eyes briefly, Darrin tried to picture the area around the grave. "There were trees, but the body was not far from the river, where the forest thins."

Nun mumbled and shook her head. "He has been dead for at least a fortnight. If he were out in the elements and part of his tunic had been exposed, there would be spots of worn material caused by the weather." She waved a hand over the body. "As you see, there are none. Only the corner you cut off earlier is missing. We have had rain, yet this tunic shows no signs of being wet—ever."

Darrin sat back on his heels. "What are you saying?"

Nun rose and brushed off her hands on her habit. "Sir Adrien did not die where you found him. Nor has his body been in that grave long. There is no mildew or discoloration on his clothing. This body has been kept in a cave or cellar."

"Or a dungeon?" Darrin added.

Nun shrugged. "Somewhere out of the elements."

Did this prove Theo's innocence or his guilt? After Faith and he had cleaned out the dungeon, could Theo have snuck back in with the body? The idea, though plausible, seemed impractical. There would be no way that Theo could have gotten the body into the dungeon alone. But what if he had help?

The serpent of mistrust slithered up and coiled within Darrin. Faith knew the workings of the château. She would know when to sneak in a body without others seeing. Yet why would the pair pick such a vulnerable spot?

Nun put her hands on her hips and glowered at Darrin. "I see your mind working. Faith had naught to do with this. Methinks you better look elsewhere."

But where? Sir Rollin? He found the grave and gave alert. Why would he do that if he had killed Sir Adrien? Besides, Theo had admitted that Sir Adrien's death was a good thing. Unless there was another culprit who needed to be dealt with.

"There is nothing else I can tell you about Sir Adrien at the moment. Put him in a cart. I will think on this a bit and perhaps take a closer look in the morning." Nun shuffled to the stable door. "Have no worry. The truth will come out. It always does. Even when we try to hide it."

We try to hide it. What did she speak of now? King Richard being Faith's father? Darrin almost asked her about it, but Sir Rollin strode into the stable with Father Chabot.

"We are wondering if we can have the remains of Sir Adrien," Rollin asked.

Father Chabot stepped forward. "I would like to give him rites and a blessing."

Darrin wanted to point out that Sir Adrien was long dead and his soul had journeyed either to heaven or hell already. Nonetheless, he saw no point in stopping Father Chabot from doing his duties. "Of course, do what you must, but wait until the morrow to bury him. Nun may wish to have another look." Darrin walked to the entry, trying to sort out his newfound knowledge.

"Sir Darrin, when the time comes, where should we bury him?" Rollin called.

"I have been told that Sir Adrien wanted to be buried in the chapel," Father Chabot said.

Darrin's insides froze. "Not the chapel. For all we know, Sir Adrien may have killed my father and I'll not have his remains next to my parents."

Neither of the pair said a word, though their disapproval was apparent.

"Bury him outside the château walls. I do not care where. But do not do so until Nun looks at the body one more time." Darrin glared at both men, making certain his orders would be followed. He then left; his mood dark. But as if a beam of light shone from the sky and fell upon his head, the words of Innocent came rushing back to his mind. *Pay attention as you say your morning prayers. I think you will find the answer there.*

Ten. It took Faith exactly ten steps to pace across her modest chamber and ten steps to return from where she had come.

Absurd. How absurd for Darrin to believe Sir Theodore had anything to do with Sir Adrien's death.

Puzzle. Sir Adrien dead left a puzzle. Who, then, stole

and butchered the pigs and caused the skirmish in the village?

Perhaps her theory had been wrong all along. Maybe she wasn't Sir Adrien's daughter. Maybe Sir Jean had not been blackmailing Sir Adrien. Maybe Sir Adrien did not kill Sir Jean. Through all the maybes, there was one certainty—someone wanted to erode Darrin's control of Château du Vent Doux.

There was another certainty—pacing this room helped no one. She had to get out. Faith banged on the door and demanded over and over to talk to Sir Darrin to no avail. The door remained locked and the daylight was waning. She fell back onto the bed and put a hand over her heart where Lady Angelina de Longue's note lay. Faith cried in frustration. She should have told Darrin about taking the ring and the note, but she didn't. Returning the note now would only lead to more questions and more distrust.

"Oh, what to do? Lord, I need your help." The simple prayer didn't bring any peace, only despair that the Lord did not hear her.

The thought had barely passed her mind when the door latch clicked open and in walked Nun with a trencher of food and a pair of tallows.

Scrambling to the side of the bed, Faith wiped the tears from her eyes. "What goes on in the great hall?"

Nun placed the food and tallows on the table. "Nothing. Sir Darrin has been in the chapel for at least a good hour. The rest of the knights linger about, drinking and contemplating Sir Theodore's fate." Nun gave a heavy sigh. "The longer they are kept waiting, the more mischief they will cause."

Faith stared at the plate of smoked meats and hard bread. The meal held little appeal, her stomach was a giant ball of angry, aching knots. "Sir Theodore did not kill Sir Adrien. The notion is absurd."

"That depends through whose eyes you are seeing the situation. To you it is absurd, but to a husband who sees his wife, all the time, in the company of the same knight, it is not so hard to believe."

"Sir Theodore was always with me because Darrin ordered it."

"That may have been the case, but you didn't have to like his company so much. And you didn't have to go sneaking around the keep, digging in the dungeon and hiding trunks."

A cry of exasperation fell from Faith's lips. "We were trying to help Darrin clear his name. That is all."

"You may have done just the opposite. There are more whispers than before that perhaps Sir Darrin killed his father and Sir Adrien."

"What rot. All his worry was focused on his uncle's return." Faith stopped in front of Nun and grabbed the older woman's hands. "You have to get me out of here. I have to talk to Darrin."

The older woman looked doubtful. "Perhaps I could say you wanted to pray and repent...in the chapel."

Hope rose in Faith's chest. "Try. I am sure the guards would listen to you. After all, you are a nun and a servant of God."

Nun flashed another skeptical look. "Let us not use God's name to gain personal gratification."

"We're not gratifying ourselves. We are helping Darrin and Sir Theodore." Faith pushed Nun towards the door. "Now go!"

Nun left and Faith put her ear to the wooden entry. There were mumblings, but she could not make out a single word. Within moments, the door popped open and Nun motioned for her to follow. Quickly, the pair took to the stairs with the guards behind them. They skirted the edges of the great hall to avoid attention. Seconds later, they stood outside the chapel door. The guards stood without as Faith and Nun scurried inside.

A heavy breath of relief escaped Nun's lips. "Praise the Lord. We made it."

But any rejoicing rapidly vanished when the women were

met with Sir Darrin's stiff stance and cold glare. "What are you doing here?"

Faith rushed forward and dropped into a deep curtsy. "Forgive me. I know you wanted me to remain in my chamber, but I must have a word with you."

Darrin folded his arms across his chest. "Can this not wait until later? I am in prayer."

Fighting fear, she dragged in her breath and gave a hard swallow. "Hear me out and then we can pray together or you can send me back to my chamber or wherever else you wish to send me."

His gaze scanned her face, yet she could not discern his thoughts. Finally, his shoulders relaxed and his gaze slid to Nun. "Leave us."

"Won't your guards be suspicious if I leave without Lady Faith?" she protested.

"I care not what my guards think. If I wish to stay in here all night with my wife, that is my decision. Leave please."

Nun flattened her lips at his abrupt dismissal. Obviously, prudence and spending the beginning of her life behind convent walls had taught her control and submission, for she turned toward the chapel door without a word, but her posture gave away her disapproval.

Like a hawk, his gaze returned to the prey in front of him. "Lady, speak your piece and then I shall tell you where you will spend your evening."

Goosebumps popped on her skin as his words were delivered in a cruel, cold tone. "I want you to release Sir Theodore from the dungeon. He would never go against you. He is a man of honor. I am certain someone else manipulated Sir Adrien's death to implicate Sir Theodore."

Darrin turned to face the wooden cross above the simple altar. "I know," he said quietly.

The digesting of his two words did not come quickly or make any sense. She almost asked him to repeat them, but feared she would receive a different answer. "If you know, then why did you imprison him?"

"At the time, I did not know the truth. I have come to recognize it now. Sir Theodore is not the sneaky type." His gaze slid from the cross to hers. "At least not until recently."

She looked down at the floor and folded her hands as if ready to do penance. "You have a right to lay this and other sins at my feet. Sir Theodore did my bidding because I took advantage of his honor and loyalty to you."

Darrin lifted her chin with two fingers, raising it until her gaze met his. "Did you want his heart too?"

The pleading search within his eyes held a small measure of vulnerability. Tears from the past clogged her throat and begged to be spilled. "It is not *his* heart that I seek."

He pulled away with a groan. "Lady, why do you torment me? What will you gain by taking my heart?"

She dropped to her knees before him. "I do not wish to gain anything other than what most wives have—trust and love."

His head rolled back and cynical laughter echoed off the chapel walls. "Love and trust. Years ago, you threw my trust away, and when I first came to your bed, you denied me love. Yet here you are, expecting me to give you both freely when I have seen neither."

Faith stayed on her knees and beat her fist against her chest, against the note hidden under her shift. He spoke the truth. She did not stand by him when he was accused of murder and she had first denied him her bed. "I am sorry for both. I should have chosen you over Nun and it was wrong of me to deny you. I so desperately wanted you to regain your faith."

He dropped to one knee in front of her. "You did right to save Nun. Hatred wouldn't let me see the truth or believe your words. As far as consummating our wedding, there are things you must know first. I have learned something while I have been sitting here and talking to God. Trust is something given freely between friends without certainty."

She could not hold them back; the tears poured over her cheeks and he gently wiped them away. He leaned forward and kissed her lips lightly, then slowly, he searched for more, the kiss grew deeper. Her heart shattered any doubt she had ever harbored. She loved him and would stand by him in innocence or guilt. If he would have her, she planned to be the best wife. But first she had to tell him the truth—all of it.

Faith broke the kiss; his face filled with hurt. She placed a hand on his cheek. "There is something I must show you."

Before she could reach in her shift to produce the note, the chapel door slammed open and Sir Rollin entered. "The stable is on fire!"

Twenty-one

The secret things belong unto the Lord our God: but those things which are revealed belong unto us and to our children forever, that we may do all the words of this law.
Deuteronomy 29:29

WILD FLAMES FLEW UP THE SIDE OF THE STABLE AS Darrin ran pell-mell into the bailey. Thick smoke bellowed in the air and singed his nose. The stable master and stable boys were quickly getting the horses and livestock out. Peasants, servants and craftsmen were heaving buckets of water onto the burning structure. Animals brayed, squawked and nickered as they ran freely about the bailey. Mothers scrambled to get their crying children out of the way before they would be trampled. Darrin dashed into the fray and closer to the flaming inferno. The extreme heat stalled his steps near the stable door. A ball of fire engulfed a cart next to the stable.

He raised his arms to shield himself from its intensity. "How did this start?" Darrin asked a stable boy, who was desperately trying to pull a soot-streaked mare to safety.

The lad motioned with his head. "That cart. By the time it was noticed, flames be kissin' the stable."

The fire crackled and sizzled, blocking the stable entrance. The mare jerked, refusing to go farther. Darrin tore off his outer tunic and gave it to the lad to cover the animal's eyes.

"Are all the animals out?" Darrin shouted.

The boy shrugged, nudging the horse to safety.

Out of the corner of his eye, Darrin spotted Faith organizing people to form a water-chain from the well to the stable. Leave it to her to keep her head when pandemonium ruled. Rapidly, Darrin surveyed the whole situation. The other side of the stable was still intact. Flames started dancing on the roof. In moments, the whole stable would be a glowing firestorm. Swiftly, he made his way to the far side of the stable and began kicking at the boards. The wood groaned but did not give way. Murky smoke poured from the stable and filled the air. Out of nowhere, a man with an ax appeared and began hacking away on the unrelenting boards.

A grey wall of cinders and smoke engulfed them when the boards gave way. Both men coughed and wheezed as the dark, billowy villain burned their throats and lungs. With haste, they covered their faces with their scherts before they plowed into the cloudy chaos. Darrin's eyes stung with tears as he tried to feel about on his hands and knees. A whimper and small yips caught his hearing and led him to a stall. There, deep within the straw, sat a small boy with his hands wrapped around a pup.

Darrin crawled up next to the boy. "We have to get you out of here, now."

The lad nuzzled his sooty face into the pup's black coat but did nothing. On his knees, Darrin wrapped his arms around the boy and the pup. But the lack of strength and weakness in Darrin's shoulder prevented him from holding on to the pair. The pup bolted from the lad's lap. The child screamed and lurched for the fleeing animal. With lightning reflexes, Darrin grabbed the boy's legs before he could follow the dog into the black wall.

"Let go of me," the boy wailed, trying to kick free.

Darrin grabbed the boy at the waist and hauled him upward, every muscle in his back and body screaming with agony. "The pup is lost, boy. We must leave now."

The child would not give up the fight. Darrin endured punches to the face and ribs and struggled to hold on to the child's breeches. All seemed to be lost, when the other knight emerged from the murk with the pup in hand. Immediately the boy gave up his fight and grabbed for the whining animal.

"Out first, lad," the other knight instructed.

Instantly, the boy gave up the fight and Darrin and the child stumbled out into the light. The boy immediately raced for the panting pup, who lay next to the sooty knight. The child hugged and kissed the pup until he gave out a small yelp of annoyance. With worshipping eyes and a grimy face, the boy turned to the filthy knight. "You are the bravest knight, sir. I will always be in your service."

The knight grunted and pointed to Darrin. "You should be thanking Lord de Longue, boy. He saved your life."

The lad rubbed his eyes but did not say another word. Instead he grabbed his pup and took off toward the château gate.

Darrin rolled over on his back and glanced over to the so-called bravest knight, Theo. "Who let you out of the dungeon?"

"Nun. She told your newly appointed jailer the place was ablaze. He took off as if his breeches were burning."

"I guess I will need a new jailer," Darrin rasped.

"Or you could just thank the bravest knight," Theo croaked.

The pair started laughing, but their laughter rapidly turned to hacking and wheezing. When his breath returned, Darrin rose to his feet and held out a hand to Theo. "Come then, let us finish this before the whole château is ablaze."

An hour later, they stood among the timber of the burnt and charred stable. Peasants still threw buckets of water on glowing embers. All in all, they had been lucky. Sir Rollin had spotted the fire early enough and only a few chickens and a goose had been lost. But Darrin's trials were not over—a phantom lurked about and needed to be found.

Theo kicked at the remains of the cart. In the ashes lay a skull. "Sir Adrien's?"

"Aye," Darrin said. "I guess we have less to bury."

"No great loss." Theo grinned and ran his hands through his grimy hair.

"You think not?" The pair turned to see Nun standing behind them, her face streaked black, her habit as filthy as the rest of her. "The stable wasn't the target. Whoever set this fire wanted to make sure all secrets died with Sir Adrien. I would say the villian was quite successful."

Darrin and Theo glanced now at the smoldering cart. Besides the skull, all they saw of Sir Adrien was one lone shoe.

The next morn, cleaned and refreshed, Faith found her husband picking through the smoldering remains of the stable, his hair greasy and his clothes caked in soot and ash. Another tragedy. Her heart reached out to him. This was his home and someone was hell-bent on taking it away from him. If they did not find who caused all this mayhem soon, the whole château could be lost.

The scent of scorched wood filled her nostrils as she approached the wreckage. "Are you not going to join us for morning prayers?"

Darrin wiped his grimy hands on his blackened schert. "My lady, surely you do not want me kneeling next to you as I am."

"It is not me you offend but God if you do not come at all. He will understand your worries and your answers may be given to you there."

Darrin stared at her as if she had spoken in holy Latin or ancient Greek. "An old man once told me the answers were in the chapel."

She held out her hand, not caring if it became soiled. "Then come. I will call for a bucket of water in which you can wash your hands and face. Perhaps a fresh schert and tunic also."

He held up his hands. "Nay, I will not touch you until I

am fully clean, but I will attend prayers and hope Father Chabot does not die at the sight of me."

A soft laugh left her lips. "Then let us be off, for Father Chabot and Nun will be cross if we are late."

In the hall, Faith called for the water and clean clothing. With miraculous speed, Darrin stripped off the old schert, washed his face and hands, then took the rest of the bucket and dumped it over his head. After scrubbing his hands through his tawny hair, he slipped on a new schert and tunic. He still smelled like a smoldering hunk of wood, but at least he was a little more presentable.

The chapel was full by the time they arrived with the usual people, plus one. Sir Theodore sat in the back, sparkling clean. He laughed when his gaze fell upon Darrin's rumpled appearance. However, one disapproving look from Father Chabot squelched any further guffaws. Darrin and Faith made their way to the front of the chapel and knelt.

Father Chabot did not begin with his usual prayers; instead he looked around the full chapel. "The Almighty God has spared Château du Vent Doux from utter destruction. Not one of His precious flock was lost. Let us give thanks to the Lord. I would like to begin with Psalm 147. "Praise ye the Lord: for it is good to sing praise to our God…"

Thankfulness did fill Faith's heart; Darrin was safe and finally seemed to be letting the Holy Spirit soften his heart. Yet something stood between them.

Father Chabot finished the Psalm and then began another, but Faith's mind began to drift. She squeezed her folded hand to help her concentrate. The ruby in Lady Angelina's ring dug into Faith's skin. She offered up her own silent prayer. *Oh, Lord, open my eyes and heart to your will.*

Father Chabot cleared his throat and then continued, "Lead me in thy truth, and teach me…"

Angelina's note seemed to burn against Faith's skin. *Lead me in truth.*

In truth.

Faith raised her teary eyes to the cross above the humble altar. No more putting off the truth. She needed to finish what she tried to start yesterday. With that settled, she focused on the words Father Chabot spoke. "Let integrity and uprightness preserve me..."

When the prayers had ended and the others started to leave, Faith placed her hand on Darrin's sleeve. "Do not go. We must have some words."

"Very well, but can we at least stand?" The shadows below his eyes had grown; the long, terrifying night had caught up to him.

She smiled and stood. "Of course."

Father Chabot and Nun lingered, but one stern look from Faith sent the pair to the door. When they were truly alone, Faith played with the ring on her finger. The confusion on Darrin's face caused her to falter, but if she did not do this now, she never would. She took off the ring and handed it to Darrin. "I know not how it was returned, but I took this ring from your father's trunk before the chest was brought to your chamber."

He tossed the ring in his palm before he closed his fingers around it. "I know. It must have fallen out of your cloak. I saw you searching for the jewel the night you brought the trunk in. I found it first and placed it inside."

Guilty heat rose up her spine. "Then why did you give it to me if you knew I had stolen it?"

"I wanted to see your reaction," he said quietly.

A tinge of annoyance grew within her as her hand started to curl into a fist. "And what did you learn?"

"That you did not really want the ring. Methinks you find it gaudy." A glint of humor entered his eyes.

She dropped her gaze and said not a word.

He gently raised her chin. "Faith, it is all right. You are forgiven. Worry not over this."

His enjoyment would soon flee when he realized what else she had taken. "There is more," she said softly. Her heart hammered out of control. She reached inside her gown and pulled out the small note. "This was wrapped around the ring."

His face morphed into chiseled stone as he took the note and slowly unfolded it and read. Time stood still; his gaze fixated on the words. "'Sorry. My love wasn't strong enough.'" He looked up. "What did she mean by that?"

"I was hoping you might know," she whispered, uncertain he was even speaking to her.

His mind seemed to drift away. "You didn't find a trunk for my mother in the dungeon, did you?"

An ache settled in her—he still believed she was hiding things from him. "Nay, nothing of your mother's. Only the ring and the note."

His stare was steady and even, then he looked down at the note again and read. "My love wasn't strong enough." Suddenly he looked at her and blinked, then hurried over to his parents' gravestones.

Faith fearfully followed, worried that the stress of last night and this new piece of knowledge might have pushed his mind over a cliff.

He dropped to one knee. "Look here," he said excitedly, running his hand across the words on the stone that marked his father's grave. "'Love is never strong enough.'" He then pointed to his mother's stone. "'An angel must fly.'" A glow filled Darrin's eyes as if he had been given divine knowledge. "Do you know what this means?"

She hadn't the foggiest.

Darrin rushed to the chapel door. "You there," he called to a passing servant. "Find Sir Theodore, Master Gouch and the smithy. Tell them to come quickly with pick, trowel and axe. Anything that can cut through stone!"

Twenty-two

For our fathers have trespassed, and done that which was evil in the eyes of the Lord our God, and have forsaken him, and have turned away their faces from the habitation of the Lord, and turned their backs.
2 Chronicles 29:6

A FEW HOURS LATER, A DUSTY AND DIRT-COVERED Theo, Gouch and Darrin had removed his mother's gravestone and hauled out her coffin. It had not been an easy feat. Father Chabot had already pronounced Darrin's soul doomed for hell's fire for desecrating a tomb. And doubly so for causing such destruction in a chapel of the Lord. Nun stood by shaking her head and saying prayers over and over again. But Darrin could not hide his enthusiasm and anticipation.

Grabbing a pick, he quickly pried off the lid, ignoring the strain in his shoulder. The gasps that left everyone's lips were Darrin's affirmation. The coffin was empty. "As I expected," he said triumphantly, though a small ache began to grow in his heart. His father had sent his mother away after she had given him a son.

Faith, who resembled a marble angel through the whole ordeal, dropped to her knees and peered deeper into the coffin, as if the body would magically appear. "I do not understand. How could this be?"

"The note gave me the clue. I had always thought my father carved those words because my mother had died young. But when I saw the note, I wondered if he had meant something else." Darrin placed his hands on his hips. "She didn't die. She left."

All in the chapel started talking at once and Darrin held up his hands to gain silence.

"Then what happened to her?" Faith asked.

Darrin's gaze slid to Nun. "That is a good question."

"What? You look to me." Nun thumped her chest. "I didn't even know your mother. I came to this château two years after your mother's death."

Darrin narrowed his gaze. "Aye, but mayhap you knew my mother when she entered the convent."

"Entered the convent? What kind of drivel is this?" Nun cried.

Theo chuckled and jabbed Gouch in the ribs. "This is getting better and better."

Darrin frowned and handed Theo the pick, while Gouch leaned against the chapel wall.

"Nay, that cannot be right." Faith rose to her feet. "Sir Jean was getting coin from the convent, to pay for my keep. If Lady Angelina were living there, wouldn't Sir Jean be paying the convent? Or if my care was given for her care, then no coin would have exchanged hands. Nay, you cannot be right, unless…"

Faith turned pure white and stumbled backward. Darrin caught her about the wrist, feeling the rapid beat of her heart. "Faith, what's wrong?"

Her eyes were wide with fear, as if she had seen the spirit of death. She placed her other hand to her head. "I have been struck with a terrible headache. I need to lie down."

"Then I shall take you up to your chamber," Darrin said.

Faith's body tensed when he wrapped an arm around her shoulder. She tried to pull away. "Nay, you must stay here and work this out with Nun—"

"Me? I have naught to say," Nun said, coming toward Faith. "I shall take you upstairs while this fool figures out his words are nonsense."

Faith pulled away from Darrin and held up a hand to Nun. "Stay. I do not need you. Father Chabot can escort me to my chamber."

Disappointment shone on the priest's face, for clearly he was more interested in the mystery of Lady Angelina than taking Faith to her room, but he relented with a nod of the head.

Nun rolled her eyes and folded her arms across her chest. "I'd be better off with you, but if you prefer Father Chabot, then I shall stay and listen to what other stories your husband can come up with."

A bizarre gasp left Faith's lips as she took the priest's arm. Concern pushed away Darrin's personal thoughts. His gaze followed her out the chapel. Something had frightened Faith. Surely she had not figured out her parentage? Yet something had upset her. Though Darrin wanted to soothe her, first he had to deal with the problem before him.

"Well, Nun. What do you have to say? Do I speak the truth? Did you know my mother?"

Like a sharp arrow, Nun turned and jabbed a finger in his chest. "I thought a man of your age would have outgrown silly notions. I have never met your mother. I'm here because..." She threw up her hands and let out a cry of exasperation. "Oh, you wouldn't believe me if I told you."

Oh, but he would. But he wasn't ready for Gouch and Theo to learn that Faith was King Richard's legitimate heir. "If my mother didn't go to the convent, where did she go?"

"Beggin' your pardon, but she might have gone... She might have found..." Gouch cleared his throat and coughed.

"Out with it, man."

"Well..." Gouch stretched his neck to the left and then to the right.

"Well, what?" Darrin asked, his patience thinning.

Theo threw the pick over his shoulder. "She might go to her lover."

Nun gasped and Darrin felt his gut drop to the ground. *A lover!* Never would he have thought such. Would a mother give up her son for a lover? The years of his childhood rushed painfully though his mind. He did not have a single loving memory of his mother. He spent most of his youth with servants. He balled his hands into fists and headed to the chapel door. *Aye. She would.*

That eve, Darrin sat in a corner of the great hall with a pitcher of wine and a goblet. He had started the day with optimism, hoping to solve many mysteries, but by its end, he only uncovered more secrets that had no answers. Plus, to make things worse, Faith had come up with a few conclusions of her own.

After leaving the chapel earlier, he had gone to her chamber to check on her condition. But when he entered, she turned away, claiming she was still in the throes of a painful headache. Her shaky voice and sniffs bespoke of another condition—Faith had been crying. Darrin came to the bed and sat.

"Faith, what is truly bothering you?"

With red-rimmed eyes, she turned to face him. "We must have our marriage annulled."

A few weeks ago, her words might have filled him with merriment, but now, he had hoped she had grown a little fond of him as he had of her. But then, perhaps he had been making this journey alone. A hard stone settled in his stomach "Why the sudden change? I had thought you were willing to become my wife…in all things?"

Tears rushed down her cheeks and her shoulders shook. "Don't you see? If your mother was sent to the Abbey of Sainte-Marie-des-Dames and then four years later I returned, it is because we are brother and sister. *Our* mother must have died and they sent me back here."

It took Darrin a few moments to process the preposterous tale that had grown out of Faith's mind. He shook his head and reached for her hand, which she quickly pulled away. "Nay, that is foolishness. Why would the convent then be paying my father for your keep if you are my sister? You have jumped to the wrong conclusion, just as I have."

She eyed him with suspicion. "I have always thought Nun knew something of my parents though she claimed not. This would explain why she always changed the subject when I would bring it up and why your father never wanted us to get too close."

He should tell her the truth right now, but he feared she would want the annulment all the more and then his chances of keeping Château du Vent Doux would be lost. And he could not let that happen. Besides, for some reason, the thought of losing Faith held little appeal. "That does not make sense. If that were true, my father would not have sent my mother away. Plus, I was six when she left and eight when you came with Nun. We are four years apart. If you were my sister, we would only be two years apart."

Faith pulled the coverlet tightly around her. "Mayhap she was not pregnant when she left. Mayhap we have different fathers."

So even Faith had thought his mother had left of her own accord. That she had found another who she was willing to sacrifice her son to be with. No wonder his father was such a cold, hard man. The woman he loved had deserted him, or had his coldness sent her to the arms of another man? Darrin would never know.

"It makes sense. When our mother died, my father, whoever he may be, paid your father for my keep."

Darrin washed his hands over his face. "If that were true, do you really believe my father would have taken my mother's love child to raise?"

"But the money," Faith said feebly.

"You know as well as I, my father did not need the extra coin. Rest assured, we are not related. Though I do believe my mother did indeed have a lover, one she was willing to leave her young son for." Darrin reached over and brushed away the tears on Faith's cheeks. "Talk to Nun. She will set your fears to rest on this matter."

He stayed with her until sleep chased away all her doubts. Hopefully, Nun would reveal the truth to Faith, then it would not matter who was trying to sabotage the château. Faith would leave of her own accord and the château would fall to whomever King John deemed fit. *Justice—for not telling Faith the truth.*

Now here he sat, in the shadows of the hall, pondering what he should do next. Darrin took a heavy pull from the goblet, wiped his lips and then let his gaze roam about the hall. Sir Rollin and other knights sat near the hearth, eating fowl and laughing as if they had conquered all of France. As much as Darrin loved Château du Vent Doux, the life of a hearth knight did have its merits. The simple life, like he had in the English forest. Might that have been the life God had always intended him to have? He had responsibilities there, but they seemed minor compared to the workings of a château. But he had made his decision to return home and here he would live or die. There was no turning back.

Darrin's brooding broke when Theo strode into the hall and immediately grabbed a half a chicken and a cup of wine. With little effort, he spotted Darrin and waltzed over.

"Why are you sitting in the corner like a forlorn maiden?" Theo tore off a hunk of chicken with his teeth.

"I can think better here," Darrin said, taking another drink of wine.

Theo placed his own cup on the floor and dragged over a stool. Once seated, he sunk his teeth into the chicken again, the grease dripping down his clean tunic.

"Watch it, Lady Faith will not give you her favor if you turn back into a stinking pig again."

Theo chuckled. "Speak for yourself. You smell riper than a pile of cow dung."

True. Darrin still had not bathed since the fire. Nor did he feel the desire to do so. "With you and Gouch smelling like a bunch of roses, someone has to be the mange mutt."

Finishing off his chicken, Theo tossed the bones to a pair of dogs and then wiped his greasy hands on his tunic. "Feeling sorry for ourselves, are we?"

Darrin lifted the pitcher to fill his goblet and Theo's again. "Leave off. I just found out my mother deserted me as a child and I'm no closer to finding out who is causing all the havoc at the château."

"Ah, let me cry for you. The tough man of the forest turned into a whining babe. My mother had a gaggle of children before me. Think she wanted me?" Theo waved about. "Everyone here has a sad tale to tell. God created us for a reason and only he knows why. We live, we die. And if God sees fit, we will go to heaven."

"And if he doesn't?"

"Well, then, that is a trouble." Theo raised his cup and bumped it next to Darrin's. "Come now. We shall drink to better days ahead, for as you said, things around here could not get worse."

Darrin took another hardy drink. "I can't help but think that the answer is right before us."

"So how fares Lady Faith? Is she well?" Theo asked, quickly changing the subject.

"Aye, she is fine."

"In the chapel, she looked whiter than Nun's wimple."

Darrin laughed. "When I thought my mother went off to the convent, Faith got the crazy notion that my mother was her mother. She believed we were brother and sister. Have you ever heard anything so ridiculous?"

Slowly, Theo turned his head and stared at Darrin. "What did you say?"

"She thought we were brother and sister. Absurd. I can assure you that is quite impossible."

Theo's gaze held steady, as if he were trying to puzzle out some newfound knowledge.

Darrin finally punched him in the arm. "What is a matter with you?"

Startled back to reality, Theo downed the contents of his

cup and then stared toward the hearth. "Just looking at your pretty eyes. We shall speak later. I need to warm my bones." With that, he rose and strode over to where Sir Rollin stood.

Alone again, Darrin took another long pull of wine, letting the red liquid spread a hazy warmth throughout his body, dulling his senses. Exhaustion from the last two days had finally taken its toll. He closed his eyes and did not open them until the fire in the hearth was naught but embers. Knights, servants and a few peasants had all taken to their pallets. Darrin thought he should do the same. He rose and stumbled up the stone tower steps, but he could not shake the feeling that he was being watched.

Sleep came fast and his dreams were a mishmash of the past and the present woven together. He pictured his mother leaving him, not as a boy but as a man. *I will always love you wherever I go. Do not forget me.*

Darrin woke, drenched in sweat. Were those words truth or just want? As hard as he tried, he could not find the answer in his mind. He tossed to his side and stared at the waning moonlight filtering in through the small window. He squeezed his eyes shut. "Oh, God. If you are there, please give me some answers."

He had barely finished his last word when a loud cry was heard from outside the château walls, the echo of horses galloping in the distance. Darrin sprung to his feet and grabbed his sword. A babble of voices filled the hall and a young, pale knight came racing forward. "My Lord, come quick. It is Sir Theodore."

Darrin raced out in the bailey, heading for the gate before the knight could add another word. Near the left wall, he saw Theo lying on the ground, broken and bent, half his face smashed in. "What happened?" Darrin asked the knight.

The youthful knight paled all the more. "I-I think he fell, sir."

Darrin's gaze drifted upward at the high battlement wall. No man would just carelessly fall over the edge, and Theo, being a seasoned knight, would have been very cautious.

Nun pushed through the small crowd that was forming around Theo and knelt. She clicked her tongue several times as she examined the injured knight. "Methinks he was pushed and fell on his right side, crushing it to bits." She held her hand by his nose and mouth. "Yet he still lives." She looked up at a few servants. "Quickly, help me get him inside."

Darrin reached out and put his hand on her sleeve. "Will he live?"

She shrugged. "Only God knows."

The servants brought out a large coverlet and carefully lifted Theo onto the cloth. But as they took hold of his body, Theo cried out. "Darrin. Where are you?"

Rapidly, Darrin rushed to his side, taking Theo's left hand in his. "I am here. Try not to talk."

Theo coughed and tried to work his injured mouth. "I tried to stop him, but I couldn't." A fit of coughs and wheezes overtook Theo.

"Shh, worry not. We will talk later."

"Nay!" Theo squeezed Darrin's hand with incredible strength. "Faith. Rollin has Faith." His hand relaxed and his eyes rolled back into his head.

"Get him inside," Darrin roared. His gut dropped and rocked to the floor of his stomach. With lightning speed, he ran back into the château, into the great hall, taking the tower steps two at a time. The door to Faith's chamber lay wide open and she was nowhere to be found.

Twenty-three

Behold, I give unto you power to tread on serpents and scorpions, and over all the power of the enemy: and nothing shall by any means hurt you.
Luke 10:19

"WHY DID YOU BRING HER HERE? WHY COULD YOU not stay with the plan? Now we will have to deal with Darrin de Longue. What will King John do when he finds out?"

The fog cleared from Faith's mind and her vision took focus. She lay on a soft featherbed, near a warm hearth. The chamber was lavishly draped with intricate tapestries and fine gold chairs. A large, ornate trunk gilded with gold graced one corner. If she had not known better, she would think she was in the palace of King Philip of France. But the deep baritone voice was one she was familiar with, Lord Edmund de Tosny, Rollin's father.

"We would have to deal with both of them eventually. The only difference is that instead of breaking de Longue's back through utter incompetence, we will have to fight him," Sir Rollin answered his father.

Oh, she had been such a fool. She should have been more prudent. But the events of the day had frazzled her nerves, and when Sir Rollin had knocked on her chamber door earlier, she answered.

"My lady, come quickly. Sir Darrin has discovered something of great importance." Sir Rollin had sounded so sincere, she grabbed her cloak and followed him past the sleeping inhabitants of the dark great hall. When they reached the bailey, she realized her folly. One of his fellow knights held Sir Rollin's saddled horse. He grabbed her by the upper arm. "We are going to take a little ride, my lady."

The fiendish look in his eye spoke volumes. "Where is Sir Darrin?" she asked.

"I suspect he is sleeping off the wine he drank." His jaw clenched and he bared his teeth. "Now get on the horse."

In a rush of panic, Faith slammed the top of his foot, digging her heel deep near the ankle. Giving out a loud howl, he let her go. Speedily, she raced up the battlement steps with Sir Rollin in pursuit. Relief filled her when Sir Theodore jumped out of the shadows with his sword in hand.

"My lady, behind me." Theo took a warrior stance as Sir Rollin approached. "What is this, Blossom? Did I speak the truth earlier? Must have or you would not be kidnapping Lady Faith."

Sir Rollin did not answer but charged forward with his sword poised to give a lethal strike. With fast reflexes, Sir Theodore blocked the onslaught with the flat of his sword. Equaling the vigor, Sir Theodore began to take the upper hand, laying blow upon blow on Sir Rollin's blade. The younger knight's face turned purple with rage and he aimed his sword recklessly at Sir Theodore's stomach. But swiftly, the seasoned knight twisted away and sliced Sir Rollin's tunic.

A small spot of blood shone on the young knight's sleeve and Sir Theodore's victory was at hand when one of Sir Rollin's knights came up the stairs behind Faith and grabbed her around the waist. Her cry distracted Sir Theodore. He stumbled back. Sir Rollin rushed forward and, with all his might, pushed Sir Theodore over the battlement wall.

Faith squeezed her eyes shut at Sir Theodore's scream, as if the action could change the memory and outcome. A foul-smelling rag had been jammed into her mouth, and when she struggled against the knight's bonds, Sir Rollin struck her in the face, sending her into a deep sleep. Now here she lay, the horror fresh in her mind.

Sir Rollin must have seen her fidget, for he walked over to the bed. "Ah, I see you have awakened, my dear."

Lord de Tosny followed his son. "I am sorry for the abrupt change in residence, my lady. I can assure you it will only be temporary. You will be allowed to return to Château du Vent Doux once this mess has been resolved. In the meantime, enjoy my late wife's chamber."

Faith put a hand to her aching temple. "Return me now. I do not wish to stay here at all."

Lord de Tosny gave his son an anxious look but remained silent.

Very calmly, Sir Rollin edged closer to the bed, letting his fingers glide along the coverlet. "Don't you see we are trying to help you? Your marriage was forced upon you. It is quite obvious you are not happy. You don't have to live out your life with a man that you do not love."

Though his words were smooth and even meant to be kind, an edge of viciousness clung to each word, making Faith all the warier. "I know not what you mean. I am married and there is nothing that can be done to change that situation."

Sir Rollin sat next to her and smiled. "I know your marriage has not been consummated. You were smart to deny him, my lady. An annulment will be easy to obtain...or may not be necessary if your husband does something rash."

Faith edged to the other side of the bed. "I do not know how you came by such knowledge, but I have every intention of becoming a true wife to Sir Darrin. I do not want an annulment, nor do I understand what you mean, doing something rash."

Lord de Tosny muttered something under his breath and waved off and headed to the chamber door. "Such a mess. I will see to our other guest." He bowed toward her at the entry and left.

"You abducted someone else?" Faith asked, a spiral of fear twisting up her spine. Could Darrin or Nun be here too?

A dark, lecherous shadow settled in Sir Rollin's eyes. "Come, Faith, let us be honest. We were always close friends and my heart has always been yours. I left to join King Richard's army in hopes to earn a sizable fortune to persuade Sir Adrien into allowing me to marry you. I didn't understand why he always rejected my offer." He reached across the bed and wrapped a lock of her hair around his finger. "But he may have suspected your importance," he said softly.

Either Sir Rollin was mad or his heart would not let him see the truth. Could he truly love her? Yet she had never seen his eyes glow with adoration for her. "I know not what you talk about. Aye, we have always been friends, but that is all we will ever be. I'll not leave my husband to become your wife. I am sorry."

He released the curl and gave a heavy sigh before standing. "It seems Sir Darrin has worked his way into your heart."

Faith let one foot drop on the opposite side of the bed as she gauged the distance to the chamber door. "He did not have to do any work. I gave my heart to him years ago." She had barely finished her words before she jumped out of the bed and sprinted toward the door.

But Sir Rollin's hand snaked out and grabbed her around the waist. "My lady, are you in a hurry to see us wed?"

"Don't be foolish. I'll never marry you. Sir Darrin will have your hide for this," she spat, struggling against his grip. With force, she tried to kick him, but this time her foot struck nothing but air.

He laughed and dragged her to the great hall. There, Lord de Tosny stood with a frazzled Father Chabot. "How wonderful. I am glad you have recovered from your journey, Father Chabot."

"Recovered? I was taken from my bed by force. I will recover when I return to my own pallet in Château du Vent Doux. What is the meaning of this?"

"Has not my father told you?" Sir Rollin pulled out a

stool and forced Faith to sit. He then placed his hands on her shoulders. "Lady Faith and I wish to undo a wrong and make a right. Her marriage to Lord de Longue has not been consummated. She loves me and wishes to marry me."

"I wish no such thing!" Faith said, struggling against the pressure on her shoulders.

Sir Rollin leaned over and whispered in her ear. "Lady, marry me now or I will have to kill Sir Darrin and your other faithful champion, Nun."

A vision from the past sent a wintery chill through Faith's body. Sir Adrien had said almost the same the night Sir Jean was killed—betray Darrin to save Nun's life. Only this time, Sir Rollin threatened to kill Darrin too. She had spent ten paralyzing years with the threat of Nun being sent away or killed. When would this end? *God, give me the answer. What should I do?*

The hall door drifted open, but no one entered. A soft breeze floated through the room and blew out a lone candle that rested on a trestle table. The answer came as clear as the sun's morning rays shining through the entry.

Faith turned a determined look on Sir Rollin. "Kill who you must. I will not marry you." Nun would be proud of her and she suspected Darrin would also.

"Well, there you have it," Father Chabot said. "I cannot wed a person against their will and one whose marriage has not been annulled. You have gone mad."

Sir Rollin hauled Faith up off the stool and handed her to his father, then he strolled over to Father Chabot, rapidly pulled out a dagger and held it to the priest's throat. "Do you wish to have a priest's blood on your hands as well?"

The tables had turned. It was one thing forfeiting the lives of those who were not present but another thing to forfeit the life of an innocent man. "You would not kill a priest," she said, searching for calm in a mass of shredded nerves.

"Oh, I would. I do not believe in things you cannot touch and cannot feel. God is a myth, my lady, to keep the rest of us in line."

"My lord, my lord." A guardsman stumbled into the hall. "An army is approaching. They carry Lord de Longue's colors."

Faith lifted her brows. "It looks like that myth has just answered my prayers."

"Now what shall we do?" Lord de Tosny said. "We are not prepared to fight his forces. Nor could we survive a siege right now. I knew this would all come to no good. You should have stuck to our original plan. We could have taken control of Château du Vent Doux and none would have been the wiser."

"Cease, Father." Sir Rollin dropped the blade from the priest's throat and tapped it against his lips. His gaze slid to her and then to the guard. "Let Sir Darrin in but no others. Tell him I wish to discuss the return of Lady Faith, but he must come alone."

The guard left and Sir Rollin stepped to Faith's side. "Now, my dear, we shall see who the better man is."

Darrin rode into the bailey alone, dismounted and took the steps to the great hall two at a time. It might be foolhardy to enter the de Tosny keep without knights to watch his back, but he didn't care. He had to know Faith was safe. After finding out about Rollin's deception, Darrin amassed every knight and fighting man he could find. None protested. Lady Faith was greatly loved by all. Even though the journey was a little over a half day's ride, it seemed like an eternity to him. The moment she was gone, the truth bloomed inside him— he had never stopped loving her. Through all her deceptions and betrayals, the truth radiated like an eternal light. He loved her. He loved her when he thought his heart was filled with hatred. He loved her when his mind was filled with distrust. He loved her when she offered none in return. His heart was forever hers and always had been, since the very first day she crossed the threshold of Château du

Vent Doux with her lower lip trembling and her hand fisted. From a young age, he had loved no one more than her.

Whatever the outcome of today, he would not leave until she knew the full truth of her birth. He owed her that much. Inside the great hall, Darrin found a grim lot. A trembling Father Chabot, a wary Lord de Tosny, a malicious Sir Rollin and an angry Faith, his wife, her hand firmly fisted at her side.

Darrin gave a slight bow to Lord de Tosny, who held Faith about the arm. "May I ask, sir, why you have harmed one of my finest knights and abducted my wife? What ransom do you seek?"

Sir Rollin stepped forward, diverting Darrin's attention as a line of guards filed in behind him. "We seek no ransom. Here are your choices. Renounce your claim on Lady Faith and Château du Vent Doux, then you can leave and slink back to the forest from which you came. If you do not, you can die here, right now."

Ignoring Rollin, Darrin turned back to Lord de Tosny. "Are you as power hungry as your son? Is that why you killed Sir Adrien? You wanted the château?"

Lord de Tosny shook his head. "Sir Adrien's death was regrettable. He came here after you threw him out. He wanted me to march on Château du Vent Doux immediately. It was easy to pay off his knights. He was not a well-liked man. He was a guest in my dungeon until Rollin killed him."

Darrin's gaze slid over to Rollin. "You killed my uncle but did not tell me. Why? Did you truly think you could take away what was rightfully mine?"

With ease, Rollin stepped forward with a hand on the hilt of his sword. "I could have had it all if Theo wouldn't have been sniffing about. You trusted him. By killing Sir Adrien, I eroded that trust and gained some from you in return. But that meddlesome nun let him out of the dungeon during the fire and ruined everything. It is because of that wretched knight we are standing here now."

A fusion of rage and contempt burned within Darrin, but

he held his composure. Faith's freedom depended on it. "Theo was a comrade. And now because of you he is near death."

Faith gasped and a lone tear slipped down her cheek.

Rollin gave a cynical laugh. "You still don't see it, do you? Take a good look at me." He held a finger to his face.

What did he mean? Was he mad? Darrin looked to Lord de Tosny. "Your son is unbalanced. Please try to reason with him."

Another maniacal laugh split the air. "Unbalanced? Nay. But you are blind. Your mother ran away. Do you know where?" Rollin asked.

The hair rose on Darrin's neck as Faith gave out another surprising gasp. Nay, it could not be. Not once had Lord de Tosny come to the château. Unless he was a frequent visitor years ago. A memory rushed forward in Darrin's mind; his father had done his knight's training at the de Tosny keep. His father and Lord de Tosny were close in age. Could it be?

"Your mother's trunk is upstairs." Rollin opened up his arms. "Embrace me, for we are brothers."

The pieces fell into place. Darrin lifted a sad eye to Lord de Tosny. "You were my mother's lover."

"I'm sorry. Our tryst was brief. She wanted to stop, claimed she loved your father too much. But by then she was pregnant and she refused to pass the child off as Sir Jean's. He could have killed her and me, but he didn't. He was a good man and used to be my friend. I betrayed him, but your mother was so magnificent in beauty and in the heart. Your father divorced her in private and created the illusion of her death so she could save face. The only thing he asked for was you." Tears glistened de Tosny's eyes. "She wanted to return, but I prevented it. She never stopped loving you."

"Aye, and I got the scraps," Rollin bellowed. "The half smiles, the distant stares—though her body was here, her mind was forever at Château du Vent Doux. Of course neither my father nor my mother did reveal the truth. For years I tried to please her and never knew why I couldn't."

Pain of loss sluiced through Darrin again. She had been so close all these years. "When did she die?"

"Nine years ago. She died of a broken heart after hearing about your father's death. You see, in one of her depressed moods, she told me everything. I was twelve summers old and had learned I had a half brother who my mother loved desperately. I grabbed one of my father's knight's sword and rode to Château du Vent Doux. You can't imagine my surprise when I noticed the gate was open. I took it as a sign. I snuck into a quiet hall and up the tower steps. There I encountered your father. He knew who I was and tried to soothe me. Imagine. I killed him. Though in truth, I wanted to kill you."

"Oh, no! I didn't know." Lord de Tosny slumped and Faith helped him to a chair. "I am so sorry," he said to Darrin.

"Sorry," Rollin raged. "There is nothing to feel sorry about! It was like living in a tomb here. I put all my efforts into my knight's training after that, always planning on taking over Château du Vent Doux. After all, you had run off and all knew your father planned to marry Lady Faith off to ensure the safety of the keep. But Sir Adrien denied me over and over and over again. Always claiming I was too young, not a proven knight. So I gave my service to King Richard. And I learned so much more."

Grief flowed through Darrin. He had indeed been instrumental in his father's death. He had left the gate open that night after he had fought with his father. Darrin's shoulder began to throb as he looked to Faith. Rollin knew Faith's paternity too. He must have been the knight King Richard had mentioned from his deathbed. Darrin didn't want Faith to learn the truth this way. "Let us settle this like knights." He tapped the hilt of his sword. "We will fight and whoever draws first blood can have the hand of Lady Faith and Château du Vent Doux."

Faith came to his side. "I never heard of anything so foolish in my whole life. I am not a piece of meat or a bolt of cloth to be bartered for."

Darrin didn't need her interference. She could get hurt. He lifted a hand toward her without taking his eyes off of Rollin. "Take Lord de Tosny to his chamber. He is not well."

She looked to the older man holding a hand to his chest, his breathing heavy. She turned her gaze back to Darrin. "Think of your arm." Her eyes sparkled with fresh tears. "Don't be foolish, please."

Darrin touch her cheek with his free hand. "There is no other way. Go and pray." He then directed his attention to Father Chabot. "Take Lady Faith and Lord de Tosny upstairs."

"Nay," she cried, but Father Chabot and a few of the guards took her in hand along with Lord de Tosny, leading them toward the stairs.

When they were gone, Darrin squared his shoulders and faced Rollin. "Well?"

"I will take the challenge." Rollin drew his sword. "Only it shall be to the death. I'll not have my bride dreaming of you and wondering what you are doing on cold winter nights, especially when we are ruling all of England and possibly France as well."

Darrin winced as he pulled his own sword from his scabbard. He gripped the handle as hard as he could. "King Richard told you."

Rollin laughed as he took his stance. "Aye, he told me of your possible reluctance to carry out his last desires. He told me to get rid of you if you did not marry Faith or did not fulfill all the parts of the decree. There is another document given to me that if you failed, I would get Lady Faith's hand in marriage as long as you did not die by my hand."

His arm shook as Darrin raised his sword, ready to strike. "Ah, so that is why I did not find your knife in my back when we arrived at the château. But why all the intrigue?"

"Your hatred for Lady Faith and her Christian demands on you gave me time. My father, who despises bloodshed, wanted a peaceful end, hoping you would return to England of your own accord."

He stepped closer to Darrin and continued his earlier thoughts. "I feared King John would find out the truth and would kill Lady Faith. So when you thought I was tailing Sir Adrien, I went to King John and swore allegiance to him, promising to keep an eye on you. You were supposed to fail as Lord of Château du Vent Doux. I would have gained all that you lost—including Lady Faith." Rollin stepped to his left and the pair started circling one another.

Darrin kept watch of his opponent. "Then with the French King's help you would have amassed an army and marched on King John, claiming Faith the rightful heir."

"Very good. Only now it will be said that you came to attack me, and therefore, I had to defend myself. King John will reward me and seal his own fate at the same time."

Rollin lunged forward and Darrin quickly blocked his attack, but the onslaught did not stop. Whack after whack, Darrin fought off, first with the blade and then with the edge of his sword, each blow sending needles of pain up his arm. Rollin was a superior swordsman, and Darrin, if whole, could hold his own. But in this weakened condition, he would not last long.

Darrin ducked and swerved right as Rollin avoided another attack. Rollin pushed on, every strike bringing him closer to victory. Falling to one knee, Darrin braced himself for a swift end. Hopefully, the men at the gate would succeed where he had not. He had but one prayer as he watched the silver blade approaching his head.

Lord, protect Faith. Give her the love and life she deserves. Free her from all evil. Forgive me my sins and accept me into your kingdom.

Shouts filled the bailey and distracted Rollin for a moment, exposing his midsection. Darrin took the advantage and dug his blade deep into the soft skin of Rollin's belly. A look of surprise spread across his face as his tunic turned bright red. He stumbled back. The great hall door flew open and there stood Darrin's knights and peasants armed with sticks and pitchforks.

"We've come for Lord de Longue and his lady," Gouch stated with ax in hand.

The de Tosny knights fled the room.

Darrin's sword clattered to the floor and he limped toward Gouch. "You did not follow my orders."

"Nay. They were foolishly given."

Darrin raised a hand to Gouch's shoulder. "You're a smart man, Master Gouch. Methinks you should be knighted."

Gouch gave a snort. "I'd rather not."

Twenty-four

Oh that I were as in months past; as in the days when God preserved me; When his candle shined upon my head, and when by his light I walked through darkness.
Job 29: 2 & 3

EARLY THE NEXT MORN, THEY RETURNED TO Château du Vent Doux, and a grand celebration ensued. Upon receiving word that Sir Darrin and Lady Faith were safe, every servant and peasant began to decorate the hall and pitch in with the cooking and cleaning. One would think they were celebrating the return of Christ. The festivities carried on to the next day, when all discovered that Sir Theodore would live. It seemed like the merriment would never end. Yet finally, when fatigue set in, the château returned to its familiar pace.

As he had done every day since his return, Darrin went to check on Theo. He lay in a dark room, the right side of his face heavily bandaged. His sword arm and right leg were placed between boards in hopes to straighten out the broken bones and mend the crushed joints. The knight would never march into battle again or spar in the practice yards.

"Darrin, how wonderful to see you. Please pull back those dark drapes Nun hung over the window. I do prefer the light instead of the darkness."

A hard lump formed in Darrin's throat as he did what Theo asked. Theo kept a positive attitude and a profound strong faith in God even though his recovery was slow. By contrast, when things looked dim in Darrin's life, he ran from God. When he received his shoulder wound, he grumbled at his lack of strength; not once had Theo uttered a single syllable of complaint, even though his life had dramatically changed and would never be the same again.

What made one man a strong pillar and another a weak twig? Darrin pulled a chair closer to the bed. "How are you feeling today?"

"Good, good. I am able to move my fingers. See?" The fingers on Theo's right hand twitched and moved a tad, but a frail smile shone on the left side of his face.

Theo's might of character humbled Darrin. "I pray that you grow stronger daily."

"Do you?" Theo asked. "You and I had something in common. Neither of us sent up prayers to God often."

"But you changed. I watched you change. You went from soiled and rowdy knight to a clean and good man. And even now, you remain strong and close to God when others would hold him with blame. Tell me, how did this happen?"

"Your wife. When you forced me to keep an eye on her, she made me do many things."

His words took Darrin aback. Other than moving the trunks about, Theo had never spoken of what Faith did with her days. A prick of jealousy touched Darrin's heart, but he mentally admonished the feeling. Theo was a truly honorable man. "What did she make you do?" he asked quietly.

"I would never go to chapel with the rest of you, so she would make me pray when I did other tasks. First, it was just a few prayers and then I began to pray every day—out loud. I found myself praying almost constantly. I am not sure even now how my heart changed. No matter what happens in my life, I am a new man."

Here Theo lay, broken and bent, yet he spoke of being a new man. Darrin swallowed hard and turned away for fear he might blubber like a babe.

"You have changed too. You cannot hide your love for her, but something is holding you back."

Darrin cleared his throat but kept his eyes averted to the bed coverlet. "You are most perceptive. But I must ask you first, how did you know that Rollin was my half-brother?"

"I think I always knew. Every time I saw Rollin, I felt as if I had met him long before he came to King Richard's camp. I hadn't, but I never connected the similarities between the two of you."

Similarities? There were none that Darrin could see. Rollin was lean and had dark, handsome looks. A smile tugged on Darrin's lips. He was stocky and resembled his father. "There are no similarities. We were as different as night and day."

"That is not true. You both have similar eyes—yours hazel in the middle with blue on the rim. His just the opposite." Theo struggled to sit up, a glint his left eye. "You both had the cocky saunter. Why, you even fought the same way. All this my mind saw, but my brain could not understand until you told me that Lady Faith thought you were brother and sister. Then it came to me as clear and as bold as our Savior's resurrection."

"That is why you abandoned me so abruptly in the great hall that fateful night. You went to talk to Rollin to see if he knew."

"Aye, and besides, I had no desire to listen to your woe-is-me tale. I did not come right out and ask him, but when I said I believed Lady Angelina left because she was with child, Rollin's eyes blazed with the truth. I then knew he was our traitor. From that moment on, I kept watch."

"But you did not come to tell me." Darrin raised his gaze to meet Theo's.

"You were well in your cups and feeling sorry for yourself. I would have told you my suspicions in the morning. But that never happened."

No, it hadn't. Silence reigned between them as each of them made peace with that tragic eve.

"But none of this has to do with what is troubling you," Theo said.

Darrin tapped his fingers together, debating if he should tell Theo the one secret that had not been revealed. "I fear I must let Faith go." His voice was hoarse and choked with worry.

"Why? You love her. It beams from you like a holy light. God has given you everything you have ever wanted. Why are you not grateful?"

"Because I have not given her everything she deserves."

Theo tipped his head to the side as perplexity settled on his exposed features.

Starting at the beginning, Darrin told him everything, and once the telling was done, a great relief swept through him.

"Now I understand why you were acting like a dog who had had his tail sawed off—chasing ghosts and villains around every corner. You must tell her."

"Aye." Darrin looked down at his folded hands. "But I fear her answer."

"You fear she will want to be queen or that she will kick you out on your arse?"

"Both. I fear both."

"Well, then, you are more of a cripple than I."

Both men laughed and Darrin reached over and hugged his friend.

Faith sat in her room staring out the window as another new day approached, while Nun sat with needle and thread, hemming one of Faith's gowns. Neither woman said a word, both deep in their thoughts.

With the new turn of events, Faith expected Darrin to come to her bed. But night after night, he still abstained. However, he was present every morn for prayers and often could be found in the chapel late in the eve. Understandably, he had a lot to think about and figure out—his past and where to go from here. Yet there was naught to fear anymore. Lord de Tosny had sent word to King John, accepting full responsibility for what all transpired, and a fragile peace ensued between both households.

There was no reason for Darrin to avoid her, unless he no longer wished to have her as wife. Her heart lurched. Did he still hate her so? However, when she was held captive, he came for her and had been extremely tender on their journey back home. Had he just been playing the chivalrous knight?

The birds sang in the trees and the sun's warm rays rested on her face as she peered out the window. Spring was definitely courting summer. The blooms were fresh. Daffodils had given way to the heady smell of lavender. Before she knew it, there would be lilies and roses growing in the fields. The days grew longer and spirits flew higher. Even so, Faith could not chase away her weariness.

With a heavy sigh, she stood. "Let us go for a walk, Nun."

Nun placed her mending on the table. "That is the wisest thing I have heard come out of your mouth in days."

But before they could leave, the door swung on its hinges and Darrin stood in the entry.

"I shall leave the two of you alone," Nun said.

But Darrin blocked her retreat. "Nay. What needs to be said can be said in front of you. For I think you know the truth as well as I."

Without a word or an answer to Faith's questioning look, Nun withdrew to her chair again.

"My lady, please sit." Darrin took Faith by the hand and led her to the only other chair in the room. "I have something I must show you." He knelt on one knee in front of her and pulled a yellow piece of parchment from his tunic. "I have not always been forthright with you. Please, read."

The paleness of his skin and foreboding look in his eyes did little to calm her. Perhaps it was better not to know what the message held, but her curiosity could not be contained, and with shaking fingers, she took the note and unfolded it. She read the words once, not comprehending the meaning. Something about King Richard and her mother. Faith read it again, focusing on every word. *Lady Faith de Saint Marie is my legitimate daughter.*

Faith's mind reeled forward and back. Her hands began to perspire as her heart took a rapid gallop. "What cruel jest is this?" she whispered.

Darrin reached out for the hand she had fisted without thought. "This is no tale, but truth. On his deathbed, King Richard revealed all. He paid my father for your care. It is why my father disapproved of my love for you all those years ago."

Her whole body began to shake and quiver. *King Richard, Coeur de Lion,* was her father. It explained so much. Why she was taken from the abbey, why she was brought up as a lady, why she could not love who she wanted. Tears flooded her eyes and rolled down her cheeks. Her mother was a peasant who had loved a prince who would become king. A tragic love story, indeed.

"Faith," Darrin said softly. "Do you know what this means?"

Means? She tried to force her mind to remember the day the man, King Richard, had come to the abbey. The only day she had ever seen her father.

Darrin raised her chin. "You have many decisions to make."

His words meant nothing to her. "What do you mean? Decisions?"

He seemed to ponder his answer for a long time. "Do you wish this to be publicly known? Do you wish to seek your rightful place as queen?"

Her mind swam—queen. An untitled ward, queen of England. It sounded absurd. She stared deep into Darrin's earnest eyes, hoping to find answers. "What do you want me to do?"

Confusion filled his face. "It is not my choice, but yours. I will stand by your decision or go far away from you. Whatever you please, I shall do."

Whatever she pleased. He spoke to her as if she were

queen already. Was that what this was all about? He stood by her because she could be queen? Her heart fell into dark depths and crumpled. Saving her had been an act of honor, not an act of love. She rose to her feet and wiped her eyes. "Do not give me safe answers. I wish to know one thing. Do you stay with me out of duty or out of love?"

The warring of emotions that crossed his face almost sent her to the depths of despair. Then he took her head between his hands. "I love you. I have always loved you, even when I denied it. If you wish to be a queen or not, if you allow me to be your husband or if you send me away, I will always love you and cherish you and honor you."

Piece by piece, her broken heart began to knit together. "If this be so, then husband, I wish only to be your loving wife with no crown."

He gave her a deep kiss and then another that swept away all the hurt of the past ten years. He then kissed her face and neck and twirled her around the room. "If I could, I would give you the sun, the moon and the stars. For I adore you and you will always be my queen."

"Stop," she laughed. "I am very blessed. Besides knowing who my parents were, being your wife has always been my dream. Tell me, you knew him, what was he like?"

Darrin looked at her thoughtfully. "I knew him as a warrior, nothing more. He gave orders and once in a while asked for my advice, but I did not know him personally. For your sake, I wish I did."

A soft creak from the chair behind them reminded them they were not alone. Nun stood with tears glistening in her eyes. "I can tell you what he was like. At least what he was like when he was young. He was kind and gentle. He would pick wildflowers out of a field and tie a red strip of cloth around them. He would stand up in the middle of a courtyard and sing off key and dance with anyone who might walk by. His laughter could fill your soul with sunshine. He would debate the affairs of the world with such passion and vigor. His smile would make you think of no others."

Nun unwrapped the cloth that held her wimple in place. She pulled off the headdress, revealing short pale hair. "His kisses were sweet, warm and everlasting. I will never forget him."

Faith placed her hands to her throat as Nun's words sunk in deep in her heart. "Mother," she whispered through her tears.

Crying just as hard, Nun shook her head. "I'm sorry I could not tell you. I needed to keep you safe. No one knew except for the abbess and Brother Klein. Now both are long gone. When you were little and Richard came to the abbey to see you, I was so excited. I thought surely we would be a family again. But he looked right through me as if I didn't exist. All he saw was a young nun. He did not remember me, so I said nothing. He had changed. His mind was heavy with duty and war. His love from the past had died with the young man I knew. I feared for your safety, so I hid the truth even from you. Forgive me."

Nun had bandaged Faith's scrapes and hugged her when she had a bad fall. Told her stories and taught her to read. She was there to give advice and a scolding if necessary. Taught her how to bake a meat pie and how to prune a plant. Nun had dried Faith's tears and held her tight when her heart was breaking.

She had always had a mother. Faith flew into Nun's arms. "I love you, Mother."

Nun patted Faith on her back. "And I love you too."

Epilogue

*And we know that all things work together for good to them
that love God, to them who are called
according to his purpose.*
Romans 8:28

DARRIN STRODE BACK FROM THE PRACTICE FIELD, the late summer rays beating on his sweaty back. Each day his arm had grown stronger and so had his love for his wife. If they conceived a child or not within the year, it did not matter. They would always be together, be it at the Château du Vent Doux or somewhere else. God had blessed them abundantly, for no couple could be happier.

Nun still wore her habit and continued her role as dutiful companion, but the bond between daughter and mother could not be denied. Often they would slip away and discuss King Richard and his youthful love for a peasant girl once named Louise Marie. Faith never seemed to tire of the story.

Since Rollin's death, all acts of sabotage ceased and the knights who had been loyal to him fled or pledged their service to Darrin. The whole mood of the château seemed to be lighter and when Gouch married the smithy's daughter, Monique, festivity exploded and the merriment lasted for days.

The sorrows of the past melted away as God blessed all at Château du Vent Doux. In spite of all the bliss, one man's life would never be filled with its past exuberance. Indeed, it was the only thing that Darrin wished he could change. Theo walked with a profound limp, his right arm grotesquely bent at the elbow and his fingers uselessly curled inward. His once pleasant face now frightened small children. Through it all, he kept his cheerfulness, often saying he was a two-headed coin. From the left side, he was a dashing noble, and on his right side, he was a scraggily villain—not many men were blessed to see both.

Darrin had begged Theo to stay and give advice to pages and squires who would become knights. Nonetheless, Theo wanted to return to England. On this bright, beautiful day, Theo would leave, casting a cloud over those who loved him.

Approaching a cart laden with Theo's few belongings, Darrin hugged his friend. "You can still reconsider. England is cold and damp most of the year, while here spring comes early and the warmth knits the bones and heals the soul."

Theo raised his left eyebrow. "We must remember our time here differently. Often I slept in the mud and the cold winter winds tore through my tent. If I was lucky to have a tent at all." He shook his head. "I came to Normandy and France to seek and win my fortune. That is no longer possible. It is time for me to leave."

"Lady Faith is stricken with grief," Darrin pronounced, his last-ditch effort to keep his friend here.

Theo worked his lips into a weak smile. "She has you to keep her company. Besides, she will have her hands filled now that she is with child."

Startled, Darrin thought his friend made a preposterous jest. When he said nothing, Theo started to laugh.

"She has not told you?" Theo raised his good hand and put it on Darrin's shoulder. "Do not be too angry with her. It was the last thing she whispered to me this morn."

Elation grew within Darrin and he could not contain his excitement. Not because this would guarantee their rights to the château, but because this would seal the loving and adoring bond between him and Faith. "Praise God!" Darrin hugged his friend.

Theo laughed all the more. "Go now and find her. I can let myself out. I have paid a peasant to take me to the port. You need not worry about me."

Darrin pulled back but still held Theo by his shoulders. "Godspeed, my friend. Mayhap when my wife and our child are able, we will come to visit you, or perhaps you will find England does not hold much for you. You will always be welcomed here."

"Aye, I know." A sadness entered his eyes and Darrin knew his friend still had a lot of healing to do. Suddenly he brightened. "Now go! Your wife awaits to tell you the news."

Darrin squeezed Theo once more and then ran for the great hall to his adoring wife.

Theo scanned the bailey, looking for the old man he had hired to take him to Nantes. With his injuries, they would have to stop often so Theo could stretch his aching muscles and bones. Finally, the old man strolled up.

"A lovely day for a journey, don't you agree? I cannot wait to return to England."

Theo looked at the old man's colorless eyes and could not discern if the man was serious or not. "I do not need you to travel that far with me. Only to Nantes."

The old man nodded and helped Theo up to the wagon seat. "You may change your mind as we ride along. We could discuss spiritual growth."

"You are not a priest and I am right with my God," Theo said, placing a bundle of clothes under his maimed arm.

"Maybe so, but I do not speak of your welfare, but that of another."

Theo pondered the old man's words but said nothing, for who was he to criticize the oddities of others? In truth, if the man proved to be good company, then Theo would willingly take him to England. Lord Leonard de Taine had passed away and the ownership of his keep had been given to Theo as a gift from Lady Eleanor de Maury provided that he take good care of Lord de Taine's prized possession—his goats.

"Well, Master… What is your name?" Theo asked. The old man took a long time thinking on what should be a simple answer. Only a villain would take that much time. Perhaps he should be wary of this man.

"What do you wish to call me?"

A villain, indeed. But Theo suspected the man's notorious days were over. "Well, let me see…how about… Jude, after the saint."

"Ah, a good man. One of the best. Though I do not think you need the prayers of the hopeless."

Theo laughed. "Some might disagree. For some reason, I think the name fits. Lead on, Master Jude, for we have a ship to catch and a home to claim. By the way, do you have any knowledge on the care of goats?"

Jude tipped his head and cast his clear, colorless eyes on the horizon. "They are a fine creation, are they not?"

If you enjoyed this book,
please consider reviewing it where you purchased it.

Excerpt from

Joshua's Prayer

Olivia Rae's new inspirational contemporary

One

Sam Morgan stared at the shabby sign outside the old dilapidated Victorian. In peeling paint it read:

> GRACE HOUSE WOMEN'S CENTER
> Giving women a fresh start during troublesome times

Apart from college, Sam had lived in Golden Ridge, Missouri, all his life. He'd met his wife, Vicky, there and they had their son in Golden Ridge. He thought he'd die here in this small town nestled close to Big Golden Ridge Lake. Years ago any person who spent a pleasant sunny afternoon in Golden Ridge would have thought, what a wonderful carefree place. The people are so friendly with their easy talk and warm smiles. And the homes in this town are so well-kept. What a delightful place to live in and raise a family.

Those used to be his thoughts and dreams. To live a perfect life in this perfect town. But he'd been wrong. Now this place brought him nothing but sorrow. This town reminded him of failed promises and death: the death of his parents, death of his wife, and the death of his dreams. His spirit was as worn out as the broken-down house and neighborhood before him. It was time to collect his son and try to piece together their lives elsewhere. Away from the painful memories Golden Ridge held around every corner.

A gentle clinking sound drew his gaze to a small wooden sign swinging on metal chains below the larger one. In bold black letters the words leapt off the stark white sign:

> Now Open
> GRACE HOUSE PRESCHOOL
> Serving the Community of Golden Ridge
> All Children Welcome

Sam looked at his watch. Five o'clock. School should be out and hopefully most of the kids had gone home. Well, at least those who didn't live there with their mothers. Sam walked up the path to the house. He paused at the steps and clutched the railing. The time had come for him and Joshua to start anew.

"No, I won't go!"

Sam's gut wrenched at his son's panic-filled cry. He'd known this wouldn't be easy for Joshua, but he didn't think getting his son to leave Grace House would be this hard. Like a recurring nightmare, he was disappointing Joshua again. Huge tears spilled from his son's eyes as he clung to the hem of his caregiver's skirt. Sam had tried to cajole Joshua out of Grace House and into the car. They'd gotten as far as the foyer when everything stalled.

A more direct approach was needed. He took a deep breath and took hold of his son's arm. "Joshua, I'm sorry. You can't stay here. Mommy doesn't live here anymore. It's just you and me, buddy. We're going to be okay. I promise." He buffered his gruff actions with a smile.

Unfortunately, Joshua wasn't buying any of it.

"No. No. No. I want to stay with Miss 'Cole." Joshua turned his tear-streaked face up to Nicole James. "Tell him. Mommy wanted me to stay with you while she's in heaven."

Sam's heart constricted. No child should ever have to

lose their mother. And no child should have to carry the weight of such a loss alone. Especially not alone. Sam had known that and thought of his son while he worked overseas, but at the same time he'd grasped at reasons not to return and face the reality of his wife's passing.

Some father you are, he told himself.

Miss James rubbed a gentle hand over the boy's curly, dark honey-colored hair. "Joshua, your daddy wants to take you home, but I'm sure he'll bring you back for preschool tomorrow." Her green-flecked eyes narrowed as she lifted her chin and glared at Sam, challenging him to defy her words. "Won't you?"

She had to be kidding. He had no intention of bringing his five-year-old son back there tomorrow or any other day. He had a realtor to contact and movers to talk to. Regardless of whether or not their house sold right away, he planned to roll out of Golden Ridge, Missouri as soon as possible. He postponed several surgeries in Guatemala after he'd learned of Vicky's death. People were counting on him to return, ASAP.

With Vicky gone there was nothing left for them in Missouri. He had responsibilities and Joshua—even with his disability—would adjust in time. His son would be fine once they got away from all the misery and sad reminders Golden Ridge had to offer...and the iron-spined redhead standing in front of them.

Though he didn't know her well, Sam had exchanged a few pleasantries with Miss James at church. He knew the attractive twenty-something-year-old was co-owner of Grace House, which apparently just opened a preschool. But beyond that he knew little else. In letters she wrote and during phone calls, his wife had raved about the support she and Joshua received there when they returned from Guatemala. He didn't care if Miss James was the best preschool teacher in all of Missouri. Right now she was the roadblock that stood between him and his son.

Sam gritted his teeth. "Come on, Joshua. Daddy is going

to take you back to Guatemala. You remember. You and Mommy were there for a month. Remember Jario? The man who made the wooden flutes? You liked the songs he played."

Joshua yanked his arm from Sam's grip and seized Miss James' legs like she was a buoy keeping him afloat during a dangerous ocean storm. "No. I don't 'member. I don't. I don't. I don't." There was no negotiating with him now: Once his son hit the "fit" stage, Sam knew it was all over.

"Dr. Morgan, please," the teacher said. "Joshua is having a hard time dealing with change. Most young children with his condition do. And because of his short-term memory problems, and his mother's accident and death, he's even having problems remembering you."

My God, they hadn't been apart that long, had they? Sam's mind ticked away the months. *Could five months erase a child's memory of their father?* Not normally, but a child with severe Fetal Alcohol Syndrome might forget… Guilt tightened its band across his chest.

Sam rubbed a hand across his aching forehead. "Look, Miss James, I appreciate all you've done for my son, but now it's time for Joshua and me to make a new life." *Away from Golden Ridge.* "There are only bad memories for us here."

She squeezed Joshua closer. "I mean no disrespect, but I was working with Joshua and his mother while you were gone. Joshua has made excellent progress at Grace House's Preschool and since your wife moved here she…was working very hard too."

The pause in Miss James words was worth a thousand words. Though this young teacher didn't want to admit it, in the end, Vicky had fallen off the wagon again. All the years of therapy hadn't changed the outcome. Vicky's alcoholism had finally killed her, albeit with a car and a tree. Had she stayed sober, she wouldn't have hit that maple tree and Joshua would still have a mother.

Miss James lifted her pretty chin another notch. "I think

you should consider enrolling him in the kindergarten program we're starting this fall. The more things stay the same, the better off Joshua will be. Trust me."

I love my son and am not doing anything wrong. Why should I trust her—a stranger to me—to know what's best for Joshua?

No way. He was done with those words. He'd trusted his wife would remain sober. He'd trusted God would help her stay that way too. His gut tightened. He'd trusted everyone else—his whole life. And look where that had gotten him and Joshua.

"I don't think that's going to happen."

Why had Vicky started drinking again? Going to Guatemala had originally been her idea. She'd been so enthusiastic when they thought about giving a year of service to the International Surgical Christian Outreach Program. She'd said it was God's will, His plan for their family. She'd thought a year in Guatemala would do their marriage a world of good too. Sam had hoped she was right, for their marriage could use all the help it could get after years of lies and deceit.

He'd wanted a new start just as much as she had. He wanted the fun-loving, caring wife he married years ago and he was willing to do almost anything to have her healed of her addiction. Even if it meant spending a year away from his home. But a month after arriving in Guatemala, Vicky had packed up and left with Joshua, blaming his son's FAS for why they couldn't stay. However, Sam had signed a year's contract with ISCOP. They desperately needed his services and before she left, Vicky made it pretty clear she didn't want him back home right away either.

The move hadn't changed a thing. She was still unhappy and he hadn't a clue about how to change her attitude. So he honored the terms of his contract and made a decision he'd regretted every day since Vicky's death.

The air seeped out of Sam's lungs as he eyed the young woman pensively. "Come on, Joshua."

Miss James' hand covered his. "Please, Doctor Morgan."

At one time, he'd believed this woman could keep Vicky sober in his absence and change her back into the woman he'd married long ago. He'd believed Grace House offered the answer to his prayers.

Some answer. He hadn't even been gone four months when Vicky served him divorce papers. To top it off, she had moved into Grace House with Joshua. Her letter had been pretty clear: *"I hate everything about you. Even your house."* He couldn't get rid of the niggling feeling that Miss James had something to do with that. Sam knew he should have come home as soon as he was served the divorce papers, but he thought helping a kid who had been waiting for eighteen months for a new jaw was more important. Besides, deep down, Sam knew his marriage was finished... That going back right away wasn't going to change the outcome for any of them.

Clearly his decision to stay overseas had been wrong and Joshua was suffering as a consequence. Sam pried Joshua away from the not-so-tender grip of the delicately built Miss James. "Sorry, we have to go."

His son kicked and shrieked, his wide open mouth displaying his crooked baby teeth; that too was caused by FAS. Well, at least that was fixable—if Joshua would sit in a dental chair. At the moment, his son twisted and turned, flailing his limbs. Sam mentally sighed. He could straighten teeth, but he'd never be able to fix Joshua's mind or change the past for either of them.

A second later that set of tiny teeth latched onto his hand. In surprise and pain, his grip loosened and Joshua made a beeline for the stairs and his bedroom. His son was out of sight in less time than it took a hummingbird to blink.

Beads of blood left an imprint of uneven teeth on the side of Sam's hand. The wound stung, but not as much as the pain in his heart. He'd known things would be tough when he returned home, but he hadn't expected his son to freak out at the sight of him.

Miss James took his hand in hers, examining the slight injury. "You're hurt."

Her hands were warm and soft as she gently touched the side of his hand, running her fingertip over the wound. She had all the earmarks of being a caring, loving person, but he knew better than to believe that. If it wasn't for Nicole James, he'd probably still have a wife waiting for him at home. Not to mention a son who didn't screech at the sight of him.

He pulled his hand away. "It's nothing major."

Her brow wrinkled. "I don't know. Bite wounds can cause serious infections. You really should—"

"I'm an oral surgeon—I got it."

The metal rod returned to her spine. "Of course, you know best."

Now she got it. He did know best. This town was bad news with its reminders of his parents wasted lives and his dead wife. If he had gotten his family away from this town years ago maybe things would be different now. He should have insisted that Vicky and Joshua stay with him in Guatemala. But he had trusted Vicky's judgment. He had trusted God. He had trusted the good people of Golden Ridge. Trusted all of them to watch over Joshua.

But no more blind trust. No more bad decisions. He couldn't handle making even one more mistake. Looking up to where his son had retreated, Sam took a deep breath and made for the stairs, but Miss James stepped in front of him.

"I think you should leave Joshua here for the night. This has been his home since before his mother's death and I think we should try to keep things as normal as possible for him."

Sam had managed to make it back for the funeral, but obviously not fast enough. Pastor Martin said Joshua was in excellent hands. At the moment Sam felt that statement was up for debate.

"I know this is hard for Joshua," Sam inched toward the stairs, "but staying here longer than necessary will only make things worse. You've known him for five months. I'm his father. I've known him his whole life."

Miss James didn't back down. Instead she rose up on the bottom step and looked him in the eye. "He's still very shaken up from losing his mother. Uprooting him before he can come to terms with his mother's death could mentally scar him for life. I am sure all he needs is a few more months of stability—in Golden Ridge."

Heat rushed over Sam's body and he broke out into a sweat. "I disagree. The sooner Joshua forgets this place, the better." Sam winced at the forcefulness of his voice. *Was he mad at her or at himself?* He should have been here for Joshua when Vicky died rather than leaving his son with a stranger. Things seemed clearer on this side of the equator, away from so much need.

"I'm sorry, Dr. Morgan, w-we all think it is important for Joshua to stay awhile longer," she stammered.

"We? Who's we?" He clenched his hands at his sides, controlling the urge to push her out of the way and make his way up the stairs to his son.

She shot a glance at his fists and then put a hand to her throat. "Why Pastor Martin and me—"

"I'm Joshua's father. I know what he needs. You and the good pastor think you know what is best for my son? What credential gives you that right? Well I disagree. Now if you'll excuse me." Sam made another attempt to step around Miss James, but she quickly blocked his way again.

She held out her dainty, though shaking, white palm. Bold as the angel guarding the entrance into Eden, she raised her chin. "Please, Dr. Morgan, you and Joshua are very upset. I'm sure you want to do what is best for your son. What's one more day after all? He *did* just lose his mother."

Sam should have pushed her aside and headed up the stairs, but her words took the fight out of him...and he sensed Miss James wouldn't back down. For a little thing, she sure was filled with grit. Sam pulled his hand across the back of his neck. What difference would one more day make? After all, Joshua had become used to not having his father around for long periods of time.

"All right, Miss James. Joshua can stay the night, but..."—Sam gave her a pointed look to make sure she knew he meant business—"I'll be back tomorrow afternoon. Please make sure Joshua is ready to leave by then."

Without another word, Sam stalked across the foyer but closed the door quietly behind him. Tomorrow he'd collect his son and then return with him to the surgical mission clinic in Guatemala. Obligations had to be met there before Joshua and he could move on to their new life. At least at the mission clinic, Sam knew he was doing something good. But here...in this town...his failures as a husband and father seemed to taunt him from every place Vicky and he used to walk.

What did he always pray in the Lord's Prayer? *Thy will be done.*

Cynical laughter stuck in Sam's throat. *This was God's will?* What kind of God would leave a disabled boy motherless?

He'd go back to the Guatemalan mission and do the surgical dentistry, but nothing more. He'd leave the preaching and teaching of God's word to the ministers, because deep down he finally knew the truth—God really didn't exist for him.

Dear Reader,

First off, I would like to thank all my readers and fans for encouraging me to add to *The Sword* and the *Cross Chronicles*. Without your support *Adoration* never would have been written. I do so hope you enjoyed your time in France. We will be heading back to England with Sir Theo in the last (for real this time) book in the series, *Devotion*. I love to hear from my fans so please let me know what you think of the series and which book, so far, is your favorite.

While you wait for *Devotion*, consider reading the other books in the series if you haven't done so already. You may also like my contemporary inspirational, *Joshua's Prayer*. I guarantee a good cry before the ending.

Think about becoming a Faithful Follower and getting all my latest news before anyone else does. I have giveaways every month! You can join at www.oliviaraebooks.com.

Finally, if you enjoyed this book or any of my other books, please consider leaving a review at your place of purchase—even if it is only a few words. Your reviews are greatly appreciated.

Until then…abundant blessings,

Olivia Rae

Olivia Rae is an award-winning author of historical and contemporary inspirational romance. She spent her school days dreaming of knights, princesses and far away kingdoms; it made those long, boring days in the classroom go by much faster. Nobody was more shocked than her when she decided to become a teacher. Besides getting her Master's degree, marrying her own prince, and raising a couple of kids, Olivia decided to breathe a little more life into her childhood stories by adding in what she's learned as an adult living in a small town on the edge of a big city. When not writing, she loves to travel, dragging her family to old castles and forts all across the world.

Olivia is the winner of the New England Readers' Choice Award, Illumination Award Bronze medalist, Buyer Best Book Award Finalist, a Kindle Book Award Semi-Finalist, and a finalist in many other contests. She is currently hard at work on her next novel.

Contact Olivia at Oliviarae.books@gmail.com

For news and sneak peeks of upcoming novels visit:
Oliviaraebooks.com